Ms Mia

and

Murder

at the

Italian Villa

Jennifer Branch

Villa Bella Sorgente

1

A Grand Adventure

"Are you sure that seat's all right?" Judith fussed over her daughter, as the private jet roared high above the Atlantic Ocean. "I think there's a draft coming from that vent. Wouldn't you be more comfortable next to me, dear?" She patted the empty place by her in invitation.

Francesca refrained from rolling her eyes, but couldn't stifle her exasperated sigh. "I'm fine, Mom. Just tired." She pulled the cozy plaid blanket up to her neck, covering her ankle-length flowered dress. Her wavy dark hair effectively hid her face from her family, shining like a raven's wing in the soft lights of the plane. "I'm all tucked in, see? I'm just going to sleep the rest of the trip." Deliberately closing her eyes, she shut out further conversation.

"If you're sure, darling," Judith turned to Mia, shrugging her socialite thin shoulders in apology. "I would have expected Francesca to be more social, since you're letting us borrow your company jet, but she's still so upset about everything." Her pink lips compressed.

"Maybe she's just tired," Diane suggested. Her sensible gray slacks were singularly unflattering to her silhouette, and a baggy paisley polyester blouse was unsuccessful at camouflaging her comfortably plump stomach, made worse by her slumped shoulders. Her only concession to makeup was a brief slash of a neutral lipstick, but her ruddy cheeks needed no blush. Rather, a touch of powder would have benefited them greatly. She leaned forward and sipped her drink, her no nonsense, thick brown hair swinging with the movement, and her soft brown eyes worried. Soothing the older woman at a hushed tone, almost below the noise of the engine, she added, "Francesca hasn't been getting much rest lately. Just let her sleep, while she can."

"Francesca will be fine, once she adjusts to the situation," Judith pronounced with authority. "Better to find out her husband's a thief now, than after they have children. It's a lot easier to get rid of him now." She raised an elegantly arched dark eyebrow, causing faint lines to briefly appear in her smooth oval face.

Mia remembered when Judith had been stunningly beautiful, the belle of every gathering. Now, she was best described as well preserved.

"Can you imagine?" Judith complained. "I'm so grateful she can get a divorce from that fraud before he goes to jail. She's back home safe with me, just as if nothing had ever happened. We're lucky everything came out when it did—they were only married a few months, after all. It will be easy for her to forget him, after she gets over the shock." Her beautifully manicured hands clenched on the chair arms, then deliberately relaxed. She added in carefully modulated tones, "We all need to simply forget about the entire distasteful incident."

Diane added sadly, her wide mouth twisting, "She did love Ryan very much, poor girl." She glanced at Francesca, quickly averting her eyes before the young woman felt her stare. "And they're both so young."

"Love a thief?" Judith said sharply, superciliously arching her eyebrow. "Nonsense. She's much better off without him." She repeated, as though convincing herself, "much better off."

Mia quickly looked over at Francesca, who appeared to be fast asleep under her dark curtain of hair. She hoped the girl wasn't listening to their discussion of her disastrous marriage—she'd been through a lot in the last month. She didn't need to hear it all rehashed.

"I'd hope I brought her up better than that," Judith added. "My daughter would never stoop so low as to stay married to a thief, and one who stole from the family, at that." She nodded decisively, the matter settled to her satisfaction. "She'll forget he ever existed. I won't let him ruin any more of her life than he already has."

Mia said tactfully, "A big family vacation will take her mind off her troubles. Italy in early summer is too beautiful to worry about anything."

Diane's eager smile widened in anticipation. "I was so grateful that Kathleen set everything up for us in Italy—it's hard to plan a really interesting trip in a foreign country, when I don't speak the language. All the guides steer you to where everyone else goes. I want to completely immerse myself in the real Italy." She chuckled, a soft round sound, "I've been practicing my Italian like crazy. I'm sure I'll pronounce everything wrong, but I'm going to try, at least!"

"Diane, you're wasting your time," Judith said with amusement, her brow lifting. "The Italians will all speak English, since they deal with tourists every day." Judith picked up her book, a must-read from some celebrity's reading list. She turned a page desultorily, marking travel time.

Diane shrugged uncertainly, saying to Mia, "I know it doesn't really matter, I just think it's polite to be able to say hello and thank you to people."

Mia agreed warmly, "Ciao and grazie go a long way towards making new friends. I always think it's just polite to learn a few essential words when you're visiting a country."

"Such as 'where's the bathroom?'" Judith sniffed a little, leaning towards Mia, finger marking her reading place. "You never do know what kind of place you're going to actually get when you're booking overseas. I've heard some dreadful stories," Judith added. "But Kathleen set it all up for us when I told her we desperately needed a family vacation to distract Francesca. I absolutely insisted on seeing her photos of the place." She tapped her finger on her book with satisfaction, "Kathleen's, mind you, not the rental agency's. Her photos looked like the place would be all right. The Villa Bella Sorgente, she said. It makes such a difference, knowing she checked it out for us." She paused and added, "Of course, Kathleen doesn't," she coughed, "exactly go by the same standards as we do. She's lived too much in uncivilized places, for her job." She looked significantly at Mia, her still beautiful, wide set dark eyes skeptical. "I really can't answer for what little problems might arise."

"Italy is always beautiful in the summer, isn't it?" Mia said cheerfully. "I absolutely love the Veneto— some of the best food and scenery in Italy. Those stunning ancient towns." She sighed, "I'm looking forward to immersing myself in the real Italy also."

Diane beamed enthusiastically, "And flying there by private jet, thanks to Mia! Such a wonderful start to our adventure." Her red lips curved with happiness, and she lightly stroked the butter soft leather armrest. Her unpolished nails were neatly cut across broad, capable fingers. She added ingeniously to Mia, "I've never flown by private jet before. It feels like utter luxury."

"Such a convenience, not having to deal with all the airport annoyances." Judith's expensively dark head nodded graciously to Mia, her exquisitely made up eyes showing no expression—and no wrinkles whatsoever. Mia thought to herself that Judith had a very clever botox doctor. Of course, Judith's expressions had always been micro, restrained by her natural reserve.

"It's so nice you could join us as well, dear. Quite like the old days." Judith smoothly recrossed her legs, the heavy silk of her ivory designer pantsuit swishing. She tapped her book with a discretely pink nail, darting a concerned glance at Francesca's apparently sleeping figure.

"I was happy to come along; I haven't seen Kathleen in ages. The company plane would just have been deadheading to Italy in this direction—much better that we go along for the ride." Mia smiled benevolently, looking around the sleek Gulfstream IV jet with pleasure. "I'm looking forward to our Italian adventure. I haven't been in," she thought a minute, "almost two years. Too long to stay away."

"Francesca needs a nice long trip, surrounded by her family." Judith looked lovingly at the sleeping figure. "She's been through such a lot, thanks to that brute. My lawyers can handle her divorce while she's here. She can sign on the dotted line when she gets back, not have to deal with the—" she paused, "messiness." She leaned towards Mia, lowering her voice. "She's handled it all for weeks, boxing up her things and packing up wedding presents. Crying her eyes out the whole time, my poor little girl. She needed to get away from all that. Take some time to recover." She nodded in emphasis. "My lawyers assure me it will all be finished by the time we return. She and I can go back to our old life without any further problems."

Francesca's dark lashes lay lushly on almost translucent pale cheeks, closed eyes ringed in purple circles. Her soft dark hair fell around her face. If she wasn't actually asleep from utter exhaustion, she was giving a very realistic imitation. Mia said aloud, "She'll feel like herself again after two weeks in sunny Italy. We'll all be better for it." She patted Judith's elegantly manicured hand sympathetically. "Don't worry, dear, delicious cuisine, and lots of walks through those charming old towns will perk her right up."

"I agree," Judith said, her narrow shoulders relaxing slightly. "And I've organized everything for our fresh start when she gets back home. I've arranged for her things to be moved to my guest house. They're repainting it in her favorite colors while we're gone." Her pink lips uncompressed into a small smile, and she smoothed her silk slacks, resetting their elegant drape to her satisfaction. "It will be just like she never left home."

Diane frowned, but said nothing.

"I can't wait to see Kathleen again," Mia said, redirecting the conversation. "She's been working in Padua for how long?"

"She's been there for about a year," Diane told her. "We've missed her quite a lot." Her expressive mouth twisted minutely. "I always looked forward to her coming for Sunday dinner. She'd have such interesting stories to tell us about her projects." She tucked a lock of hair behind her ear.

"Something to do with olive trees?"

"Oh, yes, an awful fungus that's attacking the olive trees in the Veneto. Such a terrible shame, some of those trees are a thousand years old, can you imagine? Kathleen's been putting in some long hours, but she tells me they're making some real breakthroughs," Diane said proudly. "She thinks they'll be able to save most of them with a new spray they're testing."

"That's a relief," Mia said. "The olive trees are such an integral part of Italy. And the villa is near Padua?"

"Yes, a tiny little town named Belruscello. It's not even on most maps as more than a crossroads. Kathleen's always so clever about that kind of thing," Diane added with a smile. "She finds the most interesting places to stay, in the middle of nowhere. Remember that house on the beach in Puerto Rico? That was lovely, like a dream."

"Like a sanitation nightmare," Judith bluntly broke in, telling Mia with a disgusted look, "There were lizards crawling in my room. Actual lizards." Her brow arched. "No glass in the windows, just that netting stuff. Anything could have gotten in. Anything at all. The diseases we were exposed to," she shuddered and took out her phone, stabbing at it with agitated fingers. "It was a miracle that everyone didn't get sick. This place better be more like the photos she sent."

"I fell asleep every night to the sound of the ocean," Diane remembered wistfully. She leaned back into the soft leather.

Judith said firmly, speaking to Mia, "Don't worry, I was very clear about my expectations for accommodations this trip."

"I'm sure it will be very nice," Mia said. And she was sure it would be.

Mia loved staying in interesting, out of the way places, just as much as she enjoyed the more obvious luxuries of Spinel Resorts, her family's hotel chain, founded by her late husband. She smoothed her perfectly coiffed ash-blond hair. "And it's so lovely your family can all join us. I can't believe young Kevin," she smiled back at him, "is all grown up with a kid of his own. I remember when he was a teenager washing cars for the football team fundraiser. And now he's built a thriving business, from what I hear."

Kevin heard his name, and grinned at her in proud acknowledgment of her compliment. "Doing just fine, Ms. Mia. Just fine."

"Oh, Kevin is doing very well now," Judith added, with a bright, encouraging smile. "He didn't want any part of the family business. It completely crushed Harold at the time—you know how Harold and his brother, John, built up Parker Perches—we do most of the big stadium seating now— from absolutely nothing. They wanted to make it a family legacy, but Kevin insisted on going out on his own." Her smile thinned. "Kevin was dead set on his little plumbing business, so Harold loaned him the money to start, anyway. I gave him a lot of helpful advice, of course," she added. "It's so difficult for small businesses to get started without capital, you know, and of course banks don't want to loan new businesses money. They want a proven track record before they loan a penny at a decent rate."

Kevin's lips straightened, and his brown eyes narrowed slightly as he cut in, "We now have fifty people working for us. The largest plumbing company in our county." His shoulders pulled back proudly, and his big hands gripped the leather armrests, his knuckles whitening. He had grown from a gawky teen to a well muscled, tall man, with thinning brown hair he clipped short to soften his bald spot.

His wife, Candace, looked up at him with adoring, wide blue eyes, "Kevin's done so well, working all hours and weekends." She tossed her long, corn silk blond hair over her shoulders, carefully arranging it. Her mascara spiked eyes fluttered their laden lashes. Her ridiculously curvaceous figure was outlined with tight white slacks and a fuzzy pink sweater. She looked like a walking Barbie doll, Mia thought with an inward smile.

"Fifty people employed, just imagine," Judith bragged. "Quite a small business success story for our family, even through it's just plumbing."

"He hasn't taken a vacation in two years," Candace continued, with a brittle smile on her candy pink lips. She patted Kevin on the knee with long nails that gleamed like armor, and snuggled up against him. "He really needs some time off to relax with family."

"Can't stop for long when it's going well, honey," Kevin smiled down at her. "I don't want to lose momentum."

"You need to spend some time with Ben too," she urged. "He won't be home with us much longer. Little birds have to fly the nest sometime." She wafted her cotton candy pink nails vaguely in her offspring's direction.

Judith looked with disinterest at her nephew slouched in the rear of the plane, glued to his phone, then her eyes returned to Francesca's sleeping figure like a homing pigeon. "Sometimes, they come back," she murmured to herself, with a complacent smile.

Ben Parker hunched down in his seat, gangly legs shod with enormous neon sneakers, stretched far out into the aisle. Mia didn't know what his voice sounded like yet, since he hadn't uttered anything except teenage grunts. He was in high school, not a talkative age for most boys. He'd grow out of it in a few years.

The last member of their party was Miss Savannah Parker, Judith's niece and marketing director at Parker Perches. She had installed bulky headphones over her ears as they sat down, carefully removing large silver hoop ear rings to do so. Her long, dark hair was looped into a seemingly casual bun, low on the back of her head, and a tiny silver nose ring pierced her right nostril. She wore formfitting black Lululemon pants and a slouchy soft cashmere sweater, also in her signature black. Her lips were painted in so dark a red, they also might be considered black. Her dark eyes were rimmed in heavy kohl—black—and glued to her phone screen. The only note that jarred her wan Goth persona was her warm, tan skin. It made her look far too healthy.

"So what have you been doing lately, Diane?" Mia asked.

"Not much," Diane said, her mouth turning down. She ran a hand through her heavy brown hair, faintly streaked with whispers of silver threads. "You know, I took care of Mom when she had cancer. Dropped out of nursing school when she needed full time care." She blinked hard. "I was glad I could be there with her, at the end." Her eyes held Mia's a minute, then dropped to her capable hands, stretching her fingers out, as if they ached.

Mia said with sympathy, "I was so sorry about Sadie passing." She smiled at Diane, "I know it meant a lot to her that you were with her."

Diane nodded and shrugged minutely, brushing off sentiment. "I felt pretty lost afterwards. It took everything we had, just to keep her at home like she wanted it, not in one of those hospices." She sniffed, her eyes filling with unshed tears. "After I sold the house and paid off the medical bills, there wasn't anything left for nursing school afterwards." She shrugged again, resettling her fussy blouse around her middle and looked at Judith, "Judith kindly offered me a job helping her. I've been there ever since."

"It's not so long as all that," Mia said gently. "It's been what, two years?"

"Four, in August," Diane said, pushing her thick hair back.

"My, how time flies," Mia said, with surprise. "Have you ever thought about going back to school?"

Diane looked down at her hands, stretching the fingers out again. "I plan to eventually, but things keep coming up. I'll get around to it, maybe next year." She glanced quickly at Judith, then looked up, and smiled hopefully at Mia. "I'm looking forward to seeing Italy for the first time. I've always wanted to travel there."

"It will be a nice vacation for everyone," Mia said kindly.

Kathleen greeted them with a wave as they walked down the stairs leading off the big Gulfstream IV at Aeroporto Internazionale di Padova Gino Allegri. Bright sunlight radiated off the concrete, and the Italian sky was blue and clear.

"Mia!" Kathleen called from across the tarmac. "It's been ages!" Kathleen caught Mia on the last step, giving her an enthusiastic hug, then held the smaller woman out at arm's length, grinning. "It's good to see you, Mia."

"It's good to see you too, Kathleen. You haven't changed a bit."

"Like fun I haven't." Kathleen patted her rounded belly, sticking out like a pea in a pod on her tall, athletic frame. It was the only sign of fat on her otherwise lean figure. "Italian food is just too good not to eat."

"Why ever would you deprive yourself?" Mia smiled at her. "You look good, Kathleen." She did, too. Her luxuriant gray hair was neatly clipped in place at the back of her neck. She wore well cut gray trousers and a fitted turquoise blue polo shirt with a coordinating teal blue leather belt, stalwart staples of her quintessential preppy wardrobe, unaltered in decades.

The two women had been the best of friends since kindergarten, when Mia had politely shared her crayons with her new classmate. Kathleen carefully colored in the assignment's lines with a precisely even stroke, while Mia had treated the printed lines as mere suggestions to her artistic ability. By the end of the day, the two girls were inseparable.

They spent nights at each other's houses, vacationed with each others' families, their lives intertwined with laughter, clothes swapping, teenage tears and boyfriend angsts. At college, Mia had majored in hospitality management, and Kathleen had piled advanced science degrees on top of each other with the ease of children's blocks. They had danced at each other's weddings. Mia marrying her husband, Leo Spinel, and raising her two stepsons and their daughter together. Kathleen had only two blissful years of marriage with the love of her life, abruptly ended by an icy road and a drunk driver. After the hurricane of grief had passed, Kathleen had thrown herself into her work, publishing scientific papers as if they were her children. Now, they were both widows.

They had lost touch, then reconnected more times than Mia could count. Every time they met, it was as if they had never been apart, after the rapid chatter of catching up.

When Kathleen had asked Mia to join the Parker family in their rented Italian villa for two weeks, Mia hadn't been able to resist. Staying connected with

Kathleen was much easier now with texting and phones always in reach, but Mia had gradually lost touch with the rest of the Parker family, who'd been so much a part of her childhood, just exchanging Christmas cards or attending weddings now.

She'd adored Harold, Kathleen's older brother, with the fervor of the young child who'd been swung in the air and played ball with. Harold had always been patient with his much younger sister and her friend, throwing himself into the fun of sand castles and bike rides with visible enthusiasm. He'd been the big brother she'd never had, and always wanted.

Harold's enthusiasm had carried the rest of his siblings with him when he founded Parker Perches, going from a small local business building benches for local high schools to an international company producing stadium seating for massive arenas. His brother, John, had joined in the hands-on building, then supervised construction, while his sister, Sadie, had manned the company offices. Even Kathleen had contributed, using her chemical expertise to devise new coatings that made the seating last decades without visible wear.

The business had thrived, and the Parker family had too, for a while. John and his wife had been the first to fall, leaving their sons, Jeffery and Kevin, in Harold and Judith's care. Childless, they had raised them as their own, taking Jeffrey into the family business, and supporting Kevin when he started his business. Sadie's daughters, Diane and Judy, had expanded the pool of cousins, until family vacations took place in sprawling rentals.

When, after many years of raising her nephews, Judith had Francesca, the couple had been over the moon with joy. Nothing was too good for their adorable baby daughter, and the built-in older brothers and cousins had thought the same.

Judy, Diane's sister, had had her daughter, Savannah, very young, then left the girl orphaned in her teens. Harold had stepped up again, sending Savannah to the best boarding school and college money could buy, eventually welcoming her under the protective wing of the family business.

After Harold had died several months ago, Judith had taken over the reins with firm, capable hands. She and Jeffery, as the senior family members, had guided the business, into a continuation of their solid success. There might be gaps in the family business tree, like Kevin's plumbing business, but each generation of Parkers planned to participate in Parker Perches, keeping the family company strong, generation by generation.

Mia had joined this family trip, not just because she loved Italy, and looked forward to seeing her dear friend Kathleen—both true—but not the real reason. She'd come because Kathleen had an unusual note of worry in her voice when she'd asked Mia to come. Kathleen was not a worrier by nature, taking each crisis with scientific detachment. Mia had only seen her collapse once, on the death of her husband. She'd recovered, as much as anyone ever does from a great tragedy, and deliberately moved on, creating an ideal life for her altered circumstances.

It had not been merely her imagination that Kathleen was worried. As she greeted her family with hugs and cheek kisses, Mia noticed tension in her jaw, a crease between her eyes. A new restraint was in her hugs, her back pats more deliberate, not as casually eager as she'd been in the past. Mia wondered what was going on.

Francesca had wakened on the approach, yawning like a sleepy cat, unfurling her blanket cocoon. She looked like she'd needed a good long sleep, to eat well, then perhaps another sleep or two. She stood blinking, her striking, long lashed gray eyes hidden behind oversized dark sunglasses, her airy sundress dancing brightly in the hot tarmac wind.

Mia wondered if Francesca's abrupt divorce was the reason for Kathleen's invitation. If so, she didn't know what she could do to help. Perhaps Kathleen just wanted her to help smooth over an awkward family vacation? She would know soon enough.

Mia nodded to the captain as he descended the stairs, a straight backed young man with flyaway brown hair. "Thanks for the smooth flight, Nate."

"No problem, Ms. Mia. I'll see you back here in two weeks, God and weather willing."

"Are you sure you don't want to spend the night at our villa before you leave?"

He grinned, "No, thank you. We're going to treat ourselves to a nice Italian dinner, and turn in early at a nearby hotel. The crew needs to get going early tomorrow to get to the conference pickups. Tomorrow will be a tour of Europe, pretty much, while we pick everyone up."

"Ciao, then," Mia said.

He tipped his captain's hat to her with a grin. "Arrivederci, Ms. Mia." He and his crew strode off with the haste of the young, eager to explore a new city.

She smiled at his cheerful enthusiasm, and turned back to the Parkers.

Kathleen had rented a large Mercedes van—the only vehicle that could hold the entire family. Kevin and Ben loaded the considerable weight of luggage into the back. Kathleen took the wheel, driving the unwieldy vehicle around the curving Italian roads with precision and verve. She was clearly used to the fast pace of the twisting Italian roads. Judith, as the matriarch, perched in the prime viewing seat up front, with Francesca ensconced directly behind her.

The landscape changed from swathes of flat fields with crops growing to the green covered mountains of the Parco Regionale dei Colli Euganei. Massive villas popped up in every terracotta roofed village, like so many roosters guarding their flocks, intricate ironwork gates leading to elaborate palaces. Most of the warm array of stucco houses fronted directly on the street, ancient wooden doors painted and peeling in layers, revealing colorful centuries.

They skirted the mountainous park through terraced vineyards unfolding on every hillside. Kathleen waved her hand and shouted back something unintelligible over the engine. Mia guessed they were nearing their destination as the roads narrowed, and towns became smaller. She looked with interest as they passed through a charming town piazza. A massive fountain splashed in the center, and a motley crew of kids intent on a ball game took up half the piazza. Cars slowed to drive around the game, seemingly used to the detour.

At the outskirts of the small town, a solid stucco wall went on for miles, before it was broken by ponderous wrought iron gates, open graciously wide for their visit. Smoothly raked gravel crunched under the van tires. They climbed the gently sloping hill, the drive bracketed by manicured lime trees, and hazed by golden streaks of sunlight filtering through their bright green leaves. The drive ended in a sweeping courtyard, surrounded by a sprawling villa of a warm ochre stucco. A venerable well, massive stonework girded by ancient ironwork, dominated the courtyard. Terracotta pots of red geraniums made bright splashes of color against the age softened walls.

"What a lovely place!" Mia told Kathleen, as she cut the engine. "I feel like we stepped back in time a few centuries."

"It has a wonderful atmosphere, doesn't it? One of my colleagues had his family reunion here last year. He couldn't stop talking about this villa. I thought it'd be perfect for our family gathering."

"It looks very nice, Kathleen," Judith approved. "Very well kept."

"He said the meals were fabulous." Kathleen winked at Kevin. "That growing boy of yours will be well fed."

Kevin grinned back at his aunt. "You would not believe how much Ben can eat at a sitting—then be back for snacks in an hour."

They piled out of the van, all laughing with excitement. They'd traveled around the world for this family adventure. After the sterile sameness of the airport and car ride, the warm sun and the ancient building felt like they were finally arriving somewhere very different from back home, truly starting their adventure.

The large courtyard, big enough for a dozen cars or more, was ringed by low outbuildings and another wall. In ancient history, it must have been defensible once the substantial gates were closed, with the smooth stucco walls against the perimeter, and windows facing the safety of the courtyard. Only easily shuttered windows had been presented to threats from the outside, though Mia could tell there had been new vista windows added to make the villa more pleasant for modern life. One side of the square had clearly been the stables in a past generation, the stall doors replaced by neat garage doors in the same green as the shutters on the main house, and the upper haylofts converted into apartments. Two more buildings looked like additional guest cottages carved from older uses. Mia noticed, to her delight, one round stone tower had dovecote holes at the very top.

The main villa building was fronted in an arched columned veranda, with a balcony above. The stone tiles of the veranda met the gravel of the courtyard seamlessly. Round humps of terracotta tiles quilted the roof in a range of colors and ages, from faded and pale, alive with moss, to crisp and new, in the colors of the setting sun.

A single Alfa Romeo 4C was parked like a shiny red toy in front of the garage, looking terribly anachronistic, as if it'd traveled there through a time machine. "Nice car," Ben commented with glimmers of passion appearing in his eyes, as he walked over to the little two seater for a closer look. It was the first thing he'd said the entire trip.

A tall, lean man with close cropped gray hair, striking silver eyes, and a commanding posture strode out of the villa, closing the heavy, carved wooden door with a thunk. "Hi, Ben, like my rental? Have to drive an Italian car when you're in Italy, you know."

"Hi, Uncle Randall. Can I drive it?" Ben asked eagerly.

"Not unless you have a valid license here," Randall Green easily rejoined. "How're you doing, Mia, Kathleen? Judith, good to see you. And Francesca," he paused a beat, then quickly asked, "How was your flight, honey? Smooth?"

"The flight was fine, Uncle Randall. Slept like a rock the whole way." She put both arms around the big man, and hugged him like she was drowning, and clinging to a rock in the ocean for dear life. "Nice to fly private, huh?" She kept one pale, but well muscled arm wrapped around him.

Randall pulled Mia to him with his other arm, for a bear hug. Smiling, she hugged her old friend back. "Little Mia, lovely as always. Glad you came along with the rest of our gang." He slapped Kevin on the back. "Good to see you, man. I think Ben's shot up a foot since I saw him last."

Kevin slapped him back. "Uncle Randall, glad you're here."

His wife came up, and pecked Randall on the cheek with a loud smack, leaving a bright lipstick print on his stubbly cheek. "Me too, Randy. Oops, sorry."

Smiling, he wiped the pink splotch off his cheek. "Looking good, Candace. You'll enjoy someone else cooking for once, eh? Get some ideas for back home."

"I'm looking forward to learning new Italian recipes to wow the girls with," she told him, patting her tightly controlled stomach. "I'll have to keep up the exercise though, not let things slide."

"Kathleen, you found us a gorgeous place," Diane said. She twirled around, taking it all in, smiling from ear to ear. "A real Italian villa, all to ourselves. It's like a dream come true."

Francesca, still clutching Randall's arm, looked around at the bright sunlight and warm terracotta and smiled tentatively, as if her cheek muscles weren't used to the movement. "It's beautiful. Really old, like going back in a history book."

"Is anyone going to help us with the bags, or do we have to carry them ourselves? It looks like it's a do it yourself place," Judith commented uneasily.

Randall smoothly reassured her, "Oh, there's plenty of staff, from what I can see, but I'd be happy to carry your bags in for you. Just put mine in my room. Pretty nice, with a view of the pool."

Judith said, "Kevin can carry mine." He came forward, as ordered. "If you'd just get those bags of mine, and put them wherever they're supposed to go, I'd appreciate it, dear."

"Sure, Aunt Judith. No problem." He hoisted the three bags easily and headed for the main door, calling back, "Candace, Ben, could you grab ours and follow along?"

Without a word, Ben stopped ogling the car and got the bags, thoughtfully leaving his mother with the lightest one. He followed in his father's wake, the sullen look back on his face.

The rest followed behind slowly, enjoying their first impressions of the villa, reluctant to be cooped up inside after the long flight. Randall scooped up an armful of bags, mostly Mia's usual mountain of luggage. "Still don't travel light, do you?" he chuckled. "I remember that camping trip we went on when I had to make a second trip back just for your stuff. Your luggage always stacks taller than you do."

Mia answered pertly, "I hope you remember I was the only one who brought marshmallows to roast, too. And the chocolate and graham crackers."

He laughed heartily. "That I do. Harold and I made ourselves sick eating most of them."

"It's because you burned them to torches, not roasting them evenly like you're supposed to. Who'd want to eat char?"

He kept laughing, as she opened the heavy door for him. His hands were full with her luggage, after all. "Mia, you haven't changed. You might as well be ten years old, with pigtails."

"I never wore pigtails," she informed him, to more laughter.

They spilled into the grand entrance hall. After the bright sun and heat of the courtyard, the stone and stucco of the thick walls felt cool and dark, a cocoon enveloping them in dim history. Ancient oak beams structured the room, with terracotta tile floors spanning

24

their spreads. Faint ochres and greens from medieval stencils decorated the cornices and highlighted the windows.

"Isn't anyone here?" Judith questioned, a note of annoyance in her voice. The men dropped the luggage, waiting for the next step of their journey without encumbrances.

"Teresa, that's the housekeeper, was here a minute ago," Randall said. He peered around as if she might appear from thin air, then tried calling, "Hello?"

Silence. A few dust motes danced in the rays of sunlight leaking in, giving a slight shimmer to the light.

Savannah walked around the room, her long black hair swinging like a dark sheet. She'd stripped off her sweater in the warm sunlight, and was wearing a black spaghetti strapped top that enhanced her tan skin. She opened one door, then another, looking inside the magnificent rooms curiously, the taller Ben peering over her shoulder. "I don't see anyone here."

"Where'd everyone go?" Randall tried again, louder. "Ciao? The rest of the group's arrived. Anyone?" His voice echoed in the massive hall, floating up the stairs, and dying away to nothing in the still quiet.

He tried again, booming through the tall rooms, "Hello!"

The strident roar of a mower started up outside, far away in a field. Sunlight hazed the dim darkness of the hall and trickled down from windows slit into the upper floor walls. Ben fingered a gong and the mallet beside it suspiciously.

"Don't even think about it," his mother said quickly. "That's probably to call guests to dinner."

They heard footsteps hurrying down the hall, a quick rap tap tap on the hard tiles, and harsh breathing as if someone had run up the stairs in a hurry. Still breathless, a welcoming "Buona sera! Buona sera!" proceeded the bouncing ball of a woman with short, chubby legs and a white apron moving rapidly toward them, hands outstretched in heartfelt welcome. Her thick hair, unfortunately a rather obviously dyed black, was pulled back in a heavy, smooth bun low on her neck. In perfect, but thickly accented English, she rapidly added, still puffing for air between words, "The Parker family, here at last! I am glad you have made it. Those roads," she crossed herself, "you never know when you arrive. The young men, they drive like maniacs." She held out her plump hand to Kevin. "I'm Signora Teresa, la governante of Villa Bella Sorgente." She beamed at them, unreservedly.

Kevin shook her hand briefly, "Kevin Parker, nice to meet you," then gestured to Judith, "This is my aunt, Judith Parker."

Judith nodded to Teresa, saying limply, "It has been a long trip. I'm afraid I'm ready to see my room."

She did look tired, Mia thought. Judith might be any age, from her appearance. She hadn't changed much in the decades Mia had known her, her perfect oval face unmarred by wrinkles, due to expensive treatments and meticulous care. But she must be feeling her actual age after the journey, especially after Kathleen's enthusiastic driving.

"Oh, of course, of course. Our guests often like to wash and lie down for a few minutes when they arrive," Teresa said with an easy smile. "Let me see, your apartment lies on the courtyard, as you requested, the other rooms are upstairs in the main building. Except for," she looked around the group for individuals, "Signora Kathleen Sutton? She is also on the courtyard, with you. You are all a family, yes?"

Kathleen stepped forward, "I'm Kathleen. Yes, it's a family vacation."

"Ah, good. We will make a wonderful celebration, then. To come so far together as a family is quite an occasion!" Her crisp white apron rustled as she drew out enormous antique keys from among its many folds. There was no chance anyone might wander off with one of these weights in their pocket. "Let me show le signoras to your rooms. "Salvatore, my husband, will bring your luggage when he is done mowing. Will the others prefer to wait in the sitting room or the veranda?" she gestured outside.

"The veranda would be lovely," Mia spoke for the group. She always preferred being outside in the sunlight after being cooped up traveling. Leaving the luggage in a pile in the hall, they trouped back outside.

Chairs scattered with pristine white cushions and nearby tables were carefully placed under the shaded veranda spanning the building. "I thought there was a pool?" Judith questioned as she looked around. The smooth stone floor felt cool in the shade.

"There is, there is, to the side of the villa," Teresa answered quickly. "It is still too cold for me, this early in the season, but your young people will enjoy it."

"It's not heated?"

"It is," Teresa gave a dramatic shudder, "but if the sun is not very bright, it still is not warm to me."

"I see," Judith agreed, with a satisfied nod, as if checking the villa features off a mental list. "Kevin, dear, would you mind bringing my bags to my room now? I can't wait to change out of travel clothes."

"Sure, Aunt Judith," Kevin obediently trailed the little group with Judith's bags as they headed for the small buildings skirting the main courtyard. As they opened Judith's door, Mia relaxed into one of the comfortable cushioned chairs to wait.

Candace collapsed into the chair beside her, commenting, "Wouldn't you know she'd have Kev fetching and carrying for her from the start?" She crossed her long legs with a petulant look.

Mia soothed, "It's been a long trip." She stretched her arms, feeling the tightness ease a little. "Judith is probably feeling her age and doesn't feel up to lifting luggage. I know I don't, and she's older than me." She stretched in another direction, twisting in the chair.

"Yeah, you're right," Candace agreed. She visibly forced a smile back onto her deeply dimpled cheeks. "It's been a long trip. And Judith is getting old." She tried to keep the slight flicker of satisfaction off her face at the thought, but failed. Instead, she added, with her toothy smile, "We'll have to take really good care of her this trip." Her bright blue eyes strayed to her son.

Ben leaned over Savannah in a mock monster pose, photo bombing her. Savannah, oblivious, had pursed her mouth until her lips looked like a blood dark trout gasping for air, and snapped multiple photos of herself, with red geraniums against the warm stucco of the building for a backdrop.

Candace said, forcing a laugh, "Savannah just loves adding to her socials, you know? Kids." She shook her head. "She's a sweet kid, really. Just likes the goth bit, right now."

"My daughter was the same way when she was younger," Mia said. "She's one of the media contributors at Spinel Resorts now, besides her accounting job there."

"Really?" Candace laughed. "I wouldn't have guessed accounting would have pretty things to share."

"Oh, she takes photos of hotels on business trips, not her paperwork," Mia laughed. "We like having several different points of view for our hotels. That way it's always fresh, not such an over processed feeling. It feels more like a big family, with a lot of our team contributing."

"Makes sense," Candace took out a shiny gold lipstick case. "Of course, Parker Perches doesn't really need to advertise to the masses, like hotels do. You need a good quality bench, you buy a Parker." With no need for a mirror, she carefully touched up her already perfect lipstick, mimicking Savannah's pucker. Mia refrained from her own instinct to touch up her lips too, just a little.

"What's Ben planning on for his career? Is he going in with Kevin or something else?" she asked instead.

Candace snapped her lipstick closed. "Kev wants Ben to join the plumbing business, of course. Start their own family dynasty, not be dependent on Parker Perches forever," she added with a little laugh. She shrugged, her prominent round breasts jiggling with the movement. "Plumbing is hard work, and someone has to show up whenever a client calls, no matter the time of night. When we started, I made all Kev's appointments, and did all the paperwork. Made sure Kev had the supplies he needed. And raised Ben too." She smiled with the memory. "Those were some days, let me tell you. I never stopped to breathe once."

"You must have been busy."

"I know. Now he's successful, he's hired a business manager and a service for appointments." She grinned, showing white square teeth around her perfect pink lips. "Now, I get to play. And raise the kid, of course. Ben graduates from high school next year."

"It sounds like you've earned a break. That must be a nice change," Mia told her.

"Yeah, it sure is. After working my butt off, it's nice to kick back a little—" she broke off as she saw Kevin's easy stride returning across the courtyard and smiled her toothpaste ad grin. "Oh, good, Judith is settled in." She raised her voice in a slightly nasal whine, "Did the room meet her standards?"

Kevin leaned down and pecked her on the cheek. "Yeah, they put her in the best room in the place, like Kathleen asked. Pretty view of the vineyards on the other side of the building. She's happy with it. Hope our room has a view that good."

Candace leaned back against him and smiled, curving into his body suggestively. "Trust me, you'll like the view."

He smiled down at her, then said, "So, we'll all get together for dinner tonight? Will there be time to explore this place before that?"

Mia smiled and looked at the golden sunlight hazing the distant trees. "I think it will be nearly dark by the time we get to our rooms—we should be able to see the sunset before dinner, at least."

"Yeah, we'll have to check the grounds out tomorrow," Candace agreed. ""I'm not twisting an ankle in the dark, on the first day!" She swung her pink strappy sandal with its little kitten heel.

"I'm looking forward to walking down to that town we passed through on our way here. I think I'll stroll down in the morning," Mia said.

Candace laughed, a slightly grating tone, "I'm not exactly a bright and early morning bird."

"No, you like your beauty sleep, honey," Kevin agreed, with an affectionate smile. He patted her shoulder. "Plenty of time to see everything. We're here two weeks, after all."

2

Dinner Party

Before dinner, they met back on the veranda for drinks and appetizers, under the flickering light of gas-lit torches. The heady perfumed white roses draping the porch columns wafted through the air, mixing with the sweet scent of citrus blossoms. The night sky seemed very blue and deep next to the wavering light of the torches.

"Whatever drink you want, we've got it," said a skinny girl with unwashed, but carefully styled hair. An orange miniskirt and a candy apple red strapless top sagging inward at her clavicle did nothing to enhance her figure. She forcefully proffered a startling array of drink options, wheeled out on an antique brass bar cart, as Mia approached the gathering.

Mia smiled at the girl in greeting. "Buona sera. I'm Mia."

"Mia. I'm Anna. What do ya want?" she demanded impatiently, nasal voice slightly muffled as she rolled candy from one side of her mouth to the other. Under a heavy coat of makeup, her face was pockmarked with acne. She was much the same age as Savannah, but seemed older than the American girl, by her manner. To the world, she presented a been there seen that blasé attitude, where nothing novel would be found under the sun. Not a trace of a welcoming smile lurked on her face, just a desired to serve Mia her drink, and move on to the next person, so she could finish her assigned task.

"Hmm, Anna, I think I'd like something local tonight, something a little light. Can you mix me a spritz Veneziano?"

Anna tapped a foot impatiently. "You mean an Aperol Spritz—Prosecco and Aperol?" Her blunt English was American accented, by way of Hollywood.

"With a splash of soda water and slice of orange, please."

"Yeah, yeah, I know. No problem." Anna turned to the polished drinks cart, and Mia heard hard candy crunch in her mouth as she mixed the cocktail with practiced ease. She smoothly sliced a fresh orange, adding the final garnish to the faceted lead crystal glass, and handed it to Mia.

Mia took a sip. Bitter and sweet, with the fizz of refreshing bubbles. "Perfect. Thanks, Anna." She sat down in a chair next to Francesca. "What are these delightful looking little things?" she asked about the colorful spread of creations speared with toothpicks.

"Spunciotti," Anna told her. "The baccalà is good." She shrugged expressively. "Everything, but everything, Signora Teresa makes is good. She is a fabulous chef." Her sudden enthusiasm made obvious her primary reason for working at the villa.

"Teresa is the chef? I thought she was the housekeeper?"

Anna shook her head, correcting her. "I do cleaning and serve the meals. She tells me and the others what to do. And tells Salvatore what to do, as well," she grinned wickedly. "Her husband, Signor Salvatore, is the head gardener. Signora Teresa cooks so beautifully." A smile flashed briefly on her narrow, thin face at the thought of those meals.

"I see." Mia took some of the creamed cod, whipped to a froth with olive oil, and spread on dainty slices of white bread. "Oh, you're right, the baccalà is very good."

"I told you. Everything she makes is good." Anna hurried back to make Randall his drink, a simple soda water topped with one of the fresh orange slices.

Francesca was gazing across the courtyard, obviously lost in her head. "So, Francesca, which appetizer do you like best?"

Francesca looked at Mia, as if she'd forgotten she was there. "Which appetizer?" She looked down at the tray. "Oh, I guess the cheeses. That one's really good," she pointed with a delicate pink polished finger.

"Monte Veronese?" Mia took an exploratory bite of a sliver of the hard white cheese. It was good, slightly sweet. She tried some lemony Morlacco cheese, next to it. "Very good as well."

Randall came over to join them. "I'm sticking with meatballs. You can't miss with meatballs." Perfectly brown and juicy meatballs were on their own plate, with just a sprinkling of parsley brightening them. He popped one in his mouth, then grabbed another.

"So, what have you been doing, Uncle Randall?" Francesca asked, taking another piece of cheese.

"Still based in Germany," he told her. "Love it, great country. Best bread in the world." He took another bite with gusto. "Italian food is pretty damn good, though. But German bread, can't get enough."

Francesca laughed a little. "We'll eat all we want this trip, and take some long walks to burn it off."

"I run five kilometers every morning," he patted his lean stomach. "Never gain an ounce with that routine. All about routine."

"I don't think I'll start that routine this week," Francesca laughed and took a sip of her white wine. "Too much like work." Her wavy black hair shimmered with orange highlights in the flickering torchlight.

"Want to walk into that charming little town with me tomorrow, Francesca?" Mia asked.

"Love to. We can have breakfast in town, if we leave early," she suggested, swinging her neatly shod foot under her flowery gossamer dress.

Mia wondered why Francesca didn't want to have breakfast at the villa with her family. "Sounds like fun," she agreed, a little curious at the suggestion. Perhaps

Francesca wanted a break from her family after the long trip together, like any young woman might.

Kathleen joined the group, then Savannah and Ben came around the corner, laughing. "Fantastic pool," Ben told them enthusiastically. "I'm taking a dip first thing in the morning."

Savannah had arrayed herself in a tight fitting black gown, dripping with black lace, and had added another layer to the kohl rimming her eyes. Her white powdered face was all big dark eyes and blood red lipstick, like a young, beautiful vampire in the medieval setting, which was probably the look she was going for.

Savannah told Ben, "I'll be there watching. I bet you jump out again from the cold."

"Not unless you go too."

"Oh, we'll both jump in at once," Savannah told him. "We can always get back out. I don't mind the cold."

"Fine," Ben agreed. He eyed the well stocked bar with an anticipatory gleam.

"No alcohol for you," Randall told him pointedly. "You're underage."

"We're in Italy," Ben whined. "Don't be so lame, Uncle Randall."

"Doesn't matter," he told him. "Up to your parents whether you have a glass of wine with dinner."

"They're not down yet. It's not fair," Ben continued whining until Randall made a firm cut it out motion with his hand.

Savannah, noticing Francesca's wine, told Anna, "A cabernet, per favore," in a very superior tone. She sipped the red wine with her matching blood red lips, smirking at Ben.

Diane entered in a rush, her cheeks scarlet from hurry. "Am I late? I just unpacked. Judith needed a little help."

"Never late for a good thing," Randall told her, with a smile. "Have a seat, honey."

She sat down next to Francesca. Anna hovered, demanding, "What do ya want?"

"Oh, I don't know," Diane looked around for inspiration. "What's everyone else having? White wine?"

Anna took that as her order and poured it out, handing it to her, with a disdainful shrug.

"Thanks." Diane sipped the cold wine with pleasure, and looked around with obvious enjoyment. "Isn't this the most amazing place? I feel like we stepped back in time a hundred years. Dinner by torchlight, even. So romantic..."

Judith called out from across the dim courtyard. "Hello, everyone! Looking forward to our first Italian feast?" She hesitated, then asked, "It's so dark—I can't see a thing out here. Can you turn on the lights?"

Anna looked like she hadn't heard the request for a second, then sauntered over to flip the switch. The flickering warm glow of torchlight was suddenly overpowered by bright white security lights, illuminating Judith's path across the courtyard.

"It looks like everyone's started without me," she commented. "I'd better catch up. What is the wine?"

"Oh, just have a glass. Have another if you like it," Randall said with a grin, holding his glass up in a toast, "Now you're here, we can start the party."

Anna took that as Judith's order, and handed her a wine glass.

"Oh, really," Judith looked confused, then came over to sit by Francesca. She leaned over, "I've been thinking, dear, that after dinner you should change rooms with Kathleen, stay on the courtyard next to me. I don't like the idea of you all alone over there."

Francesca looked up, startled. "But I just unpacked. And Kathleen's probably unpacked too. I can't do that to her."

Kathleen heard Francesca's exclamation, "And Kathleen what?" she asked in a warm, pleasant voice.

"Kathleen, you wouldn't mind trading your room for Francesca's, would you? She'd rather be next to me, under the circumstances."

"Oh, but," Francesca weakly protested.

Kathleen shrewdly glanced at Francesca's face, and chuckled lightheartedly. "Don't be silly, Judith. We're all settled into our rooms and no one wants to repack all over again." She added, "It's just two weeks, not like we're moving here permanently."

"I really think," Judith began, her brow furrowed.

"Oh, Judith, everything is just fine as it is," Kathleen laughed deliberately. "Don't be such a perfectionist. Everything is great."

"If you're both sure, then I wouldn't dream of changing a thing," Judith smiled at Francesca, warm concern in her eyes. "As long as you're both happy."

Francesca took a sip of wine and another bite of cheese. Her smile didn't quite reach her deep set gray eyes, luminous in the shadows.

"So, what shall we do tomorrow?" Judith asked the little group, a bright smile on her face. "Let's see, we're having dinner again at the villa tomorrow night, but we'll have lots of time for activities all day. Maybe tour Padua? Or Vicenza? So many sights to see in both, and neither is very far away." She looked for a hint from Francesca.

Francesca took another bite, chewing thoughtfully, noncommittal.

Kathleen glanced around at the group, most of whom clearly didn't want to get back into another vehicle anytime soon, then said, "Let's play it by ear. It's nice to just drink in the relaxing atmosphere here." She stretched out her arms.

"It's all very well for you, my dear, you live in Padua," Judith told her. "The rest of the family doesn't have that long in Italy. We have to see everything while we're here."

Kathleen smiled mischievously, "You can always come back to visit me, if there's something you missed. I do have a spare room."

Francesca chuckled, "Watch out, I might take you up on that. There's so much to see here, isn't there?"

"Any time." Kathleen looked around the group. Judith's finger tapped on her wine glass. She clearly wanted a firm itinerary for tomorrow, so she could check that off her mental hostess list. "Let's plan a few things in the area we can't miss." Judith's mouth relaxed from its thin line, and she leaned back in her chair a little. Kathleen thought aloud, "We're staying at this amazing place, a once in a lifetime experience, really. Let's plan to explore the villa and grounds tomorrow, walk to the village, go swimming, all the unique things we have right here."

Judith nodded pleased agreement.

Kathleen continued, "Then, we can explore farther afield the next day. We definitely want to see the Scrovegni Chapel, Giotto's masterpiece. The ceiling is a deep, deep blue, true lapis ultramarine, with gold stars. Looking up into it, you feel as if it's a million years of history—all the way back to the fourteenth century. And we'll absolutely go on the Palladian villa tour in and around Vicenza. We can walk the Palladian route through Vicenza, and end up at the Basilica di Monte Berico, stopping for gelato on the way." She laughed and shrugged, "And anyone who feels like driving, instead of walking can meet up at the villas in the van. We can do either, depending on the weather forecast."

Judith nodded in agreement, taking Kathleen's plan as her own. "Excellent itinerary, Kathleen. It's not as if we get to stay in such a unique place often—I want to make sure our young people get to see everything."

"A little immersion in la dolce vita is nice too," Randall added. "Good for the soul," he added, smiling at Judith.

With a look at her watch, Anna broke in, "It's time now to go in to dinner. Is everyone here?" She looked around, "I thought there were more in your group?"

Judith answered, "Kevin and Candace aren't here yet." She smiled tightly, "They're usually late."

"The food will get cold. Signora Teresa will not like that," Anna warned, clearly nervous about a delay.

"Oh, but surely she can wait a few minutes, so we're all together," Judith started to object, but Randall stopped her.

"If the chef says it's time for dinner, then we'll go in. I know I'm hungry," he told Judith, "They'll meet us when they get there, and catch up. Let the parents relax a little by themselves." He held out one arm to Judith and the other to Francesca. "May I escort you in to dinner, miladies?" he asked, smiling.

A small smile on her face, Francesca took his proffered arm. "Why, yes, please, Uncle Randall."

"If you're sure they won't mind," Judith began, with concern.

Mia told her, "Just relax, Judith. It really doesn't matter when they get here. If their food is a little cold because they're tardy, that's on them." She followed Anna's skinny figure into the villa.

"I suppose not," Judith agreed, adding brightly, "It is a vacation, after all." She followed on Randall's other arm.

The dining hall, far too grand to be called simply a room, was paneled in dark wood, pockmarked with ancient worm holes, and gleaming with polish. The fireplace surround met the high ceiling. At the far end, a beautifully veined stone, replete with acanthus leaves

42

and ancient heraldic devices, was worn by time. Diane went over to the massive centerpiece and lightly traced the outline of a leaf with her finger. She said, almost in a whisper, "So old...I wonder how many families have dined here, children grown old with the room?" She looked around her with awe.

Judith scanned the majestic room with a satisfied smile, "Very nice, very nice indeed." She took her place at the head of the table as Randall smoothly pulled out her chair for her. As the oldest man of the family group, Randall sat at the opposite end, next to the fireplace.

Savannah spoke up, "It's a good thing that huge fireplace isn't lit, Uncle Randall. You'd fry." She grinned at him, the smile breaking the rigid perfection of her face into the less angst ridden simplicity of a pretty young woman, her smooth sheet of dark hair looped and braided in an intricate updo that fitted well in the medieval setting.

"I expect they move the table a little during the winter," he replied, looking into the massive stone opening, near enough to engulf him in its maw.

"How?" Diane pulled up on the table, curiously. It didn't budge a millimeter. "This thing is solid oak. It must weigh a ton." She hurriedly sat down with a thump, as Teresa bustled into the room. Diane's face went beet red at being caught trying to move the furniture, even if the housekeeper didn't notice.

With a triumphant flourish, Teresa placed a huge platter of risotto directly in front of Ben. "See, we feed you lots, don't worry, I know how to feed young men.

Lots and lots." She laughed heartily. "Risi e bisi, il primo piatto." Tiny little spring peas cascaded down the slowly oozing rice. Ben practically drooled at the sight. She smiled with satisfaction at his expression as Anna brought in a second platter, brimming with pasta. "Bigoli in salsa," she announced proudly as Anna placed the heavy platter at the other end of the table. She watched Ben's expression closely as his eyes followed the plate, and beamed at his blissful look, "They love to eat, the young men, do they not?" Chuckling to herself, she bustled back to the kitchen.

Anna slinked around the room, filling glasses to the brim with a crisp Soave, then paused, hand positioned on her narrow hip. "Everyone good?" daring them to reply. Everyone's mouth was too full to answer, so she followed Teresa back to the kitchen.

Utter silence ruled the room, while the food got its due of appreciation. Platters passed around the table, there were happy murmurs of delight at the superb cooking, and cutlery clinked.

Ben helped himself to seconds for the bigoli, asking as he heaped pasta onto his plate, "What is this stuff? It's really good."

Mia answered, "Anchovies and onions, a classic Veneto dish."

Ben froze a moment in horror, then continued chewing with a ruminative look on his face. "I thought anchovies were those disgusting things people order on pizza."

Kathleen laughed, "No, bigoli in salsa is much better than that. They're simmered down for the sauce."

Ben screwed up his face, then took another bite. "Well, I like this, anyway. As long as they aren't anywhere near my pizza."

They all laughed at the expression on his face, relaxed with the good food and wine.

For the second course, Teresa served Ben directly again, placing an impressive leg of lamb next to his plate. "Tagliata di lombo d'agnello alle rosmarino," she announced with pride. "Eat!" she ordered, as she left the room. Anna placed a tray of grilled zucchini at the other end of the table, in front of Randall, brushing her scrawny leg suggestively against his thigh.

He leaned away from her, looking across the room, and saying quickly, "Well, here come the honeymooners!"

Anna smirked, then sashayed her thin hips in her orange mini, as she left the room, managing to brush past Kevin on her way out the door. He didn't notice.

The two were glowing like newlyweds, as they entered the dining hall. "What a great place you found us, Kathleen!" Kevin was grinning from ear to ear. He pulled out an ornately carved chairs for his wife, bowing as he said, "Milady."

Candace sat, smoothing her gossamer blonde hair back on her shoulders, and helped herself to a slice of lamb. "Looks delicious."

"You missed the first course," Ben told her. "They had anchovies in pasta."

"Oh no," Candace commiserated with a laugh that deepened her dimpled cheeks. "You hate anchovies."

"This was good," Ben told her appreciatively. "I had seconds."

Candace chuckled, "I never thought I'd hear you say that!"

Judith added, with a smile, "Teresa is quite a good cook, as you can see. It's too bad you missed the first course."

Candace smiled at Kevin, and he smiled back, "Oh, we don't mind."

Dessert was two trays of fritole, small, round fried doughnuts, filled with a rich cream. Teresa clearly intended one tray solely for Ben, placing the golden mound in front of him, her dancing dark eyes watching for his reaction.

He dove in, licking sticky fingers as he inhaled half the little doughnuts in a quick attack. "Wow, Signora Teresa, those are good. Really good. Thanks. Grazie."

"I knew you would like them." The little round woman looked around at her guests with approval. "Tomorrow, breakfast is at eight-thirty. Please arrive on time so the food is hot."

"I'll be there," Ben told her fervently. They all laughed.

"We'd all better be there," Savannah eyed Ben's personal platter of doughnuts, already almost gone. "If we want anything to eat."

3

A Nice Walk

Mia woke the next morning to a quiet tap on her door. She wrapped her luxurious silk bathrobe around herself and opened the door.

Francesca stood waiting outside. "Are you still up for a walk to the village? If you'd rather sleep in or have breakfast with the group, don't worry about it." She smiled at Mia, uncertain of her reception.

Mia opened the door wide. "A morning walk sounds delightful." She headed for her bathroom. "I'll need about fifteen minutes to get ready."

"No problem. I'll see if Aunt Kathleen wants to come too."

"Good idea." Mia was already arranging her soft blond hair. "I'll meet you in the courtyard." She placed delicate apricot colored spinel earrings in her ears, then chose an airy top to match. She smiled at herself in the mirror, and felt ready to start the day.

When Mia arrived downstairs, Kathleen waited with Francesca in the shimmering golden light of an

Italian morning. Their feet crunched on the gravel as they made their way down the long drive, light streaming through the alley of pollarded lime trees. The world was touched by a haze of golden glamour.

Francesca seemed almost giddy, enjoying escaping for a few minutes from her loving, but concerned family. "Don't worry, I told Teresa we were going to the town, so we won't worry anyone. I really felt like a morning walk in this beautiful landscape."

"I did too," Mia agreed. "It was a long plane flight yesterday." Walking was always Mia's favorite form of exercise. She loved exploring the world around her.

"There's sure to be a place we can get a brioche and espresso," Kathleen said. "That's all I ever eat in the morning, in Italy."

"I think Teresa's mainly cooking for Ben, not us. She seems to appreciate a teenage boy's appetite," Mia laughed, remembering her two sons inhaling meals and asking for seconds—and thirds and fourths—during their teenage years.

The sun rose, as they walked down the ancient road, smoothly asphalted now, but with traces of an older road remaining along the cut stone edges. Old cobblestone ways led up tiny side streets, climbing straight up the steep mountain side. An ancient watering trough sat beneath a trickling spring, spitting from a contorted face of a stone creature. Green ivy curled around the carved hair, as if it grew from the laughing little creature's head.

Their steep vantage point high up in the mountains revealed rolling fields and forests, sprinkled with bright terracotta tile roofed villages. The vista lay before them like a magnificent quilt, showing the countryside for miles around.

Belruscello, the nearest village, wasn't far from the villa, only about a half mile. Very few cars passed the walkers. One of the local buses careened by, swerving far into the other lane to give them a wide berth. The village was still waking up as they arrived. A dog barked in a distant house. A shopkeeper swept the cobbles in front of her store in a furious attack that clouded the air around her, and a neat little man turned the shiny key of his hardware store, leaving the door wide open for air and customers.

A group of old men gathered around a table outside a cafe, placidly swirling espresso, and people watching. Two young women in animated conversation pushed strollers with bundled babies, headed for the produce stand on the far side of the piazza. The shopkeeper carefully placed ripe plums on a tray, turning the fruit to show its best.

"Oh, those look delicious," Francesca said. "I'm getting a few to take back."

"I'm getting strawberries," Kathleen agreed. She looked around. "It looks like those venerable sages have found the best place for coffee. We'll follow their lead." She directed Francesca and Mia to a table outside, while she went inside the little cafe. The tiny store was dominated by a gigantic gleaming espresso machine. An elderly woman, wearing a cheerful orange scarf, peeked over the top of the scarred countertop, waiting for orders. She filled them with efficient hands, deftly taming the steaming dragon of an espresso machine.

They heard the steam churn as their brews were made. The elders at the next table nodded affably at them, clearly appreciating Francesca's dark haired beauty. She smiled back at them, ducking her head a little, embarrassed by their attention.

Kathleen returned with three thick white china mugs balanced in her hands. "The brioche are just coming out of the oven," she told them. "They'll bring them to us."

They all sat and sipped their coffee, relaxing in the timeworn ease of the piazza. The fountain splashed, catching the morning light in fiery orange. The old men talked, gossiping about their town, enjoying the sunshine, in no hurry to go anywhere.

As she sipped, Francesca visibly relaxed, her intensely cheerful chatter slowing. Finally, she sighed a little, "I'm glad we came." She gestured around the piazza, "Everything's so old here, it feels like, well," she shrugged, "all the small things I've been worrying about don't really matter, you know?"

Kathleen nodded, "Italy puts life in perspective, that's for sure." She smiled sympathetically at her niece. "Divorce is a difficult thing, Francesca. Don't let anyone tell you to just get over it. Move on at your own speed. Take your time healing."

Francesca's eyes teared up, and she blinked hard. "Thanks, Aunt Kathleen." She shrugged a little. "It's just that Mom takes it all so, so personally. She's so mad at Ryan, she still can't think about anything else." She swallowed hard. "I can't just forget about it for a while."

Kathleen patted her hand. "I'm sorry, I know it's rough right now. You'll make it through to the other side, but there's a lot of anger and grief." She looked at the young woman. "Judith is bound to feel betrayed at his theft too," she held up her hand quickly. "I know, it's nothing compared to what you've been through. But she's mad for you, and for herself."

Francesca burst out, "Don't you think I know that? My husband stole from my family." She shook her head in disgust. "Thank goodness they caught it, before he did too much damage, but," she rubbed her temples, "I still can't believe he'd do such a thing."

Kathleen asked, hesitantly, "Are you sure he did?" She carefully didn't look at Francesca's face, but out over the piazza, as she sipped her coffee.

"Yes," Francesca told her, her eyes heartbroken. "The auditors traced some of the money directly to an offshore account he had. He claimed he didn't know about it," she rolled her eyes expressively, "but the account is in his name, no one else's. I don't want to believe my own husband would steal from my family, but all the evidence points to him. Jeffery said that Ryan was the only person with access to steal that money." She held out her hands, palms down, "He did it, no question."

"If the account is in his name, he must have stolen the money." Kathleen sighed heavily. "I wouldn't have believed it of him, either. If that gives you any comfort."

Francesca let her breath out in a whoosh. "Well, at least it keeps me from feeling like I'm the only gullible one."

Mia took a sip of her cappuccino, then said, "Who hasn't been fooled by a man, one time or another? You're doing the right thing in moving on, if you're absolutely sure he's guilty. Learn from your mistakes, and rebuild your life."

Francesca nodded, "I know, it's the only thing I can do. That's why Mom constantly telling me how awful Ryan was, how much better I am without him, is driving me crazy." She held out her hands, bare of rings, tulle pink nails sparkling in the bright sunlight, and scolded herself, "And what do I do when I escape for a few minutes? I talk about Ryan again." She laughed harshly, driving away the hurt, and plastered a smile across her face. "So, Aunt Kathleen, tell me about the area. Do you like living in Italy?"

She looked around the piazza, breathing deeply, clearly forcing her body to relax. "It's really beautiful. Like something you read about in history class, an entirely new world."

A shopkeeper wheeled a rack of pretty sundresses out, bumping over the cobbles, singing as she worked. Children laughed as they tossed a soccer ball back and forth, bouncing it off their feet and knees. Francesca sighed deeply, "It's all so beautiful, such a simple life, here in the sunshine."

Mia said gently, "It is beautiful, dear, but we're tourists here. Life is much the same everywhere. Hopes and dreams, safety for yourself and your children."

"Oh, I know, it just seems—" Francesca broke off, looking wistfully at the children laughing as they played. "I know."

Kathleen cleared her throat a little. "Well, to answer your question, I do like living here, Francesca. I think we're making headway on our olive tree problem, but we're not out of the woods yet," she chuckled, "so I expect I'll live here at least two more years." She looked around the piazza, smiling, "And that's about right, I think. After a year, I'm starting to miss home. I hear of a family party, think of the Fourth of July, and enjoying a fried chicken picnic, listening to the symphony on Piedmont Park's lawn, all my family around me, and I miss that. I love Italy—I'm thoroughly enjoying my experience here. Living in a place is completely unlike visiting there. But when my project here finishes, I'll head back like a homing pigeon." She looked around the square again, drinking in the now sparkling sunlight gracing the piazza. "Not that I won't return as often as I can. Gorgeous, isn't it?"

"What's your favorite thing to do here?" Francesca asked.

"Well, I know I should say museums or something very erudite and professorial, but really, this is. Just sitting in the sun, drinking coffee or a glass of wine, and enjoying the experience. I love the museums and cathedrals, but to me, this is the best of Italy."

"Just enjoying the experience," Francesca repeated. "That sounds nice."

"La dolce vita, you know. We could all do with a bit more of that in our lives."

"Too true," agreed Francesca, nodding her head. "Okay, so that's going to be my new attitude—enjoying what comes my way."

A handsome young man, his shiny black locks of hair artfully messy, set their brioches in front of them with a flourish. "Buongiorno, signore."

They thanked him in a chorus.

"Ah, Americanas." He looked meaningfully with big dark eyes at Francesca, "There is much to explore here. I would love to show you all its hidden beauties."

Francesca blushed and tore a bite of flaky pastry off her brioche.

"I would love to show you around Belruscello. Any time you'd like," he urged, with a toothy smile at the only woman at the table he was interested in.

"Thanks, I'm not here for long, though," Francesca deflected.

"You can find me here, on the piazza, most days." He beamed appreciatively at Francesca, and disappeared back into the little cafe. "Arrivederci, signoras."

They laughed as he left. "He was sweet, don't you think? Very handsome," Kathleen commented, with a sly smile. "He might take your mind off your troubles."

Francesca laughed and swept her glossy black hair off her shoulders, turning her pale face up to the sun. "I don't think so, Aunt Kathleen. La dolce vita and all that, but vacation romance isn't really my style, even if I wasn't getting a divorce."

"Probably too soon," Kathleen agreed. "Though his suggestion of exploring Belruscello is a good one." She pulled a map up on her phone. "Let me see, we're staying in the big villa attached to the village. That really is the main tourist site here, but some of these streets of the piazza look very intriguing."

They finished their brioches and espressos, and left the old men taking in the morning sunlight. All three women were generally brisk walkers, but the uneven footing of the cobblestones forced them to slow down, and the gorgeous scenery slowed them still more.

Belruscello was very much a working village, not the tourist centered facade you might find in more accessible locales. The narrow streets, never designed for cars, twisted and turned, highlighted by narrow rays of morning sunlight. A three wheeled Piaggio Ape truck bounced by on the cobbles, the driver waving merrily, as they flattened themselves against a hard stucco wall with an inch to spare.

Laundry flapped across the street overhead, the squeak of wheels turning as it was cranked out to dry in the sun. They glimpsed local life in slivers of courtyards, lushly green behind thick walls.

Francesca fingered soft silk scarves, blowing in the breeze, outside a little shop. "I want something new to treat myself," she said, with a laugh. They walked down a few uneven steps into the shop. Bright cotton dresses garlanded the walls. She held up one, a warm terracotta rust, with lovely lines. "Not my style, but wouldn't Diane look fabulous in this?" They all agreed, and walked out with a few colorful scarves as well.

Meandering slowly, they eventually looped back to the piazza, now bright with midday sun. "Time to head back to the villa?" Kathleen asked, looking at her watch. "I wasn't expecting to be gone this long. Judith will be worrying."

"We might just get another espresso," Francesca suggested, then her face froze as she looked at the cluster of cafe tables.

The old men still sat around their table, pleasurably enjoying life, but behind them, half hidden, a younger man waited. His rough blond hair looked as if he hadn't taken the time to brush it this morning. His long legs were spread out, propped on a chair seat in front of him, and he scanned the piazza restlessly, hungrily searching. His roving eye alighted on Francesca, as if a magnet drew him. He stood up abruptly, knocking the chair over, stretching to his full height, tall enough to stoop to avoid hitting the cafe's low umbrellas.

Francesca saw his quick movement, and her face blanched, sheet white under her dark hair. "Ryan? Here?" she choked out. Then, she abruptly turned and ran, chiffon dress floating in her wake, not pausing to wait for the others.

With an angry jerk, Ryan headed to intercept her, but before he reached full stride, Kathleen moved to block him. "Ryan?" She adroitly moved to where he had to stop, or knock her down. "What are you doing here?" she demanded.

He looked down at her, his scowl fading, as Francesca disappeared into the distance. "Aunt Kathleen. How nice to see you, too." He didn't look very happy about it.

"Less of that aunt stuff, Ryan. I get the benefit of the divorce, too, you know. We are no longer related, and you're not using me to get to Francesca. What are you doing here?"

"Kathleen." He looked after Francesca anxiously, shifting his feet on the cobbles. "Look, I just want to talk to her. Explain everything." He looked down the street. "I just want to talk to her." He stepped to one side.

"Haven't you done enough, Ryan?" She moved to block his path again. "Francesca's been through enough, thanks to you. She was just starting to relax, on a family vacation surrounded by people who love her, and you show up. Stalking her into the middle of Italy. She deserves a break."

He ran a hand through his hair, setting the shaggy blond hair on end. "What else am I supposed to do? She hasn't talked to me. I can't get hold of her." He shifted again. "I just want to talk with her. She's still my wife. We're not divorced yet."

"Talk to her lawyers."

She turned away, and he grabbed her arm quickly, "Please, Kathleen. I love her. I need to talk to her."

The old men watched the two combatants, heads moving back and forth between the two, avidly watching the game play out. One dapper elderly man started to slowly rise at the insult to a woman, obviously trying to determine whether to intervene.

Kathleen pulled her arm out of Ryan's grasp, and quickly stood back a pace. The old man returned gratefully to his comfortable seat. "You should have thought of that, before you stole that money." Her voice softened and she told him, "Francesca was going to inherit most of it, anyway. Why did you feel you had to steal it? It was basically her money."

"It's basically Judith's money, you mean," he countered bitterly, lips twisting. "She used it to control Francesca. Always kept her just a little short, telling her it would all be hers someday, just wait for it."

Kathleen stopped backing off. "Is that why you stole it?" She shook her head. "I know Judith can be bossy. I should know, she's been my sister-in-law for decades." She barked a laugh. "But she means well, she really does."

"Like hell she does," Ryan snarled. "Anyway, I didn't steal that money."

"Oh, Ryan," Kathleen's tone hardened into brittle steel. "No one's going to believe that. The auditors..."

"The auditors what?" Ryan shouted. "They never found it all, did they?"

"Ryan, I assume you're intelligent enough to hide money in a secret bank account," Kathleen said impatiently. "That's not exactly complicated. And they did find a lot of it in your bank account."

"That wasn't my bank account. I didn't do it, I tell you I—" his voice faded away and he ran his hands through his hair, making it stand upright in blond clumps. "Look, I need to talk to Francesca. I haven't even seen her alone, since that awful day when the accountants told me I was a thief. She's my wife. I need to see her. I have a right to see her."

"And you're not going to," Kathleen's voice was firm. She turned back to Mia, "Let's head back to the villa."

Mia nodded agreement, feeling the stares of everyone on the piazza. She disliked public scenes. It was time to retire as gracefully as possible. Francesca had had time to run back to the villa by now.

Ryan was clearly not ready to let them go. He held out a hand, not touching Kathleen this time, but pleading and blocking her way. "Look, Kathleen—"

He was interrupted by a polite cough from a compact middle aged man in a battered Panama hat, laugh lines serious on his tanned face. "Signoras, I thought I recognized you." He grinned widely, "I am Salvatore, from the Villa Bella Sorgente." Maneuvering his wiry frame between Ryan and Kathleen, he blocked the younger man off from the women. "May I have the honor of accompanying you back to the villa?"

Ryan glared over the man's head, but wasn't quite willing to shove him out of the way.

Protected, Kathleen took a step away from Ryan, then started walking rapidly, her steps jerky with anger. "That would be lovely, thank you, Salvatore," she said with gritted teeth. They passed the town wall in a few minutes, and Kathleen started to relax a little.

"Salvatore, you must be Teresa's husband?"

"Yes, Teresa is my wife. I manage the gardens at the villa."

"Not by yourself, surely?" Mia asked. The well manicured grounds were extensive.

Salvatore laughed, showing very white teeth in his tanned face. "Oh no, I have several helpers. None full time, the boys now have many things they like to do better, but I have help."

As they moved down the road, Mia looked back. Ryan stood there with his face twisted into a grimace. In grief or anger, Mia couldn't tell. Either way, Francesca didn't need to talk with him during a family trip, taken for her to recover from the stress of an impending divorce. Any discussions should take place with her lawyers on hand, at the very least. But it was too bad that she hadn't had those discussions before the trip, instead of postponing them until afterwards. Ryan was right—Francesca did need to talk with him.

"I'm sorry to ask, but was there a problem back there? You seemed to know that man, who yelled and grabbed your arm?" His tone was hesitantly curious, wary of intruding.

"He's my niece's husband. They are getting divorced. You saw her leave as soon as she saw him." Kathleen walked a little faster. "It's a very ugly story, but the family came to Italy, so she did not need to be around him. He has been—" Kathleen searched for the right word, "persistent."

"Yes," Salvatore slowly considered the problem, while his legs remained quick. "Well, I can close the main gates, and he cannot get in that way, at least." He suddenly grinned and shook his head. "You cannot get out either, unless you get me to open them. But if you tell me when you want to go somewhere, I can have them open."

"We would very much appreciate it," Kathleen told him. "The poor girl needs a break." She took a few strides ahead. "Now, let's talk about something more pleasant. What can you tell me about the plants near the villa?"

The rest of the short journey, Salvatore pointed out local sights that the women would never have noticed on their own on the beautiful road back.

Diane wandered through the beauty of the villa gardens, feeling as if she was in a dream.

Breakfast had been uncomfortable. Teresa served Judith, Diane and Ben a delicious meal, blithely saying the other three women had walked to the village for breakfast. When she heard Kathleen and Mia had left with Francesca, Judith frowned. "I really do think they might have stayed for our very first breakfast in Italy."

"I'm sure they just wanted to stretch their legs a little," Diane easily explained. "We sat all day yesterday. They're ready to explore."

"Then why in the world didn't they ask us to come?" Judith stabbed at her perfectly scrambled eggs petulantly. "We might have joined them. I don't even know if Francesca slept, her first night in a strange place."

"I expect they didn't want to wake you because they thought you were sleeping in. Yesterday was a long travel day." Diane added, "Francesca is such a considerate daughter."

Judith said nothing, just stared at the courtyard, concern and annoyance written on her face. Ben wasn't a much better companion, shoveling food in his mouth, as if he hadn't eaten in a month, not bothering to talk. As soon as she could, Diane excused herself, and escaped to the peace of the beautiful gardens.

The extensive grounds around the Villa Bella Sorgente were lushly planted with bright flowers, dazzling in the warm sunlight. Butterflies danced on the jeweled blooms, and bees buzzed their appreciation. The soft pastels of angel trumpets dangled pendulously, the sweet scent wafting through the air. Diane felt her jaw unclench as she smelled a rose's intricate bloom, enjoying the rich fragrance.

It was truly beautiful here in Italy. She'd always dreamed of being able to travel someplace like this, with ancient buildings and breathtaking landscapes. Until the past few years, traveling to exotic destinations had seemed a matter of time. She had just needed to get through school before she could embark on her own adventures.

Then, her mom had gotten sick, and it had taken everything she had to keep going. At the end of it all, she'd been so tired she could barely put one foot in front of the other. She was in no shape to restart the intense nursing training, not did she have the heart for patients, at least not yet.

The past few years with Judith, she'd tried her best to heal from the hard times. Diane felt better, but every time she had tried to resume her classes, something had come up that made it impractical to do, just then. But now, at least, she was here in Italy, like she'd always dreamed, exploring the world.

She strolled through the gardens, enjoying the juxtaposition of frothy flowers framed by formal, rigidly clipped topiaries. Lemon trees, in antique terracotta pots, hung heavy with bright yellow fruit. Cheerful red geraniums bloomed everywhere, happy notes brightening the most formal of hedges.

The precise lines of the hedges must be a lot of work, to keep them perfect. She helped out in the garden at home. It took a man coming every week, just to keep the hedges clipped to Judith's specifications.

Right now, a gardener clipped away, with tanned, capable hands, meticulously removing any trace of deviance from the round topiary ball. The repetitive snip, snip was soothing in the morning sun, and Diane wandered over to look at the work.

"That's beautiful," she told him. "Umm, bellissimo."

"It is lovely, isn't it?" he replied in English, stepped back from his work, cocking his head to examine it for stray sprigs. "It's been here three hundred years, so I mustn't clip it wrong." His English was the British variety, under a light Italian accent. His trousers were worn, patched at the knees. He wore a heavy cotton shirt, protecting his arms from scratches. A battered straw fedora sat jauntily on his head, protecting it from the hot sun.

"Three hundred years. Imagine." Diane stretched out her hand to pat the springy leaves gently. "Everything is so old here, even the plants."

"Quite a change from America," the gardener agreed. "I went there once, years ago. Everything was fast and new, especially the buildings. It was an interesting experience, but I prefer a slower pace, except in cars, of course," he added with a grin.

She told him, "The cities in America are like that, but out in the country is quieter. We don't have very old buildings like this, though." She gestured at the villa. "This is beautiful."

"Ah," he agreed. "I was in cities, that whole trip."

"Then you haven't seen the real America," Diane told him. "I grew up in the country, but I live in the city now. I only get to visit the countryside occasionally," she added. Then she laughed, "I expect it's the same thing as an American thinking they've seen all of Italy, since they went to Rome's tourist sights."

He laughed, a warm, heartfelt chuckle. "That it is." He examined the topiary. "I think that one is finished for this year." He smiled at Diane, laugh lines crinkling his tanned face. "Would you like a tour of the garden?"

"Oh, I don't want to keep you from your work," Diane demurred.

"It's not a problem," he told her. "I'm finished with this, for today." He gestured down the long, narrow grass path. "Please, after you."

Diane smiled in pleasure. She had a few minutes to herself, at last, and how better to spend it than to get a guided tour from the gardener of this gorgeous garden? They walked in single file down a long pathway, their steps crunching on smoothly raked gravel. The path was flanked by tall, sweet smelling hedges. Diane sniffed, asking, "What is that wonderful smell?"

"Lauro rosa," he told her, gesturing to the tops adorned with bright pink flowers.

"Oleander," said Diane, recognizing it. "I've never seen it clipped like that." She breathed in the intoxicating fragrance surrounding her.

Stucco walls, mottled with moss and age, lined both sides of the wide path, in a long hallway. She caught glimpses of walled gardens from openings, bright flowers, lush greens, a chattering fountain where birds splashed.

He directed, "To the right, please."

She turned, ducking her head under the low arch of the doorway, and laughed out loud for joy at the sight inside. Roses spilled over every wall, in a profusion of colors, from yellows to deep, dark reds, punctuated by white froth. Heavy, luscious scent hung in the air, better than any perfume. She turned around slowly, soaking in the sheer beauty of the garden.

He laughed a little at her rapt face, "I thought you would enjoy this. It is beautiful, is it not?"

"Incredible," she breathed in the roses. Birds sang, rustling in the vines.

He clipped a red rose, and presented it to her gallantly. "For a lovely lady." He grinned boyishly at her.

She almost said no, then smiled wholeheartedly back at him, taking it with the spirit it was given. "Thank you." She buried her nose in the blossom. "Beautiful."

He smiled into her soft brown eyes, clearly admiring. "Here, allow me." He took it from her and tucked it in her hat band. "There you are. Almost as beautiful as you," he told her, lightheartedly.

"Oh," Diane said, feeling suddenly awkward. "Thank you."

He deliberately took a step back, gesturing around him. "This is my favorite of the villa gardens. It's where I come to unwind, at the end of the day."

"I can see why," Diane agreed. "It's incredible."

"My mother would garden in here for hours," he told her. "I think it was to be around the roses. They were her favorites. I remember playing in here as a little boy, smelling the roses. My mom loved this garden the most." He touched one red blossom, trailing his callused finger delicately on the petals.

"I don't blame her," Diane agreed fervently. "If I could go to a garden like this, I'd never leave." She buried her nose in a soft yellow bloom, breathing in deeply. She felt herself relax with this kind gardener.

"Do you have a garden at home?" he asked, curiously. He tipped his battered hat back a little.

Diane looked around her at the dream of a garden. "No, not anymore." She smiled in memory. "And never anything like this." She waved her hand around. "We had a bench with a pink climbing rose climbing on an arbor. New Dawn, it was called. It bloomed like crazy once a year. For that month, Mom and I would spend all the time we could just sitting there, surrounded by roses."

He smiled at her. "That sounds like a very good memory."

Diane said simply, "It is." She looked around her. "This garden is much grander, but it reminds me of that. That bench there," she gestured at a sturdy wood bench framed by a profusion of roses, "looks like the perfect place to read a book."

"It's one of my favorites. I've spent many a pleasant afternoon there, reading until the light was gone." He smiled at her approvingly. "Would you like to see more of the gardens?"

A call rang out over the wall. Judith called shrilly, "Diane! Diane! Where are you?"

Diane shook herself a little, waking from a dream. "She wants me. I'd better go." She looked around her, then into his kind brown eyes. "Thank you for showing me your garden." She touched her hat with a quick grin. "And for the lovely rose."

"It was my pleasure, Diane," he told her.

She reluctantly headed toward the demanding call, then turned back to the gardener, and boldly asked, "May I please come back to see the roses?"

"Of course you may," he told her. "I hope I'm able to show you more of the gardens while you're here."

Judith's calls were getting louder. She smiled quickly at him, "I hope so too," and ran for it.

Judith was on the hedge lined path leading to the walled gardens, calling. "Diane! Oh, there you are!" She frowned, "Where ever have you been?" She looked past Diane.

"I was looking at the gardens," Diane said, guiltily. Somehow, she didn't want to show Judith the rose garden. It was too sublimely serene for everyday complaints and worries.

"Is that the gardener over there?" Judith asked, as a figure disappeared rapidly around the corner. "A garden tour might be interesting. I want to see all of this villa, while we're here." She looked disapprovingly at Diane. "Is that a rose from the garden in your hat? You shouldn't pick someone else's flowers, you know. Your mother raised you better than that."

Diane blushed, "No, he gave it to me."

"He gave it to you? The gardener?" Judith asked, curling her lip in disgust. "Diane, you have to watch out for these Italian men, you know."

Diane didn't know how to reply, but it wasn't as if Judith gave her a chance to. Judith continued, without a pause, "Now that you're here, we can find the others, and arrange for that tour of the villa. There must be some interesting history here." She called to the gardener, collecting his tools next to the topiary. "Excuse me, signore? Signore?"

The man turned, and Judith wrinkled her nose, looking at his old, patched clothes. "Can we get a tour of the villa today?"

The gardener looked at Diane, not her. Diane shrugged a little, embarrassed by Judith's abruptness, and he nodded with understanding. "Of course. Do you wish to gather the rest of your family?"

"Oh, yes, that'd be best," Judith replied. "We can see everything together. I know Francesca will love seeing all the history!"

"Perhaps before dinner?" he suggested. "It will be cool in the gardens, then."

"Oh, I think we want to go ahead and see everything during the day," Judith said. "We're only here for a short time, you know."

He nodded agreeably, "I can meet after lunch."

"That will work for us," Judith agreed. "Come on, Diane. Let's tell the others our plan."

"Arrivederci, Diane," he told her.

She flashed a quick, wide smile at him, touching her rose in thanks. "Arrivederci."

As they crossed the courtyard, Francesca ran up the driveway, panting hard. She stopped for breath when she saw them. Her face was bright red with angry exertion.

"Francesca! Where have you been?" Judith asked sharply. "I've been looking all over for you, so we could get started for the day."

Diane, more observant, asked, "What's going on, Francesca? Are you okay?"

Francesca shook her head, wordlessly, then burst out crying. Her movements were jerky with intense emotion.

"Francesca, dear, what's wrong?" Judith demanded, going to her. "Don't cry, out here in the middle of everyone."

Kathleen, striding fast into the courtyard, answered for her. "It's Ryan, Judith. The jerk followed her here. Unbelievable."

"After what he's done to the family, he comes here? Follows us all the way to Italy?" Judith's face went white with anger, her fists clenching into hard, tight balls, her manicured nails digging into her palms.

"Let me take you back to your room, honey," Diane offered. "You'll feel better, after you get over the shock."

"No, dear, you come to my cottage, it's right here," Judith put her arm around Francesca, shepherding her toward the door. "You just relax. I'll take care of that man for you," she spit out as if it was an epithet. "He's not going to bother you again. There must be laws."

Francesca swiped her hand across her face, clearly annoyed with herself for breaking down. "No, you're right, you're right. It's was just the shock of seeing him here."

She gently broke out of Judith's grasp, plastering a smile on her face. "I haven't even seen the gardens. Are they as gorgeous as they look from here?" She rubbed at her eyes again, then handed Diane her package, "Here, I found the prettiest dress for you in town."

"Oh, you shouldn't have," Diane said, peeking into the package. "I love the color! Thanks, Francesca!" She hugged the package to herself.

Francesca smiled in return, calming. "Let's go see the gardens."

Diane said, a little too cheerfully, "They're even prettier close up." She tucked her new dress under her arm, happy for the treat.

The bright flowers dancing in the breeze would cheer any heart. Francesca stooped, burying her nose in a pink rose, then laughed as it tickled, rubbing yellow pollen off her face. "This place is like a botanical garden, all to ourselves," she enthused. She wandered down the terraced hill, admiring the flowers. Judith followed her, watching her solicitously, commenting on the landscaping.

Diane felt a little relieved that they weren't going to the lovely rose garden. She touched the flower on her hat briefly, with a little smile. The garden room full of roses reminded her of The Secret Garden book. She wanted to keep it all to herself, even if just for a little while. She had to make sure the others saw the enchanting garden before they left.

Francesca seemed more relaxed now, moving with ease through the graveled paths. Diane couldn't believe that Ryan had actually followed her here, all the way to Italy. He must want to talk to her very much. Still, he should know there wasn't anything more to discuss, especially in front of the family he'd stolen so much from. Diane caught herself idly tearing a leaf up, shredding it into little pieces, floating away to the ground.

"Let's walk around the villa before lunch," Kathleen suggested. "It looks like there's a great view from that hill over there."

Diane hurried to catch up with Kathleen.

As Francesca turned to join them, Judith placed a gentle hand on her arm. "Just a minute, Francesca. We need to talk."

Francesca's face fell, the smiling mask wiping off in a second. "What is there to talk about? We've rehashed the whole thing a million times already." She scuffed her toe in the gravel path.

"I just want you to know that man doesn't have power over you any more," Judith told her, smiling gently at her daughter. "Your divorce paperwork will be ready to sign by the time we get back, and this whole distasteful episode will be over. We'll have our old life back, just like it was."

Francesca looked after the other women, disappearing down the path, then turned back to Judith. "It'll never be over for me, Mom." She shook her head hopelessly. "I let that man into the family. I let him steal money from all of you. It's all my fault." The last word ended on a sob, and a tear fell down her cheek. She wiped it away angrily, then let her hand drop limply. "It's never going to be over, until I pay you back."

"Don't worry about that, dear. What's done is done," Judith smiled at her daughter. "And don't worry about Ryan spoiling our Italy trip any more. We'll ask Teresa to have the gate locked. He can't get past that."

"I think Salvatore already did," Francesca told her. "Teresa's husband. We met him in town."

"That's good. That's very good, dear." Judith frowned faintly. "I think you'd better keep to the grounds, for now. The villa grounds are walled, so you should be quite safe if you stay inside the walls. We can tour tomorrow from the van, like we planned." She warned Francesca like the flick of a whip, "We don't want any more unpleasant surprises, now, do we?"

Francesca, looking down at the lush green grass, felt like lying on that soft ground, screaming and beating her hands on it, like a toddler in a tantrum. Her chest was tight inside, hot and angry and ready to explode. She wondered what it'd feel like to finally break out and scream.

She replied, her voice rigidly controlled, "Yes, Mom."

Candace lay across the antique four poster bed, tracing the carvings with her long, glossy nail. Her bare legs, tanned to perfection, were propped up on the crisp white sheets, and her long blond hair hung in tousled locks around her shoulders. The French doors were open onto their little balcony, and the sheer white curtains wafted in the gentle breeze.

"Oh, this is so good," she told Kevin. "I could get used to this, you know?" She smiled lazily at her husband.

She'd loved Kevin since high school, when she'd been a cheerleader, and he'd been on the football team. She'd transferred to his high school, when her dad had left the military. After being an Army brat for so long, moving constantly, she didn't know how to make real friends, just the usual facade of getting along, and blending in. She'd tried out for cheerleading for fun— she'd always loved gymnastics—and to her surprise, she made the team. At her first practice, the guys were doing their thing, and she'd happened to get water at the same time as Kevin. His slow, genuine smile as he handed her the little paper cup melted her heart. She'd never looked at another man since.

Of course, she'd never let him know that back in high school. It was always better to keep your boyfriend guessing.

Kevin stood, looking out the sunlit window, far enough back from the curtain to be out of sight. He ran a hand over his short, thinning hair. "I know honey, I could too." He stepped back further. "Everyone's walking through the garden with Aunt Judith. We should probably go down, and join them."

"Aunt Judith," Candace pouted. "Always Aunt Judith this, Aunt Judith that. We've made it, Kevin. We don't have to be at her beck and call all the time."

"She paid for the trip, after all," Kevin told her, with a shrug. "It's only right to join everyone while we're on a family vacation."

"Can't we have just a little more time to ourselves?" Candace leaned against him suggestively.

He half heartedly pushed her away, and she pouted her full lips. "We need to go down for lunch, at least." He pulled her back to him, and kissed her, tracing her bare shoulder, then sighed and turned away. "Okay, honey. Let's go."

Candace knew when she'd lost. She said, more cheerfully than she felt like, "Okay, just a sec," as she went to change into something that would make Judith green with envy.

4

An Unexpected Guest

After Teresa's fabulous lunch, they waited on the long veranda for their villa tour. The tall, slightly stooping gardener strode over the courtyard, changed from his gardening clothes to tailored trousers, a beige linen sports coat and a crisp white shirt, the top two buttons unbuttoned, like most Italian men. His dark head of silver threaded hair gleamed in the sunlight. He walked directly to Diane, smiling at her, his kind brown eyes solicitous. "I did not introduce myself earlier, Diane. I'm Pietro Schiavon, owner of the Villa Bella Sorgente."

"Oh, well," she looked down at her sensibly shod feet, then back up into his eyes, her round cheeks blushing apple red. "You know that I'm Diane, Diane Parker." She smiled back, looking directly into his eyes. "Thank you for showing me your roses."

"It was my pleasure." His eyes lingered on hers for a moment, then he turned to the rest of the group.

Judith briskly told him, "I'm Judith Parker. You're the owner of this hotel?"

"Yes, I'm Pietro Schiavon, the owner of the Villa Bella Sorgente. My family has lived on this land for five hundred years."

"Oh my," breathed Diane softly.

He nodded to her with a quick smile, "It's a long time, yes?"

She nodded in awe.

"Let me show you my villa," he said to the group. "While you can see the gardens and public areas of the villa while you are staying here, there are several sights our guests do not commonly see." He took Diane's arm casually, guiding her through his home. The others trailed behind.

"My favorite room is the library," he told her, opening the door with a grand gesture. Diane and the group entered, then stopped in awe. The high walls were lined with intricately carved bookcases, reaching to the ceiling, and accessed by a tall ladder hooked across one long rail. Narrow windows, set in deep walls, streamed light into the center of the room, setting the Oriental rug alight with color. An ornate red marble fireplace was flanked by cozy red leather chairs. The books varied wildly. There were easily accessible bookcases, full of recent best sellers for guests' reading. More precious books worn with age, in ponderous leather tomes, were shelved behind polished brass grills, safely away from sticky, careless fingers.

"Your family must have collected books the entire five hundred years they've lived here," Diane commented appreciatively. "I don't think I've seen this many books, outside a library."

He chuckled, "Not many books here are that old. Collecting stepped up during the eighteenth century, when a famous botanist led the family." He opened the lock on one case with a key and Diane saw the brass grill was lined with protective glass. He took out one, "Antonio Stoppani's *Il Bel Paese.* The natural history of my beautiful Italy." He smiled, returning it carefully to its home, and took another out with loving care, "*I Promessi Sposi*, by Alessandro Manzoni. A work of true love, and obstacles overcome by love and perseverance."

"Very nice," Judith gave her disinterested approval, her eyes glued to Francesca, who strolled around the room, peering curiously at book titles.

Savannah shifted her feet on the carpet. "They're very old," she contributed. "Do you have any really creepy ones, like witches, vampires, and stuff?"

"Sadly, my family was more interested in the sciences," Pietro responded with grin.

"Oh well." Savannah looked out the window at the streaming sunlight, clearly bored. Her gossamer black dress was layered in ruffles that dripped down to the floor.

Mia thought Savannah was probably looking for some Victorian goth dress inspiration.

Diane asked, "All these books have been here, in your family, for centuries? That's amazing."

Pietro held up his hands. "What can I say? My family loves books." He stood for a moment in thought, looking at Diane, then seemed to make a decision. "I want to show you a special book." He pulled a panel back, revealing a safe. "This has been in my family since before this villa was built." His body blocked the view of an elaborate safe entry, which seemed to include a retina scan as well as long multi step codes.

Mia wondered what precious objects he kept in such a well fortified safe, but also in a room open to guests. She planned to avail herself of the chance to examine this extraordinary library at length later, when she could take the time to appreciate its wonders.

Pietro, from his intense expression, was trying to impress Diane. And from Diane's rapt attention, it was working. Mia smiled, glad to see Diane beaming instead of looking like a beaten dog. Diane was a very pretty girl when she was happy—and it was obvious Pietro agreed.

He removed a heavy tome from the safe, bound in rich chocolate brown leather, worn by age. "La Divina Commedia, by Dante Alighieri." He set it carefully on a carved wooden book stand. "This one was transcribed by monks, by hand, in the year 1467, before mass printing. It is truly a work of art." He opened the gilded pages with care, touching them as little as possible. Bright flowers, in vibrant reds and blues, gleamed on the pages, framing the heavy, dark letters.

"Oh!" Diane looked at the pages, carefully not touching the antique paper. "Dante." Pietro turned a page for her. "I've read it, not in Italian, but the translation, I mean. With my mother." She turned to him. "I read to her a lot, when she was sick. She said she'd always wanted to read it. So we did."

She pushed her glossy brown hair back, tucking it behind her ear, examining the antique page with rapt enjoyment. "It was complicated, but beautiful too. A journey of redemption."

Pietro turned a simpler page or two, then revealed more bright, intricately painted illuminations. "Men will go through hell and back, for the right reasons." He turned another page. A haunting illustration of a figure in a boat, bowed under a great weight. "Dante, rowed by Charon across the River Acheron," Pietro told them. He closed the book lovingly and returned it to the safe, to Mia's intense disappointment.

"Would you like to see the wine cellars next?" he asked the family.

"Ooh, you have wine cellars here," Candace enthused. "That's much more my style."

Pietro laughed, taking Diane's arm proprietorially. "I warn you, they're dark and damp."

"With spiders?" Diane asked, with a sly grin at her host.

"Oh no, Teresa would never tolerate spiders in her house."

Laughing, the party made their way down to the damp, dark cellars.

They emerged from the shadows into the bright light of the courtyard. The afternoon sun glared, white hot against their eyes, after the cool dark cellars. Savannah, her long dress trailing in the dust, looked like a particularly well preserved vampire emerging from a long sleep, her dark rimmed eyes huge and unfocused.

Pietro sat down in one of the comfortable veranda chairs, shading his eyes from the sun. "Anna will bring drinks out soon," he told them.

"After seeing all those dusty old bottles, I could do with one," Candace told him. "They sure made me thirsty."

Kevin laughed, putting his arm around her. "Beautiful place, Pietro. Thanks for showing it to us."

"It was my pleasure," Pietro told him. He smiled at Diane, as she sat down next to him.

When Anna came out with her bar cart and plates of stuzzichini, Judith quickly requested a white wine.

"Spritz Veneziano, again, please, Anna," Mia requested, taking a sliver of Soprèssa Vicentina. The salty cured sausage contrasted nicely with the refreshing spritz.

Pietro ordered the same, saying, "Nice choice, a Venice classic."

"Oh, then I want to try that too," Diane said. She raised her glass to Pietro. "To classics." A broad, happy smile lit her face, the rosy apples of her cheeks glowed, and her eyes sparkled. She sat back in her chair, basking contentedly in the sunlight. Mia noticed how pretty Diane was looking, her skin warmed by the Italian sun. Her shoulders were uncurling from their habitual slump, as she talked animatedly with Pietro and Kevin about the villa.

To the family's surprise, a compact car drew up to the courtyard, spitting gravel in an abrupt stop. Francesca jerked up, backing toward the open villa door. "I thought the gate was locked."

"It is," Pietro stood up alertly, his tall figure looking less scholarly as he straightened. "Relax, your family are my only guests. Salvatore locked the gates, as you requested, this morning. He must have let this car in."

A man got out of the car, standing there a minute blinking, adjusting to the bright light of the courtyard. Francesca recognized him, slowly sitting back down. "Why, it's Uncle Jeffery," she said, with surprise. "I thought he wasn't coming this trip?"

"He said he wasn't able to," Judith said levelly. "Well, isn't it nice he could come, after all." Her voice was flat, without a hint of surprise. She stood up to greet the new arrival, shaking out her trousers.

"Aunt Judith, I hope you don't mind me coming," Jeffery said, as he came their way.

Judith said smoothly, "I'm so glad you were able to come."

She allowed him to ritually kiss both her cheeks. He stooped down to do so, his tall, trim figure showing his marathon running routine. "We've been touring the villa this afternoon with the owner. I'm sorry you missed it."

Ever mindful of her social duties, Judith next introduced the villa owner. "This is Pietro Schiavon, whose family has owned this villa for centuries."

Jeffery, unimpressed by anything that wasn't a clearly tabulated asset, said, "Jeffery Parker, pleased to meet you."

"Please, sit down, sit down." He glanced around at the assembled group. "Afternoon drinks? Nice. I'll have a gin tonic."

"Jeffery, what a surprise," Candace said, her smile not quite meeting her eyes. "We didn't expect to see you here."

"Candace, looking good as always. Sunny Italy suits you," he complemented her, with a swift look up and down her figure. He acknowledged his brother with a,"Kevin."

"Jeffery," Kevin added flatly. "Glad you could make it. "He took the proffered glass of Soave, and drained it quickly, returning it to Anna for another round. Candace tugged on his arm, pulling him to the edge of the gathering.

Jeffery turned back to Judith, and sipped the gin, cold enough to frost the glass. "Nice," he repeated. "No, with that IRS audit underway, I wasn't planning to come. Didn't have time for it, pleasant as this is. But some things came up that made it imperative I see you and Francesca immediately." He nodded to Judith. "So I thought I'd come over for a day or two, then get back to work. It's not as if I can't work on a plane or at a hotel, nowadays."

Pietro smoothly excused himself and his apéritif, walking toward the apartments over the stables.

"So, that guy owns this place, huh? Family money must be running pretty dry, if he's renting out rooms," Jeffery scoffed.

"I didn't ask," Judith said decorously, raising a delicately arched eyebrow. Jeffrey laughed, a grating sound like a triumphant macaw.

Diane winced, and looked like she wanted to follow Pietro. Instead, she put her glass down, pulling her feet under her and crossing her arms tightly over her breasts.

Randall frowned. "Parker Perches is in an IRS audit? Shouldn't you have informed us, as shareholders?" He rubbed his hand on his stubbled chin.

"I am informing you," Jeffery replied, with an exasperated sigh. "The IRS is going through absolutely everything—it's been all hands on deck, so to speak. All that business with Ryan flagged us, of course."

Francesca looked down at the ground, clearly wishing she was somewhere else.

Savannah glanced at her cousin, and quickly asked, "I thought they'd started the audit before Ryan was arrested? They wanted tons of receipts—it was a real hassle in marketing." She swirled her wine idly.

"The whole thing has brought more negative attention to our company than we needed," Judith pronounced, with a note of finality. "It really has." She patted Francesca's knee, but she didn't look up. "Not your fault, my dear."

"I thought I might have a little talk with Francesca before dinner," Jeffery continued. "Give her some idea of her options."

"No, you can discuss that with me, Jeffery," Judith cut him off. "Francesca doesn't need to deal with that, right now. She's supposed to be on vacation, getting away from that unpleasantness. I don't know why you'd bother her with this right now."

Francesca set her glass down with a sharp clink. "If you're going to treat me like a child, I don't need to be around for it. I'm going to change for dinner."

"Francesca, wait—" Judith protested. She angrily turned on Jeffery. "Now, see what you've done."

"It's not half of what I could do, dear aunt." He drained his glass. "Shall we have that little chat? It is why I'm here, after all."

"Of course," Judith said coolly. "The library will be private enough, I think."

He followed her without a word, looking around appreciatively, "Nice room. Fancy place you're staying, Aunt Judith. Must be costing a mint. Not using company money, are you? The IRS might want to know."

"You were invited," Judith reminded him dryly. "You chose not to come."

"I was busy with that damn audit," Jeffery complained. "I haven't even had time to go running this week." Jeffery ran in rain or shine, almost every day of the year.

"There are a lot of country roads around here."

"Yeah, I'll shake off the dust, before I get back in a plane." Jeffery's voice sharpened. "Look, Aunt Judith, handling this is getting awkward. The auditors are asking all kinds of questions about Ryan's access to the accounts."

"It shouldn't be that hard for them to figure out," Judith said acidly. "Poor Francesca, she didn't know a thing about it." She deliberately crossed her legs, smoothing the heavy silk.

"No," Jeffery agreed. "She didn't. Convincing them of that is another matter, however." He ran his finger along a shelf, examining the book titles, then sat in one of the red leather chairs, wiggling until he got comfortable.

"We need to keep her out of it. The last thing she needs is additional stress," Judith told him, a hard note in her voice. "Did you know Ryan showed up in town?" She sat on the edge of the opposite chair.

"In town? You mean here?" Jeffery said, startled.

"Yes, the poor girl walked down to town with Mia and Kathleen. She had the fright of her life when he chased her down in the town square." Judith glared at him, clearly holding him responsible.

Jeffery shook his head in disbelief. "I thought he wouldn't be able to travel internationally, while out on bail."

"I called my attorney. Apparently he's not a flight risk, so his travel was actually approved." Judith shook her head in disgust. "I don't know what everything's coming to when they let criminals wander around the world."

"You need to keep him away from Francesca." Jeffery tapped his thumb on the chair arm. "It's not safe."

"I know, she had to practically run back to the villa. I had the people here lock the gates. He can't get past the walls. It's practically a fortress, and we're the only ones staying here."

"Yeah, I had to argue with some Italian guy at the gate to get in. Now I get it." He pulled his laptop out of his briefcase. "Take a look at these."

Judith tapped on the keyboard, and frowned. "The auditors found this?"

"Yeah," Jeffery agreed. "You see why I had to come."

"I see." She frowned at the screen.

"I'm not going to be able to keep it a private, family affair for much longer," he told her. "Everything is going to come out. There's a lot of money involved."

Judith looked at him, her wide set dark eyes turned stormy. "As long as blame goes on Ryan, where it should, we can weather it. It's a privately held company, after all."

"Still, there's going to be some scandal. I'll clean it up the best I can, but I'll need a free hand," Jeffery told her.

Judith nodded, "You have it. Do what you need to do to get the company out of danger." She tapped her exquisite manicure on the leather chair arm. "Is that all?"

"I just needed to know what I should do."

Judith nodded again. "It's up to you, now." She stood, resettling her trouser legs back into their beautiful drape. "I'm going to go change for dinner."

Savannah quickly followed Francesca when she left the veranda, catching up at her door. "Hey, Fran, can I come in?"

"What do you want?" Francesca bluntly. "Give me a break."

Savannah slipped in the door. "I want to borrow a dress," she told Francesca airily.

"Yeah, right," Francesca said sarcastically, collapsing onto her bed.

Savannah opened the wardrobe door, flicking through soft pastels. "Sure I do." She pulled out an airy dress covered in bright pink roses, and held it up, contrasting ridiculously with her floor length black ruffles. "Don't you think it's me?"

Francesca giggled, despite herself. "It's so you."

Savannah put the dress back and returned to browsing. "Seriously, you don't have any black at all?" She glanced at Francesca, "You'd look good in black, that dark hair and those big gray eyes."

"I don't like black," said Francesca simply. "I like bright colors."

Savannah closed the wardrobe. "Well, at least it's not all pink, like Candace. She looks like a walking Barbie doll."

"Oh, Candace isn't so bad," Francesca said. "She just likes dressing up. So do you, " she added. "Just differently."

Savannah flopped down on the bed, her black skirts looking like some night flower as they floated down around her. "Yeah, I'm actually ready to change up my look a little."

"You have been out of college for a few years," Francesca said dryly.

Savannah rolled her eyes.

"No, seriously, try a dramatic red, like this." Francesca got up and pulled a dress out of her closet and swirled it around. It was a deep, dark red, like a damask rose.

Savannah held it up against her in the mirror. "Maybe," she said.

"Come on, wear it tonight," Francesca urged. "It's even kindof goth. You'd look amazing."

Savannah laughed and put it back. "Maybe," she said, touching it lightly. She turned to Francesca and asked, "You want to talk about any of that?" She motioned in the general direction of the veranda, and rolled her dark eyes expressively.

"That I freaked out because Ryan followed me to Italy like a stalker?" Francesca asked. "Or that Uncle Jeffery is hinting the IRS is after me?"

"Whichever," Savannah said, running her finger over the silver loop of her earring.

"Neither," said Francesca, with decision.

"It's going to be a long vacation with your mom making sure we see everything in northern Italy," Savannah said. "I think we would need more than two months to do what I heard her planning."

"Tell me about it," agreed Francesca.

When Jeffery came back out onto the veranda, only Kevin was still there, sipping wine, and looking like he wished he'd asked for something stronger.

"Well, little bro, how've you been?" Jeffery asked heartily. His curled lip contradicted his easy friendliness. He swirled his drink, looking uncomfortable around his younger brother.

"Can't complain," Kevin told him, responding to the words, and ignoring the sneer. "How are you, is more to the point. I remember you declaring after Costa Rica, you wouldn't go on another one of Judith's family vacations, if it was the last one you ever took. What made you change your mind and fly all the way to Italy?"

"Family togetherness, and all that crap," Jeffery told him, with a supercilious look. "Can't get enough of it."

"Yeah, somehow I doubt it, brother," Kevin rejoined. "Don't stir up trouble, okay? Candace is finally getting the trip to Italy she's wanted all these years, and Judith is pretty stressed about Francesca's divorce. We want to keep things calm, you know? Everyone relaxing together."

"You mean, you want to keep things calm," Jeffery sneered. "I've had enough trouble over Francesca's divorce too. You wouldn't believe the hours that's cost me."

"I know, I know, but it's not Francesca's fault," Kevin said. "She didn't know a thing about it, until you told her."

"How do we know that? Maybe she did," Jeffery suggested slyly, draining his gin glass.

"No, not Francesca," Kevin told him, his voice steady and firm. "She's a nice kid, always has been. Don't try to make this into something it's not."

"I wouldn't dream of it," Jeffery told him. "Well, I'm off to change, before the family dinner bonding takes place." He put his glass down, bumping it on the table. "And to find another drink."

Kevin remained behind on the veranda, sipping his wine with a frown on his face. Jeffery was going to be trouble. He always was.

Mia struggled to keep a cheerful conversation going at dinner. Judith sat silent at the head of the table, not bothering to fake polite conversation. Francesca drooped beside her, toying with her food with no appetite.

Jeffery had sat between Savannah and Randall.

Randall, after visibly fuming through the first delicious course of Bigoli al Ragù d'Anatra, a pasta with a lamb stew, finally turned to Jeffery. "Jeffery, I'm one of the original investors in Parker Perches. I built the damn things every summer for years. Why the hell didn't you tell me we were being audited?" His head glowed red with anger under his cropped silver hair.

"It wasn't your concern," Jeffery said, loftily. "I'm dealing with it." He took a bite of his bigoli, smirking.

"It is my concern, damn you. It's my company too." He banged his fist on the table for emphasis, making the silverware jump. Randall's face was beet red.

Jeffery calmly sipped his wine. "I'm the CFO, so I'm handling it. It's not as if you had children to inherit anything," he added caustically.

Randall's face inflated like a red balloon, in outraged fury. "That is beside the point. It seems like you're not handling the finances too well, if Ryan can steal us blind, and the IRS is auditing the company."

Kathleen, frowning across the table, added, "There must be a reason you didn't find the theft sooner." She tapped her plate with her knife.

Jeffery looked around the table, his narrow face lengthening with disdain for the people surrounding him. His lips narrowed, tightening. "I found it as soon as I could."

He looked at Judith. She responded automatically, "I'm sure Jeffery did an excellent job by catching the thefts before they got too big. He has my full trust."

Francesca looked down at her plate, moving her fork around her uneaten pasta. She looked nauseated.

"Because of those thefts," Jeffery added, with an undisguised smirk, "we're going to all have to trim our sails a little. I'm afraid," he looked defiantly at Randall and Kathleen, "your shares are going to be a little less this year." He repeated meaningfully, "A little less."

Kathleen nodded once, sharply, a quizzical look on her face.

Randall burst out, "Now, wait a minute, I thought business was booming?"

"Numbers don't lie," Jeffery threw the words out like grenades. "The thefts ate into our profits drastically." He looked at Savannah, sullenly eating next to him. "We're definitely going to have to up our marketing game. Get some pros on the job."

She looked up sharply. "I am a professional. I was top of my class in Marketing."

"It doesn't look like your fancy degree is translating very well to the real world," Jeffery drawled, taking a long drink of his gin and tonic. "We might need to shake that entire department up a bit."

"Sales are up fifteen percent since I started," Savannah glared at him.

"Not good enough," Jeffery told her.

"I can get a better paying job somewhere else, with my track record," Savannah told him, proudly.

"Fine. You do that, then." His smug look hung between them.

Savannah suddenly realized, Jeffery wanted her to leave. "My grandmother helped start the business," she yelled. "I'm not going anywhere!" One of her braids had come undone and hung in her face. "It's my company too."

"Only a very small share," Jeffery told her, with a grating laugh. "We all have to make sacrifices for the greater good."

"Wait a minute here," Kevin said. "The rest of us get a say in how the business is run too. And I say Savannah's doing a great job. She stays."

Savannah looked like she was going to cry. "Thanks, Uncle Kevin." She edged her chair away from Jeffery.

"I second that," Randall said, gritting his teeth.

"Fine, poor little Savannah stays," Jeffery agreed with a sneer. "But we have to cut things somewhere. What about that loan you started your business with, Kevin?"

Kevin's face reddened. "I've paid it back, every month, at the agreed on rate."

Candace cut in sharply, "He's paid every cent back, just like Harold set up."

Jeffery smiled, showing his teeth. "Yes, but that was a handshake deal, not on paper." He looked around the table, gloating at their expressions. "Not a contract."

"A man's only as good as his word," Randall said shortly.

"But his word is costing the company money. Interest rates have changed. Oh yes, they've changed a great deal since Harold made that particular deal." He looked at Kevin. "It's basically a gift, at this point. As CFO, it's almost criminal for me to be giving my brother a gift from the company funds. Let's keep this businesslike."

Kevin looked at Candace. She nodded once, in obvious answer to his unspoken question.

"Fine, Jeffery," Kevin told him. "I'll get a bank loan, and pay it all back as soon as I'm back home. Every. Last. Dime," he spat at Jeffery, sitting back in his chair. "You're not holding that over me ever again."

Candace placed her hand on his knee, and Kevin patted hers, calming down slightly at her touch. He breathed in and out, controlling his temper.

Jeffery smiled, a wide shark grin that showed his teeth. "If that's what you want to do, Kevin, but I'll be checking every penny."

After a deep breath, Kevin stated with slow force, like a wave crashing, "However, since we are being businesslike, I insist on a full, independent audit from an outside company."

Jeffery laughed shortly, "Don't you think the IRS is enough?"

"No," Kevin stated flatly. "I do not. Like you said, we should keep this very businesslike. An independent audit of everything." His wide, strong fingers gripped Candace's.

"I agree," Kathleen said, tucking a stray lock of hair behind her ear. "An independent audit is an excellent idea."

"As soon as possible," Randall said, through his clenched teeth. "It's about time we go into the company books with a fine toothed comb."

Jeffery told him, "The IRS are already doing that. I refuse to waste more company money on going over books they've already examined."

"We'll go into it when we get back to town," Judith told the group. "We really shouldn't be talking about business at dinner, should we?"

Jeffery smiled triumphantly at the group. "When we get back to Atlanta, we'll discuss this further, but we have to cut costs drastically." He looked at Savannah and Kevin. "The fat simply has to go."

Savannah curled her lip, and moved further toward her Uncle Kevin, who slung an arm around her. "Don't worry, kid. We've got your back."

She stared down at her plate, unsmiling.

Francesca's face turned white, and she looked like she was going to throw up. She shoved her chair away from the table. "Excuse me," she muttered, as she left the room.

Judith started to follow, then hesitated on the edge of her chair.

Mia patted her hand. "Just let her go. She needs a few moments to herself."

Judith's brow furrowed between her wide set brown eyes. "We're going through so much, right now. I hope it'll all be over soon." Her knuckles whitened on her wine glass stem, making the soft pink of her nails stand out starkly.

"Relax. Everything will be fine," Mia reassured her. "By this time next year, everything will be back to normal."

"We'll have our old life back soon," Judith agreed, like a mantra.

Mia sat on her balcony that night, contentedly sipping a local Grappa di Prosecco in a charmingly diminutive tulip-shaped glass. She looked across the dark fields, rolling the oaky caramel liquid in her mouth, as she went over the events of the day.

It had been quite a day, followed by that dreadful dinner. It was positively a crime to bicker at dinner, ruining such a delicious meal. Mia now understood why Kathleen had wanted her old friend with her for this trip. They might need a vacation together afterwards to recover from the rest of the Parker family.

She fixed her thoughts on their morning walk through Belruscello, remembering the charming old piazza, the lovely little shops. That part of the day had been Italy, at its best. Hopefully, the family would be too busy touring tomorrow to fight. She wrapped her pale blue silk robe around her, yawning in the rose scented air, relaxing into the night.

Below her, on the veranda, she heard the loud sound of footsteps leaving the villa.

"Still out here, Randall?" Jeffery drawled. "I do hope you're not worrying about anything."

The cushion rustled as he sat down, then Mia heard the strike of a match, and its quick flare.

Randall commented dryly, "Still smoking that stuff, huh? It ruins your lungs, you know. Can't do your running any good."

"Hasn't hurt me yet," Jeffery rejoined. "I'm a lot younger than you are, though."

Silence. Then, Mia heard Randall stand. "Well, since I'm such an old man, I'm going to bed like everyone else," Randall said. "I hope you'll be in a more reasonable mindset in the morning."

"I meant what I said," Jeffery told him.

The smell of Jeffery's pipe smoke drifted up, out of sight. The acrid sweet smell of tobacco oozed insidiously through the air, cutting through the smell of roses, and making Mia's drink bitter. With a long sigh, she got up, closing the French doors tightly behind her as she went to bed.

5

A Different Approach

Mia wakened to a scream coming from the veranda. It went on and on in undulating waves, abruptly stopped by Teresa's shriek of "Dio Mio!"

Mia slid to the floor, and began dressing rapidly. Something very bad had happened. She hoped it hadn't happened to one of her friends.

When she reached the veranda, a hushed group of people stood around the body of Jeffery Parker. He had fallen out of the deep cushioned chair, and lay splayed out on the floor, his broken pipe shattered beside him. He had vomited, then collapsed on the floor. He obviously had died quickly.

Judith came running across the courtyard. "Jeffery? Has anyone called a doctor? Maybe..." She broke off. Jeffery had clearly been beyond help for quite some time. "He had a heart attack, just like Harold. And his father." She choked a little, looking down at the still body, "Poor Jeffery. He was so young."

"All that stuff, last night—maybe he was already sick," Savannah said hesitantly. "He'd never said anything like that before. My numbers are good, not like he said last night." She fiddled with a long strand of hair, turning it around her finger. "He must have been sick already. I wish—" she broke off. Without her normal mask of heavy makeup, she revealed herself to be a more than pretty young woman, almost beautiful, even in her distress. Her big dark eyes looked anywhere, but at the body lying on the tile floor.

Judith agreed firmly, "All that running wasn't good for his heart, I don't care what anyone says. And the plane flight." She shook her head. "We won't say another word about last night. Dear Jeffery was clearly not himself last night."

Only Mia heard Diane mutter, "Then who was he? He sure seemed like Jeffery to me."

Randall asked, "I hate to say this, but he obviously vomited. Do you think it could have been food poisoning?"

Teresa volubly demanded, "Food poisoning? In my kitchen?" She gestured broadly at everyone. "You are all here—no one is sick." Her hands went to her broad hips. "No one else is sick."

Diane agreed, briefly touching Teresa's arm in reassurance. "We all ate out of the same platters. Jeffery couldn't possibly have anything we didn't have." She stared wonderingly at the body, then looked at Teresa.

The older woman nodded once, obviously grateful for Diane's statement.

Candace, crying into Kevin's shoulder, said, "We should go inside. Stop looking at him, lying like this. Oh, poor Jeffery." She sobbed again. "The kids shouldn't see him, not like this."

Kevin gently shepherded his wife into the villa, motioning Ben and Savannah to follow. The rest of the group fell into line, avoiding looking at Jeffery's glazed eyes staring into nothing, as they filed past his body.

Pietro arrived, and took in the scene at a glance. He called the police, talking rapidly, too fast for even Mia to understand his Italian, but his angry gestures at the body needed no translation. He put his arm around Teresa, who was still standing, looking down at the body in shock, gestured peremptorily to Anna, and disappeared with the women into the back rooms of the villa.

The Parkers waited inside the grand sitting room, windows shuttered to avoid looking at the Carabinieri, arriving at the emergency scene. Through the thick walls, those waiting could hear muffled conversation, the scrape of furniture dragged across the tiles, all the small ways emergencies services pay their respects to the dead.

A tiny Italian woman, impeccably dressed in a silk blouse, gold chains covering a plunging neckline, knocked softly on the open door. She carried protective gear slung over her shoulder. "I am the medico legale, Dr. Rosanna Pavan. Can anyone tell me, please, if this man had preexisting conditions, any medications, something that might explain his death?" she said in accented, but perfect, English.

Judith came forward, holding out her hand to shake. "I don't know about Jeffery's heart, but his father," she paused a moment, "and my husband had serious heart issues. They both died the same way. His father years ago, and my husband more recently."

"I see," Dr. Pavan scribbled in a notebook.

"Would you like his doctor's name? I have it right here," Judith's perfectly tinted mouth twisted briefly. "He was my husband's cardiologist, too."

"Yes, per favore." The doctor scribbled.

Diane added, "We all ate from the same platters last night, so it couldn't be food poisoning."

The medico legale looked up sharply. "He ate nothing separately from the rest of the group? Nothing at all?"

"No, nothing." Diane looked around the group, and they all nodded agreement."

"At least, nothing separately at dinner," Mia clarified. "He may have had something before or after that, without us."

The doctor nodded. "It would have had to have been during the time he was on the veranda after dinner, I think. Signore Parker has been dead since last night or very early this morning. I will know more after the autopsy." She ran her finger along her gold chains. "Does anyone have more information on his health?"

Judith answered for the others, "No, but his cardiologist should be able to tell you everything."

"Very well," the doctor said. "I will contact them, of course. Who is the next of kin?"

Kevin came forward. "I'm his brother. I will be responsible for his," he looked at Candace and Judith. His face crumpled slightly, then his jaw hardened. "Whatever we need to do, I'll handle it."

Randall clapped him on the back briefly, saying nothing.

Dr. Pavan wrote Kevin's name and information down, and left. Her departure left a hollow emptiness in the big room. Legs shifted, and feet shuffled on a rich Turkish rug. There were sniffles of muffled crying, and clicks of nails tapping on chair arms.

They avoided each other's eyes, and said nothing.

Mia gazed with interest around the high ceilinged, formal room. Long dark beams girded the room in a high coffered ceiling, faintly tinged with faded gilt traceries. Glimpses of antique brocade chairs, practically covered by summer white linen slipcovers. A large tapestry, which must have been worked by some long ago lady of the house, told a story with extravagantly dressed gentlemen and full skirted ladies, Mia wouldn't mind examining further at another time.

Elaborately carved mouldings in a honey colored marble framed the walls, with neat stacks of gilt framed landscapes, highlighted by cleverly placed lighting. Most looked like beautiful views of Italy, in both formal oil paintings and lighter watercolor sketches. Mia wondered whether they had been painted by a lady of the house.

It would normally be quite a lovely room, when the tall windows opened onto the shady veranda, cool even in the blazing heat of summer. Now, it could be a barn, for all it mattered to those sitting here.

Candace's mascara streaked her tears, dark lines slipping slowly down her face. She couldn't stop crying, even with Judith's acrid comment of, "Control yourself, dear. These things happen, but there's no use in us breaking down." Judith herself showed no sign of breaking down, just tightened lips and a slight pinching around her eyes, as if she had a headache.

Kevin sat with one arm around Candace, and his son close to him, the boy looking wide eyed and anxious, and much younger than he usually did. He had shushed Ben several times, and the boy's body was whip tense against the back of the sofa, as if it might snap.

Randall commanded one of the big linen slip covered chairs, hands firmly spread on his outspread thighs and parade ground straight posture. He stared straight ahead, mired in his thoughts. Francesca perched next to him on a small ottoman, her glazed eyes in shock. She didn't move, not a muscle, remaining limp as a rag doll, draped across the cushion. Judith frowned at Francesca from across the room, where she'd seated herself in the only upright chair, next to a tall secretary desk, but said nothing.

Diane and Savannah were almost swallowed by the large sofa, placed behind Judith. Savannah's eyes were closed and she was mouthing something. Probably a mantra like, "Keep calm. Relax. Do not panic," Mia thought. Diane was slumped back in the voluminous cushion, but her eyes darted around the room, never settling on one person for long. Her face was carefully blank, partially hidden by her hair.

Mia wondered which of the people in this room had killed Jeffery. People didn't vomit and die like that from heart attacks. After the scene last night, it was little wonder one of them wanted to kill him. And it seemed like someone had actually done it.

Her inquisitive blue eyes met Kathleen's dark ones, staring solemnly at her. Kathleen looked around the room, then back at Mia. She nodded to Mia, agreeing with Mia's unspoken conclusion—there was a killer sitting among them.

Footsteps punctuated the silence, and a handsome man, his dark hair's cut precisely controlling the wave of his hair, entered the room. Like most Italians, he was well dressed, in a sophisticated charcoal gray suit and simple dark tie. They all looked at him with a slight sense of relief, glad to have someone they could focus on, someone who wasn't a killer. Someone who might make this whole awful business go away, tell them it was food poisoning or a heart attack, anything besides murder.

"Buongiorno," he solemnly acknowledged the group, focusing on Randall as the oldest male present. "I am Tenente Antonio Zanatta, the Ufficiale del Nucleo Investigativo for this case." He spoke in perfect, American accented English. He'd either watched a lot of American movies, or spent time in the United States.

Randall stood up and shook hands, glad to move. "Nice to meet you, Lieutenant Zanatta. I'm Randall Green. So you'll be handling our situation?" He introduced the rest of the family.

Tenente Zanatta focused on Kevin. "Jeffery Parker was your brother? You're the next-of-kin?"

Kevin agreed, "I am. He was my older brother. My only brother." His hand clenched his knee briefly, his knuckles turning white from the pressure.

"I am sorry for your loss," the officer told him. "It's difficult to lose your only brother."

Kevin nodded brusquely, deliberately relaxing his hand. His other arm encircled Candace, holding her close.

Judith finally asked, "Why are the police still here? My nephew had a heart attack." She sounded like, if she said it enough, she could force it into reality.

"Perhaps," Zanatta told her. "There are some anomalies the medico legale, Dr. Pavan, is not sanguine with. While she is conducting the autopsy, I am conducting a preliminary investigation. This is the protocol in a case of sudden death, such as this."

"I see," Judith told him, frowning. "What can we help you with?"

"To begin with, who was the last person to see Mr. Jeffery Parker?" He uncapped his sleek, black fountain pen, taking out a small notebook encased in an elegant leather sleeve.

They looked at each other, all reluctant to speak first.

Randall finally admitted, saying in crisp, short barks, "I was probably the last to see Jeffery. He was there last night, on the veranda, smoking that damn pipe of his. Hate the smell. So I left." His back remained ramrod straight as Francesca clutched at his arm. He briefly put his hand on hers in reassurance.

Mia volunteered, "I was sitting on my balcony, at the same time last night, about eleven-thirty. I heard Randall greet Jeffery, then leave. I went inside my room, closing my balcony door." She smiled a little. "I didn't like the pipe smoke either."

Randall looked quizzically at her, surprised she had overheard them, then he gave a curt nod of thanks.

"His pipe and glass were found near him," Zanatta acknowledged, writing in his notebook. "Was Signore Parker depressed in any way? Does anyone know of any reason he would take his own life?"

They all sat there, stunned into silence. The only sound was Candace's continuous soft crying.

After a moment, Judith suggested, reluctantly considering the possibility, "He had been overseeing an IRS audit at work that was extremely stressful. I wouldn't have guessed it, but..."

"Now, wait a damn minute, Judith," Kevin burst out, standing up quickly. "There's no way Jeffery would have committed suicide. Not in a million years—he was too damn fond of his own skin to let anything happen to it."

"I didn't mean," Judith broke off. "I'm sure you're right," she said in a conciliatory tone. "It must have been a heart attack."

"Trust me, if he'd had a heart problem, we'd have known about that too." Kevin looked at Tenente Zanatta, spreading his hands wide. "My brother and I weren't very close, but that was one of the things he liked to talk about. We'd get together for lunch every few months, and I'd hear two hours of his doctor visits and marathon plans. He wasn't exactly interested in my plumbing business." He gave a short laugh. "Jeffery wasn't exactly interested in anyone, but himself. So there is no way in hell my brother committed suicide."

Zanatta's dark eyes glanced up from his notebook. "And the last time you saw Signore Parker was?" he paused, interrogatively.

"A month ago," Kevin glanced briefly at Francesca. "We had some family stuff to discuss." He looked off to the side, then back at Zanatta. "And he told me all about some damn stress testing he'd done to improve his marathon time. Bragged about all the fantastic results, said he had the heart of a twenty-year-old. So there is no way in a month, he suddenly developed heart problems. After Dad died at such a young age from a heart attack, we've both been very careful about checkups."

Zanatta said, "I will inform Dr. Pavan of this."

Judith said, "I already gave Dr. Pavan his cardiologist's information." She looked at Kevin, "I assumed he had problems because he had all those tests done."

He said shortly, "No. He was training for the Jungfrau-Marathon in September. 1,800 meters of climbing."

110

Zanatta said, "He was over forty, yes?"

"Forty-three."

"That is a difficult run, for a man his age. He must have been in very good condition. I did that, ten years ago now. It was rewarding, but I would not try it again now, without training for it."

The lieutenant looked like he was in his mid-thirties, lean and muscled, like a sleek panther. Mia thought if he'd train for a run, it must be a very serious challenge.

Kevin told him. "He had a rigorous training schedule. And, like I told you, he had just done stress testing. He took extremely good care of his heart and general health. He did one marathon a year, for his vacation. It was a big event for him—he'd spend ages deciding which race to run, and planning his training." His mouth flickered upwards in a brief smile. "It's about all I ever saw Jeffery get excited about. He really looked forward to those races." He pulled Candace a little tighter, and she smiled up at him, through the blur of tears.

Tenente Zanatta looked around the room. He saw white, shocked faces, but none with the obvious guilt of murder written across it. He sighed inwardly.

Dr. Pavan believed Jeffery Parker had died from poison, not a heart attack. A heart attack was much less probable now, because of the recent cardiac examination, since any weaknesses would have been exposed during a stress test or marathon training. Food poisoning was not a possibility, unless he had eaten something the others had not had, perhaps after dinner.

His digestivo glass, the most probable vehicle for poison, but not for food poisoning, was being analyzed. They would know what the glass had contained shortly, and that would quickly prove whether or not this had been murder.

Zanatta was quite certain a murderer sat here, in this very room.

6

Talking

No one felt like eating the excellent roast chicken over polenta Teresa had prepared for their lunch, except Ben, who mechanically shoveled it into his mouth, without his usual sublime expression. They were quiet, all thinking about last night's uncomfortable dinner, followed by the horror of Jeffery's death in the night.

Kevin, after shoving his plate to the side, said, "I suppose Jeffery must have had an aneurysm or something."

Judith agreed, with obvious relief at the commonplace explanation, "I think I read that high plane altitude can cause an aneurysm to rupture."

Diane said gently, dropping the words like pebbles into a pond, seeing their soft ripples, "I wonder if that was why he was so," she searched for the right word, "argumentative, last night. He must have been sick already."

"He must have," Candace agreed, with relieved eagerness. "I guess he just wasn't himself, last night. Especially after that long plane flight." She fiddled with her fork. "I wish he'd told us he wasn't feeling well so we could take him to a doctor."

Kevin added, "Jeffery always lashed out when he was hurt. I remember when he broke his leg that summer." He barked a laugh. "I spent the whole summer fetching and carrying everything for him, with him ringing that dang bell like I was a dog. He enjoyed the heck out of seeing me run around in the heat. He'd plan trips to the store at midday, just to see me sweat."

"Until I put a stop to that nonsense," Judith said with a thin smile. "He always took it out on everyone around him, when he was sick." She took a sip of wine, swirling it in the glass contemplatively. "You boys squabbled like crazy anyway, most of the time. But when Jeffery was sick, everyone had to watch out. He really didn't like feeling out of control. My poor boy." Judith bowed her head, "My poor little boy."

"Poor Jeffery," Diane agreed, her eyes glistening. "I'll miss him telling about his running adventures."

After lunch, Judith escaped to her room, saying she had a headache. And she looked like she had one, Mia thought, with her face pale, and showing lines that hadn't been there a few days before. And no wonder, this was about as bad as a family vacation got, which was such a shame in this beautiful setting.

Mia remembered Jeffery as a young boy, clinging to Judith after his father died. He'd taken as much responsibility as he could, at that young age, for his four year younger brother. Harold and Judith had raised the boys and loved them, like they were their own.

Kevin and Candace fled to their room, with Ben trailing behind them. They looked like they were in shock.

Savannah, deprived of Ben's company, went down to the pool, lying on one of the cushioned lounge chairs, her pale white skin and svelte, muscular figure highlighted with a brief, black bikini. When Mia strolled by with Kathleen a few minutes later, she already looked like she was fast asleep, behind dark glasses and large headphones. Mia thought of waking her to remind her about sunscreen, but decided Savannah was old enough to know that—and needed a break from nagging aunts.

As they walked through the bright flowers of the garden, they saw Francesca standing at the far end of the main path, looking out over the vineyards. Her brightly dressed figure drooped like a wilted flower, and oversize sunglasses hid her face. "She doesn't look like she needs to be alone right now," Mia told her friend. "Let's go over and talk about something cheerful."

They started slowly moving in Francesca's direction, but then they saw Randall striding down to the girl. He reached her, putting his arms around her, and she clung to him like a child. He guided her to a nearby bench in the shade.

Kathleen told Mia, with a look of relief, "Randall will take care of her, don't worry. Let's go to the veranda, where we're not intruding. It will be nice to get out of the sun. When I'm working in the olive groves, we always take a pisolino, a little nap, after lunch. You just don't realize how hot it gets here in the summer, until the sun's beating down."

Randall put his arm around Francesca and she leaned into him, sobbing. He let her cry for a minute, looking out at the serene greens of the vineyard. Then, he decided she'd cried for long enough. "Come now, Francesca," he chided her gently. "It's not as bad as all that."

"It's all my fault." Her voice was muffled.

Randall stiffened slightly, "What's your fault?"

She cried harder, and he felt her warm tears wetting his shirt.

"What's your fault, honey?" he asked in a soft voice, as if coaxing a hurt wild animal out into the open, where he could help it.

She drew back from him, her beautiful gray eyes blurred by tears, lush dark lashes clumping wetly together. "It's all my fault, Uncle Randall," she sniffed hard. "We wouldn't even be here in Italy, except for me."

"Now, that's just silly, Francesca. Judith takes everyone on a family vacation almost every year. She hadn't taken the family to Italy yet, and Kathleen's living here. It's a logical choice, because you all missed her."

"But Jeffery never comes along," Francesca argued. "He always says he doesn't have time. He didn't want to come—and he's dead!"

"He came because of business, honey. The IRS audit, not you," he said in measured tones.

"There wouldn't be an IRS audit except for me!" Francesca burst out. "Jeffery said so."

"You know, honey," Randall said, "I think Jeffery must have been pretty sick already last night. He said a lot of things that just didn't make sense."

"Yeah, like Savannah. She's killing it at work," Francesca sniffed, then froze, listening to what she just said. "Uncle Randall?" she asked in a small voice.

"Hmm?" he rumbled.

"Do you think Jeffery was killed?" she asked hesitatingly.

"I don't know, honey. I sure hope not," was his unreassuring response.

"Because if he was killed," Francesca went on, "that means Ryan's—" she choked, "theft, must have stirred something up."

"Maybe," Randall considered. "Or maybe not. Look, Francesca, they'll probably find it was an aneurysm or something like that. We can't let it worry us. We'll know what happened when that doc has the autopsy results. Plenty of time to worry about it then, if we need to." He coughed. "I had something in particular I wanted to talk with you about, this trip."

He looked at her, thinking of how best to approach this. He knew it was the wrong time, but it always seemed to be.

Francesca's tears had started to dry, but her face was still splotched from her recent storm. Her sad eyes drooped, and her long dark hair was dull and unbrushed. She obviously wore the first thing she'd pulled on when she'd heard the screaming outside, a bright flowered dress, flowing gossamer rayon, perfect for an Italian summer, but not for mourning. She looked at him, her curiosity still dulled by shock.

"When I heard the news about Ryan," he stopped, and cleared his throat. "When I heard about Ryan, and that you were moving back home with Judith, I just wondered," he looked seriously at her, "is that really what you want to do?"

She looked down at the grass, dragging a sandal across it, watching the leaves bend down, then spring back up.

"It's just, before you got married, you didn't like living at home so much." He forced a small chuckle. "I remember you begging me to invite you to stay, so you could get away for a while."

Francesca glanced up at him with a faint smile, "Well, you always lived in interesting places."

He coughed to hide his pleasure. "We did have a lot of fun together," he said. "But I didn't know, are you sure you want to move back home? Birds do have to spread their wings sometime, you know. You don't have to go back home. You could rent an apartment." He looked at her seriously, "You could even change jobs, you know. Move out of town for a bit. Sometimes, it's good to change things up after a rough patch. Explore new places."

Francesca shrugged a little, looking uncomfortable. "I don't know. I'll be in the guest house, not like it's my old bedroom. It's not even in the house. And it's not like I make a fortune working for Parker Perches, you know. I get paid well for a newbie industrial designer, but I'm just one of the pack, still learning."

"If it's money," he hesitantly offered.

She sighed heavily, then said slowly, "It's not really about money. I do okay. I just feel so awful for what Ryan did. Mom has been so sweet and understanding about everything. She hasn't blamed me for anything, throughout the whole mess. She's really had my back," Francesca told him. "She even paid for the divorce lawyers. Told me she'd make sure I'd get a fresh start."

"Judith does fight like a mama tiger when she has to," Randall agreed.

"And she just assumed I'd be coming back home to live, and started redoing the guest house for me." Francesca twisted the airy fabric of her dress into a hard knot, then smoothed it out. "I don't know what I want to do now, so I might as well make her happy. She's done so much for me."

"I understand," Randall said. "Well, it's probably not a bad thing, you going back home, letting her fuss over you like a mother hen again, for a while."

"It might be nice, after we get used to each other." Francesca flashed a glimmer of a smile, "And I can always go visit fun Uncle Randall in Germany, or wherever he's posted next."

"That you can," Randall agreed with a smile.

When the family escaped from the maudlin lunch and Judith left for her nap, Diane headed straight to the rose garden. The beautiful garden room was surrounded by high walls, and difficult to find if you weren't looking for it. She wanted some time to herself.

The garden was still the enchanted seclusion she remembered. The scent of roses was heavy and rich, and the blossoms spread out in a glorious tapestry of color. The teak bench, silvered by time, looked like a perfect place to gather her thoughts.

For a few moments, she closed her eyes, letting the heady scent relax her. The birds chirped in the trees on the other side of the wall. A small lizard skittered past her, pausing to cock his head interrogatively at her, as if to ask what she was doing in his garden. Diane laughed softly, feeling the tension in her jaw ease, and her shoulders relax. She reached her arms up, stretching to one side, then the other. That felt better.

She looked at the roses, their rich kaleidoscope of colors, closed her eyes, and lost herself in her thoughts.

She was startled by Pietro's quiet cough. She opened her eyes and saw his gentle smile.

"Did I catch you in a nap?" he asked, hesitant of intruding.

"No, I was thinking about Jeffery. About what happened last night, and his awful death." Diane smiled at him. "I'm glad to see you," she admitted.

"You were close to Jeffery?" Pietro sat down on the bench, looking at her with his kind dark eyes.

"We were cousins," Diane told him. "He was a bit older than me, than Kevin too." She sighed. "No, we weren't all that close. Kevin and I, we've always done stuff together, but Jeffery," she shrugged. "He was hard to be friends with. Still, he was my cousin; he's always there."

"I know what you mean," Pietro agreed. "Sometimes, my cousins are not the best of friends, but they are always family."

"Exactly." Diane smiled at his understanding. "Jeffery was family."

"What happened last night?" Pietro asked curiously. "Teresa said no one ate——you were all very upset."

Diane looked at him. "I don't know if I should say."

"If Anna was around, she'll tell everyone. Trust me," Pietro's voice was dry. "I have found that girl outside more keyholes than you would believe. If it was not so hard to get help," he smiled at Diane, "and she was not Teresa's cousin's daughter, I would let her go."

Diane laughed at his expression, "A cousin, again."

"It is always the family that nurtures us and causes troubles." He smiled at her, not urging her to talk, but clearly curious.

"Jeffery showed up yesterday, saying he had to talk with Judith about a tax audit the family company was having. He just seemed like the usual Jeffery, annoyed at having to come to Italy, when he'd rather be home working." Diane's voice choked a minute, and Pietro put his hand on her arm. She looked up at him gratefully.

"At dinner, he starts acting very strangely. Starts talking about how everyone is getting less money from the family business–Mom and I sold our shares when she was sick, so that didn't affect me." Diane grinned ruefully, "I'm not exactly an heiress like the rest of them." She shrugged.

Pietro laughed softly.

"He just said a lot of nasty things to everyone," Diane continued. "It was odd. Jeffery could get nasty, it's one of the reasons I'm not as close to him, as I am to Kevin. But he usually said snide little asides in private, not wholesale at the dinner table." She shook her head. "He must have been sick already."

Pietro looked at Diane's compassionate face, obviously trying to think the best of Jeffery, despite him being, from Pietro's brief observation, an unpleasant man. He wondered what it was like for Diane, being 'not exactly an heiress' surrounded by wealth. Her hands showed that she worked with them. She wasn't delicate and weak, but a pretty, capable woman, with a beautiful, genuine smile. He would like to know her better.

Diane looked up at him, her dark lashes unveiling deep sparks of amber in her eyes, shining luminously in her sorrow. Her grief for a cousin she was obviously trying to remember the best of touched him. She was very pretty when she smiled, with wide, naturally red lips. Her golden eyes saw the best and worst of the world, accepting it all with good humor.

He wondered why Diane was so worried, why her fear kept rising to the surface in almost tangible waves. Pietro was certain it had something to do with her cousin Jeffery's death. Well, at least he could distract her from her grief.

He rose to his feet and held out his hand to this lovely woman. "Let me show you the rest of the gardens."

Kevin looked out across the rolling vineyards, leaning against the railing on their little balcony. The doors were closed. His eyes felt grainy and hot from grief, but he couldn't let the tears run down his face. Jeffery, Jeffery was dead. His big brother, who'd always looked after him, who he'd counted on to be there for him. Sure he'd been annoying, but that was a big brother's job. Kevin had always seen it as his job to pull Jeffery down a notch when he was being a smart ass.

Why had Jeffery said those horrible things last night? He'd been downright nasty to Savannah, whom Kevin—and he'd thought Jeffery too—had always looked on as almost a little sister, after his cousin Judy had died. They'd even discussed how happy Uncle Harold would have been that Savannah was working at Parker Perches, safe under the family's protective wing.

And Jeffery asking for Kevin's loan back like that, so suddenly. If it had to be done, he could do it, but he sure wouldn't have expanded his business two months before, buying those new trucks, and hiring the extra men. He'd have to cut costs, somehow. And it wasn't as if Jeffery had warned him. Just a private, hey, bro, the family business has a cash flow problem, and we might need you to step up your payment schedule. You're going to need those cash reserves soon.

No, Jeffery had acted like Kevin was some sort of ingrate, leeching off the family, when he was anything but that. He'd been paying his loan back, with interest. He'd insisted on that when he'd made the deal with Uncle Harold.

It was one thing, Judith acting like Kevin's business was all her idea. He was used to that—Judith always liked to be at the center of everything, but she meant well.

But why had Jeffery been so hurtful, attacking Kevin last night like a venomous snake? The part of Kevin who was still a small boy, looking up to and depending on his big brother, broke inside, betrayed, but he couldn't cry, couldn't believe his big brother was really gone. His eyes burned with tears that wouldn't fall.

Candace huddled on the comfortable chair by the bare hearth, with her legs curled up protectively, her glossy pink toes bare. She had been crying all morning, and an occasional tear still slid down her nose. She'd resorted to one of the villa washcloths to dry her face during her crying bouts. Without makeup, her face was blotchy from tears, but her big blue eyes showed how beautiful she actually was, under her protective layer of paint. Her damp blond hair was pulled up into a knot, and she wore a fluffy white bathrobe from her post lunch shower, where she'd run the water as hot as it would go, shaking from cold, desperate to get warm. She pulled the thick bathrobe tightly around her, trying to stop crying.

Ben lay sprawled across the other chair, his long legs stretching across the rug, and his skinny arms hanging limply off the chair. He'd been crying too, and his reddened face looked much younger than his seventeen years old. His dark hair was messier than normal, standing up straight in clumps. "I can't believe Uncle Jeffery's dead, just like that," he said for the hundredth time. "I mean, he just got here yesterday."

"I think the plane must have given him an aneurysm," Candace suggested for the umpteenth time. "It's the only thing that makes sense."

"Yeah, and he was so mean last night. He's usually grouchy, but not like that."

"He was probably sick already, honey," she managed a small smile. "Jeffery didn't like people thinking he was sick, so he'd be a pill if he was feeling bad. He's always been—was always like that." Another tear slid down her nose, and she swiped at it.

"Yeah." Ben stared straight in front of him. "Did he really mean all that stuff he said, about Savannah's job, and Dad's loan?"

"I don't know," Candace answered honestly. "If the company is doing badly, maybe. They might need the money."

"There's no way," Ben said. "Savannah was just bragging to me about some big deal she'd just pulled off, some huge stadium in Texas. That's got to mean that they have money."

"I don't know what Parker Perches has or doesn't have," Candace told Ben. "But our family business is doing just fine, and calling in a loan early wouldn't hurt us in the least," she told Ben firmly.

"Well, now that Uncle Jeffery's dead, he won't be firing Savannah or calling in our loan," Ben told her, with a trace of satisfaction. He stood up. "I'm going to the pool to swim. I bet Savannah's there already."

"Have fun, honey," Candace told him, forcing a smile. "Don't forget to wear sunscreen."

After Ben left, the tears started trickling down her face again. She knew she needed to stop crying, and be there for Kevin.

She needed to get herself together. Jeffery was gone. Nothing would bring him back.

She'd known Jeffery a long time, longer than Kevin, really. She'd dated him a few times, the freshman dating the only senior who'd actually asked her out, when she'd first arrived at her new school. He'd been sweet, a gawky kid back then, taking the pretty new freshman out for burgers, showing her the town.

Then, she'd met Kevin, and no one else mattered. When she'd found out Jeffery was Kevin's older brother, she couldn't believe it, they were so different. She'd said no, thank you, to the next date with Jeffery, and assumed they were still friends. The first inkling that things weren't so easy was when she'd waved casually at Jeffery in the school halls. He'd ducked his head and looked right through her, like she was invisible. She'd thought he was a total jerk.

Then, they'd met at Kevin's house and, oh boy. He'd turned white in shock, and pulled her aside, hissing in her ear to never speak a word about them dating to Kevin, that it was the very least she could do for him, after dumping him for his own brother. While it was technically true she'd been on dates with Jeffery, she'd never dreamed that they were supposed to be exclusively dating or anything serious in the least. They'd never even kissed.

She'd suddenly realized those dates had meant a lot more to Jeffery, than they had to her.

Since there was no way she'd give up Kevin over a few casual burgers, she'd agreed with Jeffery to not tell Kevin. She'd regretted making that promise ever since, because it made the whole thing into so much more than it had actually been. But she'd made the promise, so she'd kept it, despite Jeffery making every attempt to make Candace uncomfortable because of their "secret." He seemed determined to make her feel as bad as possible every time they'd met. And she was equally determined not to let Jeffery know just how much his snide comments bugged her.

Candace had hoped it would all smooth out when Jeffery met someone else, but he never had. When Kevin had decided not to work at the family business, she had been so relieved at the idea of not seeing Jeffery every day, she'd worked like crazy to get their family business going. She knew Kevin's relationship with Jeffery had deteriorated because of her, and she'd never known what to do about it. Jeffery had felt like Kevin had stolen his girl, when she'd never dreamed of being Jeffery's girlfriend. If she could have gone back in time, she'd have just said "Hey, Jeffery, that diner you took me to was great. Maybe we can double date there," and the whole fiasco would have been back in proportion to reality.

She'd always felt vaguely guilty that those few, to her casual, dates had seemed to mean so much to Jeffery, and not to her. Jeffery had simmered with his resentment of Kevin ever since. Kevin had Candace and Ben, and the courage to strike out on his own, and build a thriving business from scratch. His little brother had succeeded in all the ways that mattered, and left Jeffery far behind him.

It hadn't had to be that way. It shouldn't have been that way. But it had been. All Jeffery's life since, he'd both loved and resented Kevin, his younger brother. And it all began with a few casual dates, with the new girl in high school.

Candace's eyes blurred with tears for poor Jeffery, so alone, when he could have been loved by his family, and found a girl who actually cared about him. She scrubbed her face with the washcloth, but the tears kept falling.

Mia and Kathleen were ensconced at the far end of the veranda. Neither woman wanted to return to near where Jeffery's body had been found. It was cool and pleasant in the shade, dappled shadows of leaves playing across the bright sunlight, whispering in the wind. The scent of roses filled the air. It was a sublime setting, here in the beautiful Veneto, but neither woman was relaxed.

"How are you holding up, Kathleen?" Mia asked her old friend.

Kathleen sat back, closing her eyes for a minute, then spoke without opening them. "I'm exhausted. I dreaded something bad happening on this vacation, but nothing like this."

Kathleen leaned against a chair arm, with her legs curled up next to her, and her pretty blue sandals down on the tiles. "I can't believe Jeffery is dead. I remember him as a toddler, always so serious about everything. Too serious. Most kids fall and bounce back up, but Jeffery held a grudge against the ground afterwards. He wanted to do everything perfectly, the first time." She smiled at the past. "He never really changed."

She opened her dark eyes, like pools of sorrow. "Even as a boy, Jeffery liked to get people worked up, just to watch them. He'd say something outrageous, then sit back with that damn smirk on his face." She shook her head. "He was always like that—there's no use pretending." She looked at Mia, her eyes steady on her friend's face. "Do you think he died—well, from natural causes—or was killed?"

Mia looked around them. There were no open windows and no other people within hearing distance. "I think he was murdered."

Kathleen's dark eyes were troubled. "I do, too." She twisted long silver strands of hair that had snaked out of her clip around her finger. "I don't know what to do about it, if anything." She paused, then burst out, "It must have been one of us. One of the family."

"Yes." The single syllable dropped like a stone in a pond, sending shivery ripples out.

"Last night," Kathleen spread her hands wide, then dropped them abruptly. "I'd like to say it wasn't like Jeffery, but it was, unfortunately." Her mind ran back to that little boy, crying on the floor, refusing to get up and try again. It seemed so long ago. "I think Ryan's theft gave Jeffery the chance to grab control over Parker Perches that he'd always wanted. He'd expected to be made CEO when Harold died. After all, he was the logical choice, not Judith."

She twisted her shoulder length gray hair into a knot, then loosened it. "I never did understand why Judith didn't make him CEO when Harold died. I don't think Harold planned on Judith running the business. He wanted her to ease out of the business, and his kids—he regarded Jeffery and Kevin as his sons, as well as Francesca—to take over. It's what he trained them for." She shrugged, "Harold was disappointed at Kevin not entering the business, but very proud of all he'd accomplished. He'd be prouder still of Kevin's business today."

"I think last night showed why Judith wasn't comfortable with Jeffery in charge."

"Yes," Kathleen said thoughtfully. "Jeffery didn't show himself to be a worthy successor last night. Harold would have been horrified." She tapped her hand on her knee. "Of course, I think Judith always planned on Ryan taking over as CEO, not Jeffery."

"What was Jeffery up to last night?" Mia asked.

"The same as always, I'd guess," Kathleen told her. "My guess is he was threatening Francesca with prison, to get full control from Judith. He always did want to be CEO." She shook her head sadly, "Once Ryan was out, Jeffery was the only logical choice left, so he didn't have to be so nasty about it. But that was Jeffery." Her eyes strayed to the other side of the veranda, and a slow tear trickled down her cheek.

"If Jeffery was threatening Francesca," Mia suggested. "That was why Judith let him talk to Savannah and Kevin in such a," she searched for a word, "demeaning way."

"Francesca would never steal money," Kathleen unequivocally stated. "She simply wouldn't."

"No, I'm sure she wouldn't," Mia agreed. "But if Ryan's theft allowed Jeffery to accuse Francesca of something, even if she was innocent, Judith would let him get away with anything to avoid harm to Francesca."

"Except push Francesca out of the family business," Kathleen asserted.

"Would Judith kill Jeffery over that?" Mia asked.

"Absolutely," Kathleen told her. "If Francesca was threatened, she'd kill anyone. But Jeffery was very careful to not threaten Francesca last night, I noticed. He knew where Judith's line was."

"Will it matter if your shares bring in less?" Mia bluntly asked. "I don't want you to worry about money."

Kathleen barked a laugh. "Frankly, I don't spend enough to worry about money. It's always been more of a nice cushion for me, than my income. Nice to have, but I've saved most of it. I'm leaving my shares to Diane, anyway. She's been through a lot." She looked at Mia's quizzical blue eyes and admitted, "I am concerned about what Jeffery's been doing, though. The IRS audit no one told us about isn't a good sign. And the company was running great, when Harold died. That's just a few months ago, so it's hard to believe Ryan could have stolen that much in that period of time, with no one noticing."

"It sounds like Jeffery wasn't that good of a CFO," Mia suggested.

"That's the thing," Kathleen said. "Jeffery was whip smart about money. Always was. The whole thing's odd."

"But what about Kevin? And Savannah? Harold and Judith practically raised them too."

"I don't know," Kathleen said, taking a sip of cold water. "Judith loves having a big family, but Francesca has always been her baby. Kevin wasn't really going to be hurt by calling in that loan—he has a very successful business. Maybe the family business really is in financial trouble after the theft, and needs some cash. I'm definitely going to insist on an audit," she added firmly.

Kathleen wiped a tear from her eye. "I always wanted kids of my own, but, that didn't happen for me." She waved an arm around the villa. "Kevin, Francesca, Diane, Savannah, and poor Jeffery, were like my kids. I stayed in Atlanta to help raise them, until they went to college."

"Yes, I remember you took the kids to things almost as much as Judith."

"Their activities were always on opposite sides of town, soccer, piano and ballet. I always worked my schedule around theirs," Kathleen said with a grin. "It was a blessing when Jeffery got his drivers license and could join the chauffeuring."

"I know what you mean," Mia remembered hectic times ferrying her three children to various activities. "How is Diane doing lately? I'm surprised she hasn't been back to nursing school yet."

"Yes, she was always so interested in nursing, couldn't wait to start." Kathleen paused a minute. "I think taking care of her mom really took a lot out of her. And she has a pretty good life with Judith. Judith fusses over her and treats her like one of her own, like all the rest of them."

"Maybe Diane needs a little push?" Mia suggested.

"Maybe," Kathleen agreed. "I might invite her to stay with me for a while. A change of scenery, living in another country could inspire her—The problem is Diane doesn't have the money—and that freedom that comes with money—that the other kids do. Sadie worked in the office and had a share in the business, but all those experimental cancer treatments cost a fortune, so Sadie had to sell her shares back, when she got sick. And Judith told me Diane is too proud to accept a dime from her, other than her salary. So it might be simply money that's holding Diane back."

"I wonder if we could arrange a better paying job or a loan for her?" Mia suggested. "Or a nursing school loan shouldn't be difficult to organize."

"It's something to think about," Kathleen agreed. "Sometimes we all need a little push to get out of our comfort zone." She sighed. "I just don't know if nursing Sadie took the fun out of that career for Diane. She's still young, she might simply need some time."

They saw the subject of their discussion walking up the garden path, shepherded by Pietro. His dark eyes followed her gesturing hands appreciatively, a smile on his face. "Then again, maybe what Diane needs is a little romance in her life to break out of a rut," Mia suggested, and they both laughed.

Diane came up smiling, "What are you two laughing about?" she asked.

"Just enjoying this gorgeous villa," Mia said, her blue eyes dancing. "Your home is absolutely lovely," she told Pietro.

"Thank you," he told her. "Diane tells me your family has many hotels, so that's a compliment worth having."

"It's a wonderful experience here," Mia said. "Gorgeous gardens, beautiful rooms and delicious food."

"I'm glad you're enjoying your stay," Pietro told her smoothly. Then, he frowned, "besides the recent tragedy, of course."

"It was a shock," Diane said, the smile wiping from her face. Mia realized just how much she'd missed Diane's smile. She'd always been a merry girl, her wide mouth grinning, as she giggled over some joke. It wasn't like her to be as solemn as she had been lately. She and Kathleen would definitely have to rearrange Diane's life, and give her some new interests, so she'd smile again.

Diane was still saying, "—of course, Jeffery always did love causing a fuss, but I'm sure he never meant anything by it. He just liked getting attention and having people a little upset with him."

Kathleen stiffened slightly, obviously disagreeing with Diane's charitable assessment of Jeffery, but she said nothing.

Pietro asked, "Had he been ill before this?"

"No, Jeffery was always very careful about his health. His father died from a heart attack, so he was always eating healthy and exercising," Diane told him. "Not like me," she looked down at her stomach.

Mia wanted to point out that Diane had a very charming man admiring her. This was not the time to denigrate her appearance. She held her tongue with difficulty.

"I wonder what it was," Pietro said. "The doctor will tell us soon, I'm sure. They are very quick, when it's a problem concerning tourists."

"Have you had a death before here?" asked Mia.

"No, a guest had a heart attack, though. Someone very fat, out of shape," he sketched out a round figure with a broad gesture, "he walked to the village in the summer midday heat, and ended up in the hospital." He continued, "That was the most serious illness we have had, but we have had several guests with purses or wallets stolen, in the cities, not here, you understand. The police did not find the purses, of course, but they calmed our guests, and told them to be more careful where they went."

Mia said, "Most cities have areas that are less safe than others, that locals avoid, but tourists don't realize. When I'm touring a city, I always travel with very little that matters in my handbag."

"Yes, a wise precaution," Pietro agreed.

"I'm a little nervous about going on the Palladian villas walk, now," Diane said. "Is it in a safe area?"

"I'm not sure we should even go," Kathleen said. "It seems disrespectful to Jeffery." She tucked the stray lock of hair back behind her ear.

Judith came up, "Nonsense, Kathleen. We're here to see Italy, and we're going to do it."

Diane demurred, "It just seems—" she broke off.

"We're going to continue with our excursions tomorrow. What happened to Jeffery," Judith shrugged her shoulders expressively, "It was karma. We can't do anything about it, so we need to go on with our lives." She looked around her, "It's bad enough we've had to waste another day here. No, tomorrow, we go on with our plans." She looked around at the little group, daring them to argue.

While Mia didn't see any reason not to continue with the touring, she also didn't see why the family had to be forced into going. That couldn't be a comfortable situation for any of them, especially his own brother. She said nothing, since it wasn't her decision.

Pietro took an uneasy step toward Diane, and she glanced up at him, biting her lower lip.

Judith looked at her, "Diane, dear, would you run get me an aspirin? I still have a little bit of a headache left."

"Of course," Diane obediently went to Judith's room.

Judith asked Pietro, "Have you heard from the police?"

"No, I have heard nothing yet."

"It's very frustrating them not letting us know what to do about funeral arrangements," Judith said. "Why would they take this long? I gave them his doctor's number and everything." She obviously held Pietro responsible for the Italian police's inaction.

"Just be patient, these things take time here." He shifted his feet, then looked out at the distant fields.

Kathleen added, "I'm sure they're just checking the cause of death, Judith. That has to take time, and it's not like there's an emergency."

"It just doesn't seem right him lying there. We need to send his body home," Judith demanded.

Pietro looked at his watch, and said uncomfortably, "Please let me know if there is anything I can do." He nodded to them politely, "Excuse me."

After he left, Judith said acidly, "That man is spending far too much time with Diane."

Mia said, with a smile, "Diane is very pretty."

"I suppose," Judith said acerbically. "When she takes the trouble, she can look quite nice, but she usually doesn't bother. I've quit telling her to put on makeup or fix her hair. She goes around looking like a frump. That man must think she has money."

"He seems very nice," Mia said noncommittally.

Kathleen said, "Judith, you think everyone is after the Parker money. They just aren't."

"Ryan was," Judith said bitterly. "I'm not going to let another one under my guard."

"Yes, well," Kathleen clearly bit back what she was about to say. "I'm going to the library. Pietro said I could look through his books. I understand there are some farming journals, dating back several hundred years."

Mia went inside with Kathleen, but veered off to her room. She got her handbag, then exited the house by the side door. Walking rapidly, she escaped down the drive, before anyone noticed she was going.

As she left the villa grounds, she felt an overwhelming sense of relief. The Parker family had reached the stage of grief that any person and everything said grated. They all needed to have a nice lie down, far away from each other, then return to grieve as a family. And Mia needed a break.

The town was quiet this afternoon. The piazza felt sleepy, with a few old men pleasantly napping in the shade from a balcony, and two dogs sleeping by the cool splash of the fountain. She went to the small bar, waking the elderly woman with a start from her afternoon nap. She greeted Mia with avid cheer, her network of tanned wrinkles creasing into a habitual smile, "It is very hot, no?" she asked, in accented English. An orange scarf adorned her neck, and her dark eyes sparkled in the deep wrinkles of her face.

"Yes, it is," Mia agreed. "I thought of getting a coffee, but I think I'd like something cool, instead."

The woman reached in the glass fronted refrigerator behind her, "A Crodino?"

"That sounds perfect," Mia said, taking the frosted glass bottle and paying her.

"You are staying at the Villa Bella Sorgente?" the woman asked with curiosity. The question was merely polite, her bright eyes showed she knew where Mia was staying—and what had happened.

"Yes, I am staying there," Mia agreed, playing her game.

"That poor young man, dying in the night," the elderly woman shook her head. "Are you his family?"

"No, I'm just a close friend of his family."

"Such a shame, a young man dying like that," the woman said, wiping the counter down with a clean cloth. "Ah, well, it is life, is it not? Non c'è rosa senza spine."

"It was a great shock to his family," Mia agreed.

"The carabinieri say," she lowered her voice, "they do not know why he died. It was maybe poison?"

"They haven't told us, yet."

"Dr. Pavan will find out soon, she is a good doctor. I go to her for my knee. She's given me all sorts of medicines, but finally found one that worked."

"She seemed very good. I hope she knows soon how he died." Mia thanked her and took a sip of her drink, coming to her true purpose. "I would guess you know most of what happens in town. I came here to look for a young American man, tall, with blond hair. I think he's staying in town?"

The dark eyes glittered in amusement. "You mean the young man you women had such trouble with, before?" Her mouth twitched.

Mia chuckled with her. "Yes, that young man. I really need to speak with him. Do you know where I might find him?"

"Of course, he is upstairs," the woman smiled. "The poor young man, traveling all the way here to talk with his wife, and her running away." She shook her head. "I told him to leave, let her run after him, but he wouldn't do that." The old woman laughed at the follies of the young. "The poor boy. I rented him a room. How could I not?"

"Of course you had to," Mia agreed. "Do you think I might go and speak with him?"

"Of course, third door on the right," she told Mia. "I hope you talk sense into him, tell him to go back home. He's a handsome one—his wife will follow."

"I'm going to try," Mia said. She went up the narrow stairs, and knocked on the brightly painted blue door.

"Yeah," a muffled voice said. "Come in."

Mia opened the door, and Ryan abruptly stood up from the desk that he'd been hunched over. The table tipped to the side, papers slid down to the floor, and his espresso spilled. He grabbed the nearest cloth he could find and scrubbed at the spreading pool. Mia went in the bathroom and got a towel, cleaning up the rest in short time.

He held up the stained cloth, "That was my last clean shirt," he moaned.

"I expect there's a laundromat in town," Mia suggested. "At least it was an espresso, instead of a cappuccino."

"I guess." He sat down with a thud that creaked the wooden chair. "Ms. Mia, you were the last person I expected to see."

"I wanted to talk with you, Ryan," she told him. "The best way seemed to be to find you in town." She felt absurdly pleased with herself to guess right on the first try—though she had merely thought the woman would know where Ryan was, not actually have him under her roof.

"Is Francesca all right?" he asked eagerly. "I heard there had been a death at the villa. I've been worried."

"Francesca is fine, Ryan. Upset about Jeffery's death, of course, but Judith and Randall are taking good care of her." She pulled a chair out, and sat at the table. He followed her, moving what looked like coffee splattered legal and financial paperwork to one side.

"I need to see her," he pleaded. "I have to tell her the truth."

Mia told him, with decision, "I can't make that happen, Ryan. But if you tell me the truth, I'll try to make it come out."

"I want to talk to Francesca," His chin tilted mulishly. His blond hair stood up in clumps, as if he'd forgotten to brush it after he'd showered. He leaned forward in his chair, his tall, lanky figure tensed like a bowstring.

"I can't do that," Mia repeated gently, "But I will tell you one thing," she offered.

"What?" he spat out.

"I think Jeffery was poisoned." The statement dropped in the room like a bomb.

"Poisoned?" Ryan's face went white. "The police say he was poisoned?"

"The police haven't said yet. The pathologist is doing an autopsy."

"Then, why do you say he was poisoned?"

Mia explained, "He had just had a full medical checkup before running a marathon. You know how careful he was about his health."

"Oh boy, do I ever," Ryan agreed wholeheartedly, running a hand through his thick hair so it stood on end. "He used to tell me everything bad about every lunch I ate with him. I couldn't win, restaurants were terrible, but apparently my home cooking was too. Francesca and I used to sneak off to eat, so we wouldn't get nagged."

"He vomited, before he died," Mia said.

"Food poisoning?"

"He ate the same thing as the rest of us," Mia told him, "from the same serving dishes."

"So not food poisoning," Ryan agreed, running his hand through his thick hair until it stood up even more than before. "What was it?"

"I have an idea about that," Mia said, "but what poison is not the important part, right now. We need to prevent more deaths." She looked alertly at him. "So you're going to tell me your story, right now. First, where were you last night?"

"I had dinner at a little trattoria across the piazza. Risotto and lamb," Ryan told her. "Then, I went on a walk, and eventually ended up back here."

"Did anyone see you out walking?" Mia asked flatly. "Or did you see anyone?"

"Probably," Ryan said. "But I didn't notice anyone in particular."

"Did you go to the villa?"

"Yes, but it's a fortress, you know that?" Ryan leaned back in his chair, looking smug. "I certainly wasn't equipped for climbing walls with broken glass on them."

"How'd you know they have broken glass?" Mia asked sweetly.

He shrugged. "So I did try to get over the wall, but I saw the shine—the stuff is embedded in the concrete," Ryan informed her.

"There's no way you'd let broken glass stop you from seeing Francesca," Mia told him.

Ryan laughed, smoothing his hair back down. "Of course not. But I didn't expect it, and didn't want to get myself shredded with it. I planned to come back tonight with some padding. Last night was just a—a reconnaissance."

Mia told him, with concern, "You won't do that now, will you? The police will be watching the villa."

"No, of course not. I'm not stupid." He gave her a cocky grin.

Mia wasn't sure about the latter, but she was in no mood to argue. "So tell me what's going on, what you're so desperate to tell Francesca."

"My lawyer said not to talk with any of the family," Ryan told her, his grin fading.

"You're here trying to talk to Francesca, aren't you?" Mia told him. "And I'm not one of the family."

"You might as well be," Ryan said sullenly.

"I don't have time for this," Mia tapped her finger on the table impatiently. "I'm the only one willing to listen to your side. Take it or leave it."

Ryan sighed, "Okay, okay. It's all coming out in court, anyway." He shuffled the papers. Mia noticed some spreadsheets in the sheaf.

"It's like this," he began. "I noticed some funds were missing from several of the accounts. Nothing too big, a few thousand." He ran his hands through his hair until it stood up like a shock of wheat. "I thought it was an error. At the worst, a salesman skimming a little. I never dreamed it was anything bigger."

"So I go to Jeffery, tell him, and he says thanks, he'll look into it, please don't tell anyone about it," Ryan sighed heavily. "So I keep my mouth shut like an idiot. The next month, there's a hell of a lot more money missing, and he's accusing me of taking it."

"You know the rest, they call in the police, and then they find some of the money in an account with my name on it. I can't prove it isn't mine—it has my information on it and no one else's. In fact, it's definitely my account, in my name, but I didn't open it."

"Did you check the bank videos?" Mia asked.

"I haven't gotten access to them yet. My lawyer's working on it." Ryan added, "And they used my phone for original verification, then switched to a burner."

"Who would have access to your phone?"

"For one time use?" Ryan asked, "Almost anyone. I leave it on my desk, in the locker room, wherever." He tugged on his hair again. "I never leave it for long, but running to the bathroom, across the street for a coke. And who brings their phone on a workout?"

Mia did, but she probably did a different level of workout than Ryan did.

He grinned at her suddenly, "I'm in big trouble, and I know it."

Mia had the grace to not disagree with him. "Who do you think stole the money?"

"I think Jeffery stole it."

"But he was headed to be the next CEO," Mia objected.

"I think Jeffery felt like he had been passed over when Judith took control of the company," Ryan told her. "He had expected to be made CEO when Harold died. And then—" he broke off.

"And then what?" Mia demanded.

"I think," Ryan paused, "I think Judith would have made either me the next CEO, not Jeffery. Harold had told me I would be the next CEO, actually." He looked embarrassed.

"What?"

"He'd been training me for the position," Ryan told her. "And it wasn't as if Judith would go against that."

"But what about Jeffery?"

"Judith has always been crazy about Francesca, you know. She loves the whole family, but Francesca's her favorite. It makes sense. Francesca's her actual daughter, and the others are just semi-adopted family. From things she said," he looked uncomfortable, "I think she would have made me CEO, not Jeffery. That way Francesca could stay home with," he coughed, "our kids, and still be in control of the company." He shrugged, "Jeffery would have pushed her right out of the business, if she took time off for kids." He made a queer, twisted grimace. "Jeffery loathed kids. Said they were messy."

"But still, he had shares in the company..."

"Harold always had the controlling shares, and Judith inherited them. So what she says goes." He shook his head. "I think Jeffery stole money from the company, put just enough of it in a bank account with my name plastered on it, and the rest in the Cayman Islands or a Swiss bank account as his backup plan." He shrugged, moving his whole lanky body. "Jeffery always had a back up plan."

"And you claim you didn't steal the money," Mia stated flatly.

"I didn't steal any of the money," Ryan said again, obviously not expecting her to believe him. "I can't prove it, but I'm still trying." He gestured at his paperwork.

"Do you have any proof that Jeffery did?"

"Nope," he told her. "I'm looking for it, but it's just a gut feeling."

Pietro opened the door to Tenente Zanatta with a heavy feeling in his heart. Something had been very wrong about Signore Jeffery Parker's death, from the carabinieri's solemn demeanor.

The two men had known each other since a young Antonio Zanatta had made extra money for university picking grapes in the Villa Bella Sorgente's vineyard. Pietro remembered a young man who had done his tedious job well. He wondered if working for the police was better or worse than picking grapes. It would be more remunerative, naturally, but Zanatta had not chosen easy work. Of course, most work was difficult when done well.

Without asking questions, he told the officer, "They are in the sitting room, Tenente." He asked, "May I have a quick word with you, first?"

"Of course, Signore Schiavon," the young man replied with respect.

"Can you tell me—" Pietro paused, and began again, "Teresa—you remember Teresa?"

Tenente Zanatta nodded. Everyone remembered Teresa, and especially her cooking. The feasts during the harvest season were ample, and one of the reasons young men clamored to join the grape pickers. There was so much food, the table boards bent under the weight of it. "I remember Teresa. Is she well?"

"She is worried," Pietro said, "She does not see how it could be food poisoning from her kitchen, but—she is crying all day in the kitchen because of it. Because the man vomited before he died, you know?"

Tenente Zanatta answered quickly, "It absolutely was not food poisoning, you can reassure Teresa of that."

Pietro's face relaxed slightly, "I'm very glad to hear you say that. She wouldn't accept it from me, no matter how I showed her the impossibility of food poisoning only affecting one person."

"However," Tenente Zanatta continued, his face serious, "he was poisoned, deliberately poisoned."

Pietro's whole body tensed. "You are sure?"

"We are sure," Tenente Zanatta said, with decision. "If you would be so kind as to come with me, while I tell the Parkers?" It would help to have a non official there to buffer any questions. Signore Schiavon spoke English on almost a daily basis with his guests, but Zanatta rarely had to speak English. He wanted to make certain he made no errors—and missed no words.

"Yes, I will come." Pietro Schiavon never shirked his duty. He was also extremely angry that someone had dared to commit murder in his villa.

He led the Tenente to the sitting room, thinking hard. He carefully examined the strained, white faces and tense eyes, as he opened the door, searching for any obvious signs of guilt. Catching Diane's eyes, he briefly gave her an encouraging smile, then reverted to the appropriate solemnity of the occasion. Diane's face was pale and resolute, clearly strained to her limit.

Signora Parker sat at the secretary desk, very upright and elegante. She was clearly the matriarch of this family, ready for business, with a notepad and pen ready. Her eyes were red from grief, but her rigidly composed face refused to give in to public grief. Pietro approved of her dignity in the trying circumstances. It did not seem like such a woman would poison a family member. But after all, poison was a woman's weapon. A dignified elderly woman would scarcely bash someone over the head.

One of the young women—Pietro thought in an aside that two such pretty women all in one family was a gift—the young woman, Francesca, sat with her lips compressed and long lashed gray eyes dull from shock, patiently waiting for the next blow. She slumped in her comfortable chair, like a dog who had been beaten. It was a shame to see that look on such a beautiful woman, who should have all to live for. She seemed frozen by shock. How could she have poisoned anyone?

Protectively beside her, the family friend, Signore Green, leaned forward, his hands squarely placed on his knees, eagerly awaiting the news. It would not be the news he wanted, Pietro thought. Signore Green would shoot a man, or bash him over the head, if he had sufficient reason, but Pietro doubted he would ever think of poisoning a man. Poison was not a man's crime.

Pietro wondered if a murderer would be in shock at the crime he had committed. He would pretend to be, to be sure. Perhaps the murderer would expect the medico legale to ignore the death, to avoid disrupting tourism. A murderer must be full of pride, to think he could get away with a crime that severe.

Signore Parker, the brother of the murdered man, and his family huddled together on one of the sofas. His arm was around his young son's shoulders, lending him strength. His wife, not a type Pietro admired, pretty, but troppo vistosa for his taste, leaked tears like a sieve, lacking the dignity of the other women, even the limp Francesca. Her husband patted her knee kindly, but had little effect on her tears.

The poor man, Pietro thought with commiseration, losing his only brother, and having to deal with a woman's tears. She should be comforting him. The boy, at least, sat politely, glaring under his lowered eyebrows at the room with the anger of the young. Pietro did not think the teenager would poison anyone, but of course, it did depend on what the poison was. Teenagers always found access to drugs. He might have thought it would be amusing to drug his rude Uncle Jeffery silly, and not realized what could happen.

The younger woman, the black she was wearing was appropriate, but the lace, less so, and troppo volgare as well. But the young will always wear ridiculous things. With her black rimmed eyes showing signs of watery disintegration, like a melting vampire, Signorina Savannah looked almost as bad as Signora Parker. But she was a child, still, thought Pietro kindly, and would grow into decorum. Her eyes might be full of tears for her dead uncle, but she was doing her best to keep them to herself.

The family friend, Signora Spinel, had her shoulder length blonde hair perfectly coiffed, her white linen slacks and silvery gray top, fierezza and elegante, but her wide blue eyes were narrowed, watching the room. Like Signore Green, she was not related to the Parkers. It was unlikely she would be the poisoner, Pietro thought, for she would have no reason he could think of. Her calculating expression and wary eyes said that she was very curious in why Signore Parker had died, however.

Beside her, Diane perched on the edge of the sofa, her white knuckled hands tense on her knees. Her beautiful amber eyes were partially hidden by her long dark lashes, still damp with tears. He should take her on another walk in the garden after this—a pretty woman in a garden was her most attractive setting. The news would not help her.

Signora Kathleen Parker, the one with the no nonsense gray hair, the organizer of this vacation, sat on Diane's far side. She held herself very straight and upright, her head turned politely to Tenente Zanatta.

She seemed too civilized for poisoning, but you never knew.

Pietro wondered which of these people was the murderer. His eyes wandered back to pretty Diane. He knew, at least, it could not possible be her, with her openness and cheerful attitude.

Mia looked up politely at the Tenente, while trying to watch the Parkers' reactions, for she was sure Jeffery's death had been murder. She patted Diane's knee briefly, trying to reassure the young woman.

Tenente Zanatta, dressed with care in a sober dark gray suit and sleek silk tie, abruptly began, "I have very bad new for you today. Signore Parker was poisoned."

"Food poisoning?" Kathleen asked, "I don't see how that's possible. We all ate from the same serving dishes."

"No, not food poisoning," the Tenente said soberly. "He was poisoned deliberately, by Nerium oleander, what we call ammazza asino, donkey killer. It is a very dangerous plant, you know."

Pietro frowned at the news that his garden plant had been stolen for poison.

Mia felt the blow hit Diane, the shock shuddering through her. She took the young woman's hand, holding it tightly.

"But," Judith said with confusion, "I don't see how..." She frowned, explaining, "I'm sure Jeffery knew oleander was poisonous. We have some in the garden at home. You see it all over the South."

Kevin added, "My brother would never have committed suicide, Tenente. Not under any circumstances."

"No," Tenente Zanatta agreed. "Your brother did not commit suicide. He was poisoned with oleander leaves introduced into his pipe tobacco."

"Oh!" Candace cried. "No!" Tears began to flow again, trickling dark streaks down her face. Pietro glanced at her with distaste.

Kevin stood up slowly, letting go of Candace's hand. "'Jeffery was poisoned by his pipe? Pipe smoke?"

"Yes," the Tenente said. "I am afraid smoke from oleander can poison very quickly."

"He would never have done that," Kevin stated. "Never."

"No," Tenente Zanatta agreed. "Someone murdered your brother."

7

Explorations

The next morning, they gathered around the massive dining table, staring dully into their phones, avoiding all possibility of eye contact. Conversation stuttered sporadically, no one sure of what to say, or how to say it.

No news of Jeffery's murder had reached the Atlanta news stations yet, Judith informed them, with relief. She added, optimistically, "I'm sure the police will retest their lab work, and realize Jeffery wasn't poisoned, before his death reaches the news. All this police business will all just go away. We can mourn in peace, and then get back to our normal lives."

The only one who responded to her ridiculously hopeful statement was Diane, who gave her a faint smile, and returned to sipping her coffee in silence. No one in the room cared if Jeffery's death was announced in the news now or later. It obviously would be at some point. Being in Italy gave them some isolation to prepare for the condolences and curiosity.

Oddly, no one, besides Judith, seemed to believe that Jeffery hadn't been murdered. The Parkers had accepted that everyone they knew would be gossiping about Jeffery's murder, eventually. It was hard to care about gossip, so far away, when the reality was that Jeffery's murderer must certainly be one of their family.

Mia drank her coffee, discretely scanning the Parker family. They all looked exhausted.

Savannah was the only one of the family with a clear purpose and the energy to match it. Her kohl rimmed eyes were alert, and her black hair silky smooth. This morning at breakfast, she showed that she had been up all night planning strategies. She'd start excitedly talking about a marketing strategy, then her voice trickled to nothing, as she realized no one was listening. She'd page through her phone, and look up, discussing business aloud, then give up the effort again, when no one responded. After briefly perching on a chair, eating crunchy toast heaped with apricot jam, she'd left, muttering about "damage control."

Ever since, she had typed madly all morning, comfortably ensconced on a lounge chair by the pool. She was obviously working hard, despite being on her vacation and the stressful circumstances, Mia noted. Jeffery had been wrong about Savannah's job skills, or at least her dedication to her job.

Kevin and Randall sat together at the end of the table, drinking as much coffee as Teresa would serve them. Neither man spoke. They stared blankly into their coffee mugs, and crumbled toast on their plates. Kevin had aged ten years overnight, with puffy gray circles under his eyes. He didn't seem to notice the others in the room. Mia could almost see the memories of his older brother playing through his head. Poor Kevin.

Candace had apparently remained in bed, or at least, away from this depressed gathering. Ben had come in, devoured half the buffet on offer with his shoulders hunched protectively, and his fork firmly grasped in his fist. Then he'd left, without speaking a single word to anyone. Francesca had drifted in and out, wafting a brioche and coffee out with her.

Mia, Judith, and Kathleen made polite chit chat at the other end of the table, with odd, brief pauses, broken by forced conversation about neutral topics, like the weather.

Diane said nothing. She stared across the room, as if lost in a dream, at an oil portrait of a woman, dressed in her finest clothing. The time-darkened face smiled serenely at the Parker family, in hospitable greeting. Her dark hair disappeared into the dimmed background, but her eyes and smile still shone luminously from the canvas. The bright silks of her pink dress shimmered in the soft light, and a pale hand with a delicate ruby ring rested in her lap. Diane wondered what that woman's life had been like as the mistress of this estate, in the uncertain times she must have lived through.

Diane knew from those kind, but determined eyes, that woman would not have wasted years of her life, retreating into inaction, as Diane had. Diane wouldn't be doing that from now on. She'd retreated from life long enough.

Jeffery's death, with the tight circle of his family as the principal suspects, had shocked Diane out of her lassitude. His death was sudden, and it showed that not just someone, but one of her relatives, was capable of murder. One of her family was a murderer. The statement circled in her head.

The people around her had always been just her family. Annoying, sometimes. Overprotective, demanding, argumentative. Kind, and generous, too. They'd always been there, and she'd counted on them to always be there.

She'd grown too dependent on that safety net during the past few years. The responsibility of her mom's failing life, and the raw grief of her death, had overwhelmed her. When Judith had offered Diane a home, a job running errands, and doing chores for her, Diane had gratefully collapsed into the hectic daily routine, and stopped thinking at all about her future. If she was exhausted by all the tasks adding up at the end of the day, all the better. She could sleep.

Now, Diane realized that all those little daily, unimportant tasks had wrapped up every minute of her life, in a swaddling cocoon. She'd left no energy for her future, no energy to even plan.

She had always known she couldn't stay with Judith forever. It was supposed to give her time to think about what she should do next. She needed to know what she wanted in life, and redirect her energy to building the life she wanted to have, whatever that was.

Diane thought she would like to marry and have children, have a family of her own. If she had met the right man—but the one she had planned to marry had moved on from her, while she cared for her mother. She couldn't blame him, she'd become boring and tired from the strain, while he'd wanted to enjoy being young.

She was now twenty-seven, not too old to marry, by any means, but it was difficult to meet eligible men in her circumscribed world in Judith's house. The possibility of a home with a husband and children to love and care for receded from her every year. But she had no intention of desperately seeking for a man, any man at all, as she'd seen too many of her friends do. That always ended disastrously. No, she would find a career, instead of grabbing at a lackluster marriage ring. If she met the right man after that, well—

Diane had always planned on being a nurse, from her earliest memories of carefully placing bandaids on her cousins' scratches. Never a doctor, a nurse, directly taking care of her patients, doing the little things that made their lives, and hopefully their health, better.

Now, she wasn't so sure about that career choice. Taking care of her mother had crushed her.

What would actually taking care of patients be like? Would each setback, each death—because there would be deaths—feel like her responsibility again? All of that crushing weight solely on her? Or would she be able to help the sick as part of a team, and keep her perspective on what she could, and couldn't do to help? She didn't know, but it was time for her to decide what her next stage of life would hold.

Diane listened to Mia and Kathleen chatting about the little town, planning a return to a shop they'd enjoyed. It felt good, normal, to have little things like that to do, with their absurdly abnormal situation. One of her family was a murderer. It didn't seem possible.

She glanced around the table. No one met her eye. Diane wondered if it was appropriate for them to leave the villa and explore the town, or if they should stay here at the villa, in isolated mourning?

As if in answer to her unspoken question, Judith announced clearly to the room, "Everyone, I need your attention." Eyes grudgingly met hers. "I've decided there's really no point in us moping around the villa all day." She nodded once, with determination. "I talked to Pietro, and he very kindly offered to take us on Vicenza's Palladian walk. We will be leaving in an hour."

"Aunt Judith, I don't think..." Kevin protested weakly, but Judith cut him off.

"This has absolutely nothing to do with the grief we feel for Jeffery's loss, Kevin." She patted her eyes dry with a tissue, her lips compressing firmly. "But it serves no point at all for us to sit around the villa, wondering what really happened to Jeffery." She shook her head. "I sincerely feel the police must have made a mistake, perhaps mixed up the lab work with another case. Or perhaps it was an accident. I refuse to believe it was a murder or a suicide. Dear Jeffery would never have killed himself, I'm sure we all believe that."

No one spoke. Their eyes focused on anything, but each other. Diane gazed into the dark eyes of the portrait, wanting the clarity of those strong eyes. Randall's finger tapped sharply on the table, in a slow staccato. Kevin stared at the table, biting his lip. His knuckles clenched around his butter knife.

"You see, Kevin," Judith softly urged, "we could go on with pointless speculations all day—and it would do no good whatsoever. Let's go on with our plans, with the kind help of Pietro, and let the kids see a little of Italy. It's not good for them to be cooped up all day, thinking about poor Jeffery." She paused, sniffling a little.

Kevin looked around the room at the others, noticing the absence of Ben, Francesca and Savannah. "I don't know," he wavered. He passed a hand over his wispy hair. "It doesn't seem right, with Jeffery—" His knuckles whitened on the knife.

"You know they're off sulking, morbidly upset at what's happened," Judith pointed out, reasonably. "It's not healthy for young minds to dwell on death, like this. Let's have a pleasant family day instead. No celebrations, of course. That would not be appropriate." She dabbed her eyes again, carefully not smearing her makeup. "But a normal day will do us all a world of good."

Kevin asked, uncertainly, "What do you think, Aunt Kathleen?" His brown eyes looked like a lost puppy's.

Kathleen weighed the question carefully. "Well, if Pietro thinks it would be okay, he knows what's appropriate under the circumstances. I suppose it wouldn't hurt to take the kids out for the day. It probably would be better for them than brooding on his death all day." She looked around the room. "It's probably not good for any of us to just sit here."

Mia looked down at her coffee cup, a trifle uncomfortably. She didn't relish the idea of touring so soon after Jeffery's awful murder, but Judith, as always constantly thinking of her family, had a very good point. Sitting around and thinking about Jeffery's death did no one any good. It might indeed be morbid and harmful for the younger members of the family, especially after his last evening with them. It was hard to say what was the best thing to do, but she would go along with what the Parkers decided. Of course, she'd never seen the Parkers not deciding to do what Judith wanted.

Kathleen murmured under her breath to Mia, "I also have no doubt we will have a police escort for our little trip."

Mia looked up, meeting her friend's clever brown eyes speculatively. She said nothing.

Anna appeared next to Savannah's lounge chair bearing a tray with a tall, frosty lemonade from Teresa. Savannah sipped with gratitude, thinking work days couldn't get much better than this. And she'd make sure the company marked it as a work day, too, since with the time shift, she'd been working extra hours just to keep up.

Anna had watched her sip her drink, with an odd look on her face, like she was sorry for her. The maid, sorry for her!

Savannah hated cleaning worse than anything. Her minuscule apartment was slovenly and full of dirty laundry. But no dishes, since she didn't cook. Someday she would feel financially secure enough to hire a maid to clean it, but until then, she wasn't going to do any more cleaning than she absolutely had to.

Anna had just stood there and scrutinized her. When Savannah had finally blurted, "Do you need anything?" in what she recognized was rather an unnecessarily rude tone, the skinny girl had shrugged.

"I wondered why you were working out here?" Anna asked with disapproval. "I would go to town, or something with excitement, if I were on vacation. You're not even swimming."

It's my job to take care of company publicity," Savannah told her. "And Uncle Jeffery's death has created a lot of negative publicity."

"But you are rich," Anna said. "Why do you still work?" She smiled, "I would not work, if I were rich."

Savannah laughed out loud at the statement. "I'm not rich," she told Anna. "I don't know that I'd work if I was, either." She looked around her. "I dunno, though. It's pretty nice to work here. I'm usually in a boring office. I don't even have a window."

"But if you're not rich, how do you come here on vacation?" Anna asked.

"Oh, Aunt Judith handles the money—and everyone else around her. I don't have any money of my own," Savannah reiterated.

Anna laughed derisively. "You have enough money to buy fancy clothes, and go on vacation with your family. What more do you want?"

"Oh, I dunno." Savannah sipped her drink. "I guess not to have to work. Maybe live in a really nice condo where I can see everything for miles around.."

"Me, I'd go shopping in Milan. The clothes! They're so beautiful, like what movie stars wear." She tugged at her too tight skirt. "It's where rich people shop."

Savannah chuckled. "That'd be fun too. But I really like going to thrift stores, and finding something really fantastic no one else has." She gestured at her elaborate black lace beach coverup.

"Thrift stores? When you could shop anywhere?" Anna was clearly disgusted. She left, shaking her head.

Savannah sipped her drink, and moved her fingers across her laptop. Looking at the screen, it seemed like everything was coming together.

Anna laughed to herself in the bathroom mirror, polishing the glass hard until the streaks were gone. She had seen them, cutting up the oleander leaves, on this very counter. She idly wiped down the counter, then sprayed cleaner in the bathtub. Of all days for Bianca to be gone. She was always off taking care of her mother, the fool. And always Anna had to do her work for her. Leaving a defiant streak of cleaner in the middle of the tub, Anna moved to the other side of the room.

It was perfect timing, for certain. The guest could get money today, while they were out sightseeing. It wouldn't be all the money Anna would expect to get from them, by any means, but it would be a start.

They would be back to their room soon, and Anna would remind them about the money. Anna wondered how much this rich American would pay to not go to jail for murder. She thought they would pay a lot of money, indeed.

Pietro drove the van, with Judith reigning from the passenger seat. He drove with the skillful abandon of all Italian drivers, concentrating on the road with a insouciant grin as he overtook less able vehicles, and an annoyed frown as cars more designed for speed than passenger capacity passed them by. Judith muffled her objections, clearly wishing she had chosen to sit out of sight of the excitement of driving.

Once free of the narrow mountain road, Pietro switched to his tour guide role. "Vicenza is a beautiful city because of Andrea Palladio. He put into use, in the sixteenth century, the perfect proportions of architectural beauty, that had not been used since the time of Vitruvius, in Roman times." He gestured with both hands, tracing proportions in the air, then pointed at a villa they were passing. "See? Look at those lines, those ratios. Sublime."

Judith's hands clenched her seatbelt protectively, her lips thin.

"How did Palladio know what the ancient Romans did? They lived a long time before the sixteenth century. Did he study the Parthenon or what?" Ben asked, obviously not believing Pietro.

Pietro looked absurdly glad someone had asked. He continued volubly with dramatic gestures, "Vitruvius wrote a book, De Architecture, now known as his Ten Books on Architecture." He paused to dart rapidly around a bug-like Smart car roadster, gripping the steering wheel nonchalantly with a forefinger. "It contains the three principles of architecture, Firmitas, Utilitas and Venustas. In English, Strength, Utility and

Beauty. The same principles are unchanged and in use today."

"Why would we possibly want the same architecture as two thousand years ago?" Savannah asked, disbelieving.

Pietro smiled, gesturing with both hands to emphasize his words, and the van moved with him. "My villa was designed by one of his students, three hundred years ago. We added bathrooms and larger windows, but the basic structure remains unchanged in all that time. It is still well functioning, as well as beautiful. The Villa Bella Sorgente is, of course, not a Palladian villa, but the idea is the same." He turned around to look at his audience, to emphasize his point, "All proportions of a Palladian villa are perfect illustrations of harmonic ratios applied to architecture." Judith's hand whitened, gripping hard. He chuckled and turned back to the road, straightening out the van.

"Trust me, you will see." He waved his arm out at the speedily passing landscape and Judith cringed.

Pietro bumped along the narrow streets, seeming to consider the sidewalk part of the street, when needed. Finally, he neatly pulled into a parking spot that looked far too small to contain the large van. "We are here," he said, grinning at the treat he was about to show them. "Our first stop is the Teatro Olimpico."

They clambered out of the van, looking around them at the narrow city street. It seemed very small after the largess of the countryside, enclosed by tall, narrow gray stone walls. Pietro led them briskly down the cobblestone street, and across a bridge garlanded with red geraniums. "The Teatro Olimpico is the oldest stone theater in the world, think of that." He briskly walked through an arched portico, stopping at a heavy wooden portal that was probably older than America. A woman, who looked almost as old as the door, sat beside it on a folding chair, smoking a cigarette.

"Buongiorno, Livia." Pietro gestured at the group behind him, continuing in English. "How are you today?"

"I'm well, Signore Schiavon. And you?" She discretely prodded for information, "I have heard of your trouble at the villa." Bright eyes, shining like dark jewels set in the wrinkled leather of her face, peered with interest at Pietro's group.

Pietro gave a slight negative shake of his head, continuing, "I'd like to take the Parker family, who are guests at my villa, for a quick private tour of the theater."

"Certo, Signore," The woman opened the door for the group, ushering them inside with bright eyes that missed nothing. Mia noticed Pietro discretely passing a few bills to the old woman, in return for skipping the lines.

A short walk down a dim hallway, then the theater spread out before them. Stone benches in a semicircle arranged around a massive carved relief, framing a street view, disappearing into true Renaissance perspective. Statues in niches surrounded the theater. A blue painted sky, tinted with warm afternoon sun, hung overhead, harkening back to open Roman amphitheaters.

Diane gave a soft "Ooh," of amazement as they entered, and Pietro smiled at her reaction. She wore the terracotta dress Francesca had given her. The soft, warm color, unlike her usual harsh, strident colors, suited her beautifully. Her cheeks were bright, and her figure looked pleasantly curvaceous in the flattering cut. Pietro's eyes lingered a moment on her, then he continued in his tour guide role.

"The acoustics of this room are quite amazing," Pietro told them. "Ben, run to the top row."

The teen's lanky legs quickly ran up the stairs. "Now what?"

Pietro said, in a quiet, but passionately clear, voice, "Oh luce, ultima volta ti veggo!"

"I can hear you perfectly, just like you're next to me," Ben said, amazed. His own voice carried down the rows of seats. "I don't know what it means, though."

"O light, may I look on you for the last time!" Pietro said dramatically. "This theater opened with Sophocles' Oedipus Rex, in the late 1500's. Very fitting, a Greek play opening this theater. For the Romans were inspired by the Greeks, and Palladio inspired by the Romans." He beamed at them.

"Beautiful," Diane said softly, looking around her with awe.

Savannah struck a dramatic pose from the low stage, "There's rosemary, that's for remembrance; pray you, love, remember...I can't remember any more," she broke off, laughing. Her high, clear voice carried to every corner of the room.

Francesca got up beside her, continuing in a bold voice, "There's fennel for you, and columbines. There's rue for you, and here's some for me—" her theatrical enunciation cracked. She said, in her normal voice, "It's fantastic acoustics, isn't it?"

"Modern theaters could certainly learn from it," Mia agreed. "The last performance I went to, the speakers malfunctioned, and I could barely hear the actors."

Pietro told them, "The next tour will be coming in now, so it's time for us to move on." He added in a dramatic voice, ""Non più prigioniero del mio fato, io sorgo!" saying aside, in English, "No longer captive to my fate, I rise!"

They left by the side exit as the noise from a chattering crowd grew louder in the amplifying room.

"Grazie, Livia," Pietro told the woman.

She puffed out a tight cloud of smoke, then gave him a gap-toothed grin. "Arrivederci, Signore." Mia could feel the old woman's avid stare as they went down the street.

The Palazzo Chiericati dominated the next block. Diane looked up as they passed, admiring the beautifully carved coffered ceiling and tall columns. The street, Corso Andrea Palladio, bustled with tourists and locals alike. They walked down the wide street lined with magnificent Palladian palaces, exclaiming with pleasure at the sights. Pietro strode ahead, gesturing at the buildings, telling them the stories behind the facades.

"Piazza dei Signori," Pietro told them, as the street opened. "Beautiful, isn't it? Tuesday is market day, so the perfect day to visit." He pointed, "The Basilica Palladiana and opposite, the Loggia del Capitaniato." He pointed at a truncated building with round rosy brick columns, capped with elaborate stonework. "A pity only three bays were built."

"I wonder why they didn't finish the stonework on top of the brick?" Diane pondered.

"Palladio liked the brick contrasting with the stone, in his later career," Pietro told her, walking closely by her side. "So he refused to plaster it."

"It is striking," Diane agreed.

The piazza was filled with locals shopping at the market. Tents and canopies covered everything from inexpensive clothes to locally grown vegetables. It was not a tourist market, despite the festive air amidst the spectacular Palladian buildings. It was where locals did their weekly shopping. Several booths with bright flowers scented the air. Pietro paused, buying bread, cheese, soppressata, and ripe, juicy plums. "For our picnic later."

The Parkers spread out over the large piazza, taking in the sites. Candace spotted a jewelry store with a heartfelt cry and made a beeline for it, dragging Kevin with her. Savannah and Ben joined forces, and took pictures of each other posing against the colorful backdrops of the market shops.

Judith told Francesca, "Let's go look in those shops. They look like they might have a little more select souvenirs than the weekly market. I'd like to get something to remember this beautiful place."

Francesca obediently agreed, and they wandered off to explore the shops edging the piazza. Mia followed them. She loved shopping and bringing home presents for her family. Or maybe even for herself, she thought with a smile, as she explored the colorful racks of wares.

Randall and Kathleen drifted off, and were soon sitting at a nearby cafe table, espressos in front of them.

Diane remained walking close to Pietro, enjoying the way he spoke about the city, as if it was an old, cherished friend he was introducing to her. He pointed out architectural details and interesting shops that she would never have noticed on her own.

Once, she stumbled a little on a curb, and Pietro quickly grabbed her arm to balance her. Smiling, he placed her hand on his arm, "You don't want to fall."

For a moment, Diane felt cherished, walking down the piazza, holding the arm of a handsome man. She looked up at him, describing his beautiful city with strong, calloused hands, and smiled.

They walked through the lower level of the Basilica, basically a roof covering medieval structures, surrounded by graceful, arched loggias with high, bricked ceilings. The contrast of the warm, old structures, protected inside the comparatively modern covering—four hundred years old—was striking. Diane walked along, listening companionably, feeling his warm arm beneath her hand.

She dropped her hand quickly, when Judith came into view. "I wondered where you had gotten to, Pietro," she admonished him. "I don't see anyone here. I turned around and Mia and Francesca had disappeared. I hope they haven't gotten lost. You should have kept everyone together."

Pietro did not bother to reply. Diane smiled up at him, apologizing for Judith's rudeness, and got a cheeky wink in reply. She looked quickly down, before she started laughing at his narrow, expressive face.

Candace came up, beaming from ear to ear, and holding an elegant little shopping bag up high like a prize. "Now this is what I call a souvenir! I'll show you all when we get back to the villa." Kevin smiled proudly at her happiness.

Francesca and Mia met them as the group slowly started walking back, towards the van.

Savannah and Ben weren't far behind, holding bags with t-shirts and holding large gelatos. Ben held his up, "Limone, really good. Like eating lemonade."

Judith commented, "Don't spoil your appetite for lunch." Everyone laughed. She added with a chuckle, "I suppose there's no danger of Ben doing that."

Savannah asked breathlessly, "Did you know there's a ghost tour of Vicenza? Can you imagine this place in the dark?"

Francesca told her, "Ooh, I love spooky. We should do that."

Judith said quickly with a frown, "I don't think we'll have time for that this trip."

Making a wide loop of old Vicenza, they circled back by the Palladian Museum, housed in the Palazzo Barbarano da Porto. "The only building Palladio ever saw actually completed," Pietro told them. "Now, it is about a half hour walk from here to Monte Berico, if anyone wants the exercise."

Judith demurred, "I'll ride, thank you. We've done enough walking today. Kathleen, Mia, are you coming?" It was a subtle order.

"I need to get some cash," Kathleen said. "Do you know where there's an ATM, Pietro?"

"There's one on your way back to the van," he told her.

Candace, carefully holding her little black bag with her new treasure, said, "I don't want to walk all that way in these shoes." Kevin obediently followed her. The older group took the van—and the picnic—to the Church, while the others walked. Mia would have preferred to walk, but she felt that Judith needed company.

The younger group retraced part of their route through Vicenza, enjoying the sunny day, and freedom from their recent troubles. Pietro commanded the attention of Francesca and Diane. His silver threaded hair shown in the sun, his slightly stooped shoulders straightened as he walked, and his tanned, lined face lit with energy, as he showed the pretty women his beautiful Italy. Diane's skirt flowed gracefully as she walked, and her amber eyes sparkled back at him. Francesca floated down the path, her white dress billowing.

Ben ran ahead, then back, telling them with a grin about the awesome stuff around the corner. He was clearly enjoying himself, and their brief independence from the older group. Savannah hung back from the others, but the genuine smile on her dark painted lips showed her enjoyment of the moment.

Deliberately forgetting about Jeffery's horrible murder for just a few hours, had allowed them the freedom for joy at the lovely sights and the sun on their backs. There was a collective sigh of release from the terrible strain they were under.

They walked down a long, recently built park path, pleasantly lined with pollarded trees, and bounded by a small river. The train station, with its rattling and screeching of brakes, was next, then they were outside the business districts of Vicenza, and walking on a narrow, sunlit path.

A long, arched portico, running up the small mountain, was the steep approach to the Sanctuario di Santa Maria di Monte Berico. The walled side of the path was punctuated by small, niched chapels. Light streamed through the open arches of the roadside, capped by frescos, the walkway glowing gold in the warm sun.

"Pilgrims pray at every stop on the way," Pietro explained, as they passed statues of saints.

Partway up the climb, they passed a villa decorated with small figures perched on the walls, "Villa Valmarana ai Nani," Pietro said, "Villa of the Dwarves. A daughter of the house had dwarfism, so they built the house to honor her. The story is they didn't allow non-dwarf servants, so she wasn't lonely."

"That's sad, and sweet at the same time," Francesca commented.

They met the rest of their group at the top, next to the church, and Pietro grabbed Teresa's picnic basket and folding chairs, along with the additions he'd purchased at the market. Trees offered their shade at a small park nestled next to the church.

"I'm starved," Ben told them with avid anticipation, and everyone laughed.

The picnic was simple, but delicious. Crusty bread, cheeses and cured sausages formed the base, along with the ripe plums Pietro had found in the market. Small glasses of a light Soave wine completed the offerings. After their long walk, they were all ready to eat.

When lunch had been reduced to crumbs, they wandered around the beautiful site, taking in the sublime views from the small mountain top.

A modern bronze statue of an expectant mother and her children, on a small marble pedestal, drew Francesca. "Monumento alla maternità. A monument to motherhood." She looked at the joyful face of the statue, wondering if she would ever get the chance to be a mother, now. She didn't know if she'd ever have the courage to trust a man with her heart again. Her smile drooped as she looked up at the statue.

Her mother came up beside her, and Francesca forced her smile back on her face. Judith criticized, "I wonder what that modern art is doing in a place like this?"

"The style does seem a little out of place," Francesca agreed. "But it's nice they have a monument to motherhood, in a place dedicated to Mary."

"The best thing in my life was when you came into it," Judith told her, with sincerity. "I hope you know that."

Francesca blushed, and looked down at the ground with embarrassment. "Thanks. I know I've been a lot of trouble lately."

"We'll be back to normal soon," Judith reassured her, patting her shoulder. "None of this is your fault."

"I know, but—" Francesca broke off, looking at the statue.

"Shall we go see the church?" Judith asked.

They admired the church, the massive polished columns framing the nave. Their steep walk uphill was amply rewarded by the grandeur of the sanctuary.

They all got in the van for the next leg of their journey, over the beautiful Valletta del Silenzio to the Villa Rotonda. As the van bumped and grumbled over the road, Francesca looked out the window at the peaceful fields, wishing she had walked the short journey.

The harmonious feeling continued as they walked up the rose lined drive leading to the villa. The Villa Rotonda appeared perfectly framed at the end of the drive—manifestly the destination. Today displayed the villa at its most superb, lit by bright Italian sun and framed by manicured green landscaping, punctuated by tall dark cypresses.

They slowly ascended the wide, marble staircase, looking through the villa windows to the other side of the grand building. Afternoon light streamed in the tall windows, making the marble building shimmer with energy.

Inside the cruciform shaped villa, they walked to the central atrium, capped by a massive round dome that gave the Villa Rotonda its name. A carved stone face, placed directly beneath the dome, laughed at them.

Pietro told them, "The villa is a cross on the four points of the compass, with that corner," he pointed at the far side of the building, "oriented to the south, so there is sunlight coming in through the windows, from East to West, all day long. The less candles and lanterns needed back then, the better." He laughed, "Palladio even angled the windows and rooflines, so there would be more light in winter and less in the heat of the summer."

"I wonder what they used the domed area for?" Francesca wondered.

"Parties, of course," Mia said, with a laugh. "It would be a fabulous ballroom—can you imagine?"

"Oh, absolutely." Francesca grabbed Randall's hand. "Dance with me, Uncle Randall," she ordered, taking a few light steps. Her long white dress floated around her delicate steps.

He laughed at her antics, dropping her hand. "Let's not block the views for the other tourists. I'll dance with you outside, if you insist."

"Oh, you're no fun at all." Francesca giggled, manic energy in her steps. "It'd be a beautiful place for a big party, though." She looked over at Ben. "Want to dance, cousin?"

Ben muttered something unintelligible, and practically ran to the next room, clearly pursued by horrors beyond belief.

Savannah took center stage with Francesca, and twirled in a graceful pirouette around the protective railings, displaying her years of ballet. Her black lace dress swirled around her in a wide arc. She laughed with the pleasurable movement in the beautiful space.

Francesca took her lead and twirled again, looking at the ceiling as she spun. "Just imagine." She sighed in pure enjoyment.

Judith said sharply, "Girls, cut it out. They're noticing you."

With graceful moves, the black and white dresses reverted to stillness. The young women smiled at each other. Francesca proffered her arm, "Milady." The two linked arms, and left the atrium, with a few dance steps tapped out on the way.

"Girls will be girls," said Kathleen. "It's good to see them having fun." She glanced quickly at Kevin, to see how he took their silliness. She was relieved to see him smiling at the cousins' antics as he and Candace went to round up Ben, determined that their son should experience the famous villa to the full with a guided tour.

Pietro told Diane, "Here, let me show you the mezzanine. Did you know this entire villa was designed as the country retreat of one man?"

"One person, rattling around in all this?"

He led Diane to a small circular staircase. She followed him up around the narrow stair, listening to his descriptions avidly. At the top, they peered over into the hall below.

Pietro chuckled. "He was an ecclesiastical, and made this for a solitary place to contemplate his world." He pointed at the central relief of a grinning face with pointed ears, grapevines coyly peeking out from his ears, "An odd home for a Catholic, with the face of Bacchus grinning from the very heart of the home, and statues of pagan gods adorning the walls." He pointed down at the stone face, "Not too long ago, the celebrated of this world clamored to stand there, at the center of the known universe for their highest accolade. They would ascend the stairs, and take the place of honor in the center. Kings, great artists, politicians, they stood there—if they could. Now, us tourists are politely barred from that pinnacle of civilization."

Diane stared around her, absorbing the juxtapositions, watching tourists trickle in and out of the grand, circular room. "It is odd. Very beautiful, but not a comfortable place."

"Yes, very beautiful, and worth seeing, but I prefer my simpler home to live in." He chuckled, "I started opening it to others as a hotel because it felt lonely. It's a place that needs a lot of activity going on always."

Diane snickered, adding, "It's certainly gotten that with our group."

"That it has," Pietro agreed, shrugging.

Kathleen grinned at Mia. "It's about time Diane started flirting again—a handsome Italian man too."

"That dress Francesca gave her looks beautiful on her," Mia agreed. "She's practically glowing." Though she privately thought, the day after your uncle's murder seemed an odd time to snap out of the depression Diane had clearly been in.

The group wandered into the next room. Mia exclaimed, "Isn't this plasterwork beautiful? And the trompe l'oeil? It's difficult to see where one ends and the other begins."

Kathleen agreed, "It's amazing what a few generations did. I can't believe that it all pulls together so well, when it was created over several centuries."

"I know, it's beautiful," Mia agreed. "I want to see the gardens. We don't want to miss them, and it's near closing time."

"I like that idea," Randall said. "I'm about ready for some fresh air after touring all day. It's good to see, but there's a lot of it for one go."

"The kids have enjoyed the day, at least," Kathleen said. "Judith, that was a good idea—" She looked around. "Where's Judith? I thought she was right behind us?"

Randall ducked back into the domed hall. "She's not in there. I bet she went outside for some air, too."

"I'm sure we'll see her in a minute," Mia said. "It's not like she's going to go far. Her feet were tired from walking around Vicenza, she said."

"It's all those cobbled streets—hard on the feet. She won't have gone far," Kathleen agreed comfortably.

But when they got outside, Judith was no where to be seen. Randall frowned. "It's not like her to wander off," he said, with concern.

"Especially under these circumstances," Kathleen agreed. "Okay, I'll go look for her inside. Randall, you search outside. Mia?"

"Why don't you look on the main floor? I'll look over the ground floor, see if she's exploring there? I think there are kitchens and things there."

"Kitchens doesn't sound much like Judith," Kathleen said with a laugh.

"We'll meet back here in fifteen minutes," Randall checked his watch, then strode off to circle the building, his long legs moving rapidly, his eyes scanning the formal landscape for Judith.

Mia took the side stairs down to the cellars. The vaulted rooms were cool, vented by the central dome pulling the hot air up and out, and the cooler air drafting inside. "Early air conditioning," Mia said to herself, enjoying the refreshing breeze. "At least the workers were comfortable during the summer—they had the coolest floor." A quick scan of the rooms showed no signs of Judith. Really, in the servants' domaine had been the least likely spot to find her. She made her way up to the main floor, continuing to search the elaborately frescoed rooms. After all, Kathleen and Judith might be missing each other, as Judith explored the villa.

Francesca walked to the edge of the terrace, listening to the rolling crunch of the gravel under her feet. It was a pretty view. Nothing dramatic, just peaceful fields of hay undulating across the hills. She lingered, sitting on the stone wall, looking out over the golden fields.

Everyone had been almost frantic all day, as if they were running away from Uncle Jeffery's death. She felt like running away too. She was tired of being so serious all the time, having her family look at her, watching for signs of a breakdown. She knew she hadn't handled Ryan's—call it what it was, his betrayal of her, calmly. But how could anyone handle something like that well?

She'd loved Ryan and trusted him completely. He'd been lying and scheming against her and her family the entire time. Mom and the rest of them were being annoyingly kind about it all, too. If only they'd been mad at her for letting the lying scumbag into their lives—she could have yelled and screamed back. Instead, everyone was being simply wonderful to her, and she didn't deserve it one little bit.

The past days had been weird. Uncle Jeffery's horrible death—she would never forget his body lying there, so still after excruciating pain. Then, the policeman's announcement that his death had been poison. It all seemed like some dreadful nightmare she'd wake up from soon. Francesca thought Mom must be right, they must have switched Uncle Jeffery's lab results with someone else's, someone who had been poisoned. People didn't get poisoned outside of books, certainly not in her own family.

Of course, Uncle Jeffery had acted so odd, that last night, attacking everyone in turn. He'd even been nasty to Uncle Kevin, who was as gentle as a teddy bear. It was so—she searched for the right word—uncharacteristic of him. Uncle Jeffery was always incredibly precise over expense reports and estimates. Biting remarks from him were pretty common, but they were all so—petty. That night, he'd gone straight for their most cherished feelings and cut them down mercilessly.

If he could do that, perhaps he could have committed suicide. It was obvious if that was how he actually felt about them, they must not have known him as well as they thought they did.

Or maybe he'd taken drugs. Francesca knew Uncle Jeffery was a health nut, but if some quack had offered him a "natural" supplement to improve his running, he'd have gobbled it down like a goose.

She sat swinging her foot, gazing out over the fields, hazed with the late afternoon sun, and tried not to think about what came next.

After fifteen minutes, Mia returned to the terrace overlooking the wheat fields. The others hadn't arrived back yet, so she strolled out to enjoy the view. Rays of sunlight floated over the fields, turning the landscape into a soft dream. She looked around, not seeing any of their group, and wondered where they had gone. It was time to go back to their own villa. Most of the tourists had left by now, so the guides would start shooing their group out soon.

Suddenly, the air was pierced by a drawn out scream of terror, cut off abruptly with a loud crash. Mia ran toward the sound, terrified.

She reached the far edge of the terrace and looked around, not seeing where the awful scream had come from. Francesca ran to her, yelling, "That was Mom! Where is she?" She hunted frantically.

"Judith?" Mia looked around. "Where are you?"

Francesca looked over the edge. "Mom? Oh God!" She ran like the wind around the long terrace and down the steps, yelling, "Mom!"

Mia looked down, far down. Judith lay crumpled like a rag doll at the bottom of the massive wall, her legs splayed out as if she'd been thrown. A wheelbarrow, filled with brush and tools, was overturned beside her.

Randall jogged toward her, "What was that? Someone screamed?"

Mia pointed down at the very long drop. "Judith. Francesca went that way."

Randall took off running. He really was a very good runner, Mia thought randomly. He reached Judith only a beat after Francesca did. Francesca dropped to her knees beside the crumpled body of her mom, crying hysterically.

Randall crouched down next to Francesca and placed his hand on Judith's throat. He sprang up, yelling up to Mia, "She's still alive! Get a doctor, quick!"

Mia ran toward the villa, alone in the suddenly empty terrace. She found, and managed to convince an employee to call an ambulance. She left the villa, walking briskly down the path to the side, looking for the easiest way down to Judith.

"Hey, Mia," she heard behind her. "Where are you running to?"

Kathleen caught up with her.

"Judith's been hurt badly," Mia told her. "This way, I think."

Kathleen asked no more questions, just followed Mia.

8

Aftermath

They were very kind, at the Italian hospital. The Parker family followed the ambulance in their van, with Pietro managing to keep up with the siren's frantic pace through the narrow city streets.

As she entered the hospital, Mia thought it could have been any hospital, back at home, its bland beige facade reassuringly dull, rejecting the idea of any drama under its roof.

Of course, she had enough experience with hospitals to know the festering melodramas lurking inside.

They were lucky that Pietro was with them. He was able to rapidly find where Judith was being cared for. Leaving the others in the waiting room, he went with Francesca to navigate Judith's care.

As they loaded her onto the stretcher, Judith had woken and seemed to know where she was. They had strapped her down, to avoid jarring any potential fractures. Francesca had reassured her that they would follow her, holding on to her mom's hand tightly, with tears running down her face. Judith had smiled slightly, then closed her eyes, obviously in pain.

Randall got them coffee. Mia decided it was the only bad cup of coffee she had ever drunk in Italy, as she sipped the dark brew, hoping the bitter caffeine would perk her up. She didn't know if the coffee was really that bad, or the simple pleasure was spoiled by the hospital atmosphere. She felt numb from everything that had happened. The waiting room roared with the noises of people and machinery, enveloping the senses in a humming anxiety.

All around her, people waited. Some were bored, some with their hearts breaking from intolerable strain. A child cried softly, as her mother tried to comfort her, her own face in poignant shock. A young man stared blankly at a particularly bad modern painting on the opposite wall, not seeing the travesty in front of him, only the hidden one playing out in the rooms beyond. An elderly couple huddled close, gripping each others' hands, comforting each other in the long wait.

Randall and Kathleen sat together, talking softly. Savannah and Ben stared at their phones, blocking out the surrounding tragedies. Diane hovered nearby, in case they needed someone to talk to.

Kevin and Candace sat across the aisle, his head dropped onto his hands, looking at the scrubbed clean, yet somehow still disgusting hospital floor. Candace, her blond hair clumped into locks, with even a hint of frizz, had lost her normal meticulous grooming. But her softened, loving face as she looked down at her grieving husband, and her motherly glances at Ben and Savannah, made her far more beautiful than when her makeup and hair were in perfect order.

Mia wondered what had happened back at the Villa Rotonda. Presumably, Judith would be able to tell them soon, if she remembered. You never knew with head injuries.

If Mia was going to guess, she thought Judith had been pushed off that high wall. Possibly knocked down with that heavy firewood log lying next to her. It would have been so easy. It was a long way down, and not much of a railing around the sheer drop. For a woman Judith's age, it was surprising she had survived the shock of the fall.

Why would someone push her? Who could have pushed her? That was probably the best place to start. Anyone could have killed Jeffery, his pipe had been in his unlocked room. Which of the Parkers couldn't have pushed Judith? Who could she eliminate from this terrible game of murder?

Most of the tourists had left the villa grounds by then—Mia had been the only person visible on her side of the terrace. The family had been scattered around the villa, exploring or looking for Judith. Kevin, Candace, and Ben might have still been together and touring the villa. Possibly Diane was with Pietro, as well. She needed to find out whether they had stayed together. Savannah? She hadn't seen Savannah for a while, when she'd heard Judith scream.

Why would someone want both Jeffery and Judith dead?

Well, the most obvious solution was money. Judith controlled Parker Perches, with the majority voting shares, so she controlled the family's purse strings. Even Kevin and his family were under her financial umbrella. Despite his striking out on his own successfully, he'd done it with family money backing—which Jeffery had said he was calling in.

Mia was still a little shocked at Jeffery doing that to his own brother. There had clearly been some bad feelings between the two. She looked at Kevin, hunched over as if he was in pain. Poor guy, if he wasn't the murderer. A brother you could never repair your relationship with was a terrible burden.

If Kevin had been with Candace and Ben, he couldn't have attacked Judith. Mia didn't think Kevin would ask Candace, or especially, Ben, to lie for him to the Italian police. But if they had split up after their tour, any of the three could have done it. Candace made no secret of disliking Judith, though it was usually muttered under her breath.

Ben was a teenage boy. Mia knew from her own boys that all teenage boys had tempers barely under control, ready to lash out at the slightest provocation. Ben appeared to have that temper controlled, but did he really? Jeffery had directly threatened their family and Ben's father. Judith had sat by and watched, not saying a single word to stop Jeffery.

It was also possible that Judith had seen something incriminating the night Jeffery was murdered. What more natural, especially when adjusting to a new time zone, than to look out the window or take a quick stroll? Maybe Judith had done just that, and it wasn't about money or temper, but about the murderer's self preservation?

Kathleen was looking down at her phone with a frown, texting. She was probably notifying people who needed to know that Judith was hurt. Would Kathleen have killed Jeffery?

Mia didn't like to think Kathleen would murder someone, but the truth was that she absolutely would, if she thought that person was a threat to her family. Kathleen would never dream of killing someone over money, but a threat to her loved one? Absolutely, with no compunction whatsoever. And Jeffery had never been anyone's favorite, because of his attitude. But he had been family.

Randall wasn't genetically family, but he was integrated firmly into the Parker family. His beloved wife had died young, and he'd treated the young Parkers as the kids he'd never gotten to have, turning up regularly from far flung posts.

What about Savannah? She and Francesca had wandered off together, but Francesca had shown up without Savannah later. Jeffery had denigrated Savannah's job skills, really most inappropriately, Mia thought. He had verbally attacked everyone at the table, except Judith—and Francesca.

Why had Jeffery left out Francesca from his diatribe? Mia thought it was because Judith wouldn't have allowed him to attack her daughter, and Judith controlled the money.

Would Francesca have attacked Judith, though? The horrified look on Francesca's face as she ran to Judith said no, but appearances could be deceiving. Francesca was clearly the center of Judith's world. Perhaps, Francesca was tired of so much swaddling love.

Francesca had appeared to run from the far side of the villa, but while a large building, Mia wouldn't have seen her running around the other side after pushing Judith over the edge. However, it was unlikely anyone had noticed her, and it had been attempted murder. Questions would have been asked after a death. Of course, the questions would have been directed at tourists, most of whom would have already left and not read the local news.

Maybe Francesca had been in on the theft with Ryan. Had Ryan been at the villa? He was certainly in Italy. If they had colluded to steal company money, then would Francesca have helped Ryan attack Judith? Or attacked her mother on her own?

Mia didn't think Francesca would attack her own mother, but she didn't know. She sat on the hard plastic chair, deep in thought, willing her restless legs to still and her mind to calm.

After an agony of waiting, Judith herself appeared in a wheelchair, pushed by a stout, cheerful nurse, with Francesca and Pietro following as her retinue.

Candace tapped Kevin's shoulder. He sprang up, going over to Judith and asking, "Shouldn't you stay overnight? Is it safe for you to leave the hospital?"

Judith, pale and wan, told him, "I'll feel much more comfortable back in my little cottage with my family taking care of me. I'll be fine." She managed a little smile, "I don't want to spoil everyone's vacation."

"You were almost killed by that fall! Wouldn't it be better to stay overnight, at least?" Kevin insisted.

Judith shook her head firmly, then winced at the movement. "No, I'll be fine. I'll rest better with my family around me."

Pietro told him, "Kevin, she is insisting she return now to the villa, not stay the night for observation." He shrugged noncommittally. "She has had a CAT scan. Many doctors have checked her. She is fine, not seriously hurt. Bruised and in pain, but fine." He held up his hands wide in disbelief. "It is a miracle. A miracle."

"A miracle, for certain," the nurse agreed in barely accented English. "She is fine, nothing broken. She needs rest and good food."

"Teresa would be happy to give her that," Pietro said, with a smile. "The doctor suggested someone stay with her tonight?" he paused interrogatively, looking at the Parkers.

"I'll stay with her," Diane offered. "I'd be happy to. Aunt Judith, I'm so glad you're okay." The strained look had left her eyes at Judith's reappearance. Diane smiled wholeheartedly at her aunt.

"Good, I can tell you've had experience caring for sick people," the nurse said, looking at Diane with kind eyes. "True?"

"Yes," agreed Diane, her eyes falling for a minute. Then, she raised them, meeting the nurse's inquiring gaze. "Yes, I have. I'm going to start training to be a nurse this fall," Diane added with decision.

"You'll take good care of her, I know," the cheerful nurse told her. "Good luck with your training."

"Thanks," Diane told her. She met Pietro's eyes. He smiled back at her, with a little nod of approval.

Diane and the Italian nurse helped Judith, wincing, into the van's passenger seat. She managed to fasten her seatbelt, started to turn her head, then the wincing pain made her think better of it. "Francesca?" she asked, a weak, forlorn tone in her question.

"I'm here, Mom," Francesca told her, leaning forward and gingerly placing her hand on Judith's shoulder. Judith stretched her hand up to meet it, holding Francesca's hand, a faint smile on her face. Her hand dropped to her lap after a minute, and she closed her eyes.

Judith's cottage was ideal for a sickbed. They pulled the van up to the door. Pietro and Kevin supported her for the few steps inside to her bedroom.

Diane and Francesca helped her to get comfortably into her peach silk nightgown with a lacy robe wrapped around her. Diane fluffed up the down pillows, and carefully put them to support her back.

Judith smiled up at the two young women. She looked much better now, than under the blue glow of hospital lights. "Thank you so much for helping me, girls. It's good to be back." She reached up for their hands, holding them both tight.

Francesca told her, "Of course, Mom." She sat on the edge of the bed, still holding her mom's hand. "I'm so glad you're okay."

Diane agreed, "You really scared us today."

Francesca asked, a little hesitantly, "Do you remember what happened?"

Judith withdrew her hand slowly from her daughter's. Looking down at her hands, her pale pink nails dug slightly into the crisp white coverlet. Her hands were well cared for, the hands of a pampered woman with access to the best skin care available, only a few age spots showing. An antique diamond engagement ring, with a large central stone, sparkled on her finger, somehow magnifying the hand's pale fragility and age wrinkles. Judith smoothed the coverlet with precise attention, clearly deciding whether to answer the question or let it lie.

She was saved by the door abruptly opening after a soft tap. Teresa, her bright dark eyes curious and kind, bustled in, asking, "Would you like something to eat now?" She quickly scanned the room for anything she could do to help. "Do you need more blankets or towels?" she thoughtfully added.

Judith responded, "You know, I would like a bowl of soup or something light now. After the hospital, I feel quite hungry."

"That's a very good sign. If you're hungry, you must be getting better." Teresa bustled off to help in the only way she could.

Mia came in the room as Teresa left, to see if there was anything she could do.

Judith straightened the soft coverlet around her with decision. "Now, I know the doctors said I need to have someone with me tonight, but that doesn't mean someone has to hover over me every minute."

Francesca rejoined, "Mom, that's exactly what it does mean. One of us needs to hover near you, make sure you're okay." Her jaw set firmly, and she tucked her hair back behind her ear.

"Well, you girls need to eat too," Judith told her. "You both need to keep up your strength."

Mia suggested, "Why don't the girls go have dinner? I'll stay with you while they eat. I'm sure Teresa wouldn't mind saving my dinner for later."

"Are you sure you wouldn't mind, Mia? I don't want to put you to any trouble."

"Of course I don't mind," Mia told her. "I'm happy to help."

"You were always such a thoughtful girl," Judith said. "I remember whenever you and Kathleen made a mess doing crafts, you'd always be the one to clean them up. Such a thoughtful child," she repeated, looking around the white walled room, as if searching for something missing, "It seems such a long time ago sometimes, when the house was always filled with children." She blinked her wide set dark eyes rapidly, chasing away tears. They looked sad and muted, without their usual skillful makeup. It made Judith seem unfocused, without her defined lines.

Mia made a shooing motion to Francesca and Diane, and they quickly filed out of the room. She settled herself in a slipper chair by French doors leading to a little patio, amber lights glowing in the night. Mia smiled at Judith. "Sometimes it seems like yesterday, too."

"It does indeed," Judith agreed. "Do you remember when we took Francesca to the Atlanta Zoo? She wouldn't leave the elephants—she thought they were the most amazing creatures."

Mia remembered. Her boys had been fascinated by Francesca, trailing her like she was a treasure, and Francesca had followed her slightly older daughter, Nicole. "Francesca was such an adorable little girl," she told Judith agreeably. "Always smiling at the world."

"We were so blessed when she came into our lives," Judith agreed, wiping a tear from her eyes. "I love all of my children, because, you know, the boys grew up under our roof too. But it meant so much to me to have my own little girl."

"Harold was very good with Kevin and Jeffery, wasn't he? You both treated them like they were your sons."

"That's really how I always thought of them," Judith told her. "Their parents died when they were still very young, so it was like having an instant family, with all the fun and the stress included." She chuckled softly.

"You always made it look effortless," Mia encouraged.

"I did enjoy having my family around me," Judith said. "Now they've grown up, and don't always have the time for me, of course."

"They seem very fond of you, Judith," Mia told her. "When you were hurt, they were all terrified of you dying. I've never seen them so scared." She remembered Francesca's panicked run to her mother, down that steep hill.

"I know they were." Judith looked out on the little patio into the dark, unseeing.

"What did happen back there, Judith?" Mia asked quietly.

"Oh, I don't know," Judith said deflecting the question.

"Do you remember?" Mia asked bluntly.

Judith looked at her, her unfocused brown eyes meeting Mia's sharp blue ones unhesitatingly. "It's very unclear," she told Mia. "I just remember lying on the ground, and everything hurt. I don't remember how I got there."

Mia said politely, "I'm sure you'll remember as soon as you feel better."

"Maybe," Judith told her. "Maybe I won't." She paused, then continued. "I was hit on the head in the fall, you know. The doctor said it was quite a bump. Luckily, it doesn't seem to have affected any other memories, so it doesn't matter very much." Her pink nails dug into the coverlet.

"A miracle that you survived," Mia agreed. She didn't believe for one minute that Judith couldn't remember what happened to her. However, it was quite obvious that Judith didn't want to talk about it, and Mia couldn't make her.

Mia changed the subject to a more pleasant one. "Do you remember when we took Francesca to the Botanical Gardens?"

"Oh, that child! She was used to eating salad out of the garden. I looked around, and found her with a big handful of pokeweed leaves in her mouth."

"You got them out in time, thank goodness," Mia said. "I was worried we'd have to go to the hospital." She laughed. "There was a big sign saying they were used in salad, so Francesca just assumed she could eat them. She didn't know they needed to be boiled and rinsed for poke salat."

Judith laughed, shaking her head. "The first thing I did when I went home was remove all poisonous plants from the garden. Azaleas, foxglove and especially rhubarb. Harold cried about those gorgeous azaleas, but I didn't want that happening again whenever I let her play outside."

"No, indeed," Mia agreed.

Judith smiled, "It'll be good having her back at home, especially now that it seems Diane might be leaving me soon."

"So you caught her telling that nurse she was going to study nursing," Mia said, with a smile. "You don't miss a thing, even when you're sick."

"I've been worried about Diane," Judith told Mia. "She had too much stress, too soon. I hadn't liked the idea of her being overwhelmed again in training. But I'm concerned she might be putting herself under too much stress before she's quite ready for it. She's a good girl—I don't want her to have a nervous breakdown with the rigorous training."

"You have to let them go, sometime," Mia pointed out. "She's a strong woman. She can do it."

"I hope so," Judith said doubtfully. "I just don't know that she's ready for it, quite yet."

A little tap at the door, and Anna sashayed in, flaunting a bright green miniskirt. "Here, Signora Parker. Signora Teresa made you soup." She placed a beautifully arranged tray over Judith's knees. A covered bowl wafted appetizing smells, silver sparkled, and a crystal glass held water, not wine for the convalescent.

Judith sat up a little, looking interested.

"Very good soup," Anna encouraged Judith. "Sopa coada, chicken with layers of bread to soak up the broth, It's very good," she repeated.

Judith laughed a little. "All over the world, the cure is chicken soup!"

"It works," Mia said. "Every time."

Anna agreed. "I tell you, Signora Teresa can cook anything, and make it good. But this soup is a famous one. She must like you very much indeed to make it for you. I'm sure your family likes you very much too, from all that they have said."

"I'm very grateful for Teresa making me a special meal," Judith said. "Please tell her thank you for me."

Anna nodded. "I will be back for the tray." She left, closing the door a little louder than necessary.

Judith poked at the dish with an exploratory spoon. "It looks more like a lasagna than soup, but with bread instead of pasta."

"It smells delicious," Mia told her. "I'm sure it's as good as it smells."

"Yes," Judith took a small bite. "Very good."

She suddenly put her spoon down, and a large tear ran down her face. She swiped it away, almost with anger at the lapse. "I don't think I'm really hungry. It's been quite a day."

"I know it has," Mia said, with commiseration. "I wish you'd tell me, or one of your family, what happened."

"I just can't," Judith said. "It would be a betrayal," she added with finality.

"More of a betrayal than someone pushing you over that parapet?" Mia gently asked.

"I never said that's what happened," Judith said sharply.

"I know you didn't," Mia said with calm certainty.

"I never said that," Judith repeated. "Not to anyone."

"Eat your soup," Mia gently ordered. "You need to keep your strength up."

When Anna came back to take the tray, Judith had managed to polish off most of the sopa coada and had closed her eyes, in exhaustion or to prevent further questioning, Mia didn't know. The waning light from the window softly erased Judith's wrinkles, but enhanced the dark bruise-like circles under her eyes. She needed a good night's sleep after today's fall, Mia thought.

Anna told Mia, "Signora Teresa wants you to come to dinner now, so she can clear the table. Signora Francesca is on her way, after she gets a book from her room. I will wait here with Signora Parker until she gets here."

Judith opened her eyes slightly with the noise. "I'm fine, Mia. You go eat."

"If you're sure," Mia rose and left, looking back to Anna standing, looking down at Judith. She didn't really want to leave Judith without a family member there, but after all, Judith seemed perfectly fine. And it was a member of her family who had pushed her off that wall, not Anna.

"I will stay with her," the girl repeated, looking directly at Mia.

When she arrived in the dining room, Randall and Kathleen were still sitting at the big dining table, deep into a serious discussion. "How is she?" Kathleen asked, looking up as Mia entered.

"She seems tired, but okay," Mia told them. "I'm sure she'll be sore tomorrow."

"Bruises are always the most painful two days after an injury," Randall pronounced.

"I can't believe she survived that fall," Kathleen said. "Did you find out what happened?"

"No, and she's not interested in talking about it. She says head injuries have memory gaps," Mia paused meaningfully.

"Huh," Randall grunted.

"Yes, I don't believe it either," Kathleen said. "She knows exactly what happened."

"Well, she's not going to tell us, at least not right now," Mia stated inarguably. "Did either of you see anything?"

"No," Kathleen said. "I was still inside the villa, looking for her."

"And I was on the terrace, on the other side of the villa," Randall said. "I think I heard Francesca's scream, not Judith's."

"Francesca's was a lot longer and louder. Judith's was—cut off," Mia told him with a shiver. "I was sitting on the terrace wall, but I didn't turn around fast enough to see anything," she said regretfully. "No one was there at all." She paused, then asked, "So, what do you both think happened?"

"I think she was pushed," said Kathleen bluntly.

Randall nodded, "She must have been. Judith wouldn't fling herself over some wall."

"No, she wouldn't," Mia agreed. "Which means we have a murderer with us who doesn't mind killing again."

"But why Judith?" asked Kathleen.

"Judith's the one who controls Parker Perches, and the money," Mia said. "What happens if she dies?"

Kathleen said slowly, "If Judith died, her shares are divided between all of us."

9

Blackmail

When Mia came down to breakfast the next morning, she was surprised to see Judith sitting alone at the head of the table. She held herself very stiffly, as if she was in pain, but she seemed to be recovering well.

"How are you?" Mia asked solicitously. "I'm surprised you didn't have breakfast in bed this morning."

Judith smiled, "I probably will go back to bed for a nap, at some point, but I didn't want us all wasting our time in Italy." She added, "I don't think any of us want to go touring today, but I don't want us all sitting around a stuffy room when we could be enjoying this lovely villa."

"You mustn't overdo it, Judith. That was quite a scare you gave us."

"I know, but I'm really fine, just bruised and shaken," Judith said firmly, allowing no argument.

Mia nodded. "Just let me know if there's anything I can do to help."

Judith nodded. "Diane was such a sweet girl. She stayed up with me all night. She ran to her room to change clothes, and have a little nap, after she told Teresa I was here."

"She is thoughtful, isn't she?" Mia said.

Judith continued. "Francesca wanted to stay with me last night, but I insisted she go to bed. I don't need her getting sick again, when she just started sleeping at night. She wasn't happy about it, but I made her go. I'm very lucky to have a daughter who loves me that much."

"Francesca is a very sweet woman," Mia said. "And it wouldn't do any good to have both of them staying up all night. Francesca was exhausted yesterday from what happened. Her face when she realized you'd fallen," Mia pursed her lips. "She was absolutely terrified."

A small smile traced on Judith's face. "She must have been very scared, poor girl."

"She was very scared," Mia said. "Do you remember what happened?"

Judith's face turned mulish. "No, I don't."

"Head injuries," Mia mused aloud, "can really mess with memory."

Judith raised a supercilious eyebrow, picking up her coffee cup and slowly taking a sip.

Francesca entered in a rush, her pale yellow dress floating around her, like gossamer buttercup petals. She embraced her mother, like a small child. "Mom, I went to your cottage—Anna said you were here. I can't believe you're up!" She sat down in the chair on Judith's other side. "Should you be up? Isn't it too soon?"

"Anna?" Judith asked with confusion, then laughed, "You and Mia are reading from the same script. Don't worry about me, you two. I plan on multiple trips back to my room for naps. But I don't see any reason why I can't enjoy the sunny Italian countryside, while I'm convalescing."

"Absolutely," Francesca agreed, smiling at her mom. "I'm so glad you're okay, Mom."

Judith smiled at her, reaching out her hand. Francesca took it and squeezed. "Love you."

Francesca blinked hard, then smiled as Teresa came in. "Hi, Teresa, isn't Mom looking great today?"

Teresa ran her eyes up and down Judith critically. "You look much better, Signora Parker. I hope you slept well."

"I did. Thank you so much for the chicken and rice dish you sent for me."

"Sopa coada, sì." Teresa nodded. "It was what my mother made for me when I was sick."

"It was delicious," Judith agreed.

"Now, what would you like for breakfast?" asked Teresa. "We are a little shorthanded, today. The other maid, Bianca, had to take her mother to the doctor, so Anna is cleaning rooms now."

"So nice for a daughter to look after her mother," Judith said, smiling at Teresa, then Francesca. "I don't know what I would do without my family around me." She sipped her coffee, smiling.

"May I have a cappuccino and a brioche, please," Mia requested, with a smile. "Chocolate, if you have it?"

"Of course, Signora Spinel."

"Yum. The same, please," said Francesca enthusiastically.

Teresa smiled and left the dining hall, footsteps slapping the floor as she dashed away.

After their delicious breakfast, Judith held court on the terrace from a comfortable chair, with her thin legs propped up on an ottoman topped with a cushion. Francesca sat by her side, idly turning the pages of her book, while Judith gazed out over the countryside.

Randall paid homage first, dropping his lanky figure hard into the chair. He commented, scanning her with his silver eyes, "Looking better, Judith," then looked around for a conversation starter. "That detective, Tenente Zanatta, told Teresa he would be here after lunch. I wonder if he has more information?"

"An accurate autopsy report, you mean? I hope so." Judith sniffed. "I'm ready to take poor Jeffery's body home and bury him properly."

Randall shifted uneasily. "Well, you need a few days to heal before you get on a plane, no matter what the results. Better to wait until you planned to go back. You'll get to ride Mia's private plane again that way." He avoided informing Judith that the police weren't going to let her go anywhere until they found their murderer, so it didn't matter what she wanted to do.

"Mom, you can't leave until you're healed. That's an order," Francesca smiled at Judith. She added, "I'm going to get another of those yummy cappuccinos." She headed into the house.

Randall leaned toward Judith. "We need to have a talk about Francesca, Judith."

"How can you say that now? When I just nearly got killed?" Judith asked him, straightening in her chair.

"Well, when, then?" Randall said reasonably.

Judith shook her head in refusal. "I'm worried about what might happen. She's very fragile right now."

"This isn't what we agreed on, Judith. You know it isn't."

"You and Harold agreed on, you mean," she told him pettishly.

"I have my rights, too," Randall told her.

Judith started to respond, then slumped back, looking pale. "Randall, this isn't the time for this discussion. My head is killing me."

"Sorry, Judith. You're right, this isn't the time." Randall sat back in the chair. "Do you think you'll be up to any more touring this week?"

"After yesterday?" Judith wrinkled her nose. "No, I'm definitely not in the mood for sightseeing."

"It's a pity, but I understand. Well, there's always next year." Randall sat there watching Judith, looking uncomfortable but determined to wait for Francesca's return, and searching for conversation. Judith didn't help him.

Savannah drifted by and perched on the edge of a chair. "Hi, Uncle Randall. Hi, Aunt Judith. You're looking a lot better than you did yesterday."

Randall mumbled something and escaped.

Judith smiled up at Savannah. "Hi, Savannah, I'm feeling a bit better. You look like you've been working hard already. It's a beautiful day to work outside."

"Damage control is going well. I have a plan on auto-pilot." Savannah tapped her laptop bag. "When we get back, I'll meet all our top clients, and reassure them that the business will be working as normal. As long as most of the bad news stays in Italy, it shouldn't be a problem."

"Good, good," Judith said. "I was a little concerned about Ben. He's really such a young boy."

Savannah put on a very superior tone, "Don't worry, Aunt Judith. He's okay." She added, "I've been doing lots of things with him. I'm taking him on a walk to that cute little town, since I've finished work." She stood up. "I'll drop off my laptop bag, and go find him."

Judith held out her thin, lined hand to her in thanks, and Savannah grasped it, smiling proudly at her morning accomplishments. "You're a sweet girl, Savannah. I'm proud of you."

"Thanks, Aunt Judith. Love you." She blew her aunt a kiss and went to find her cousin.

Francesca came out with her foamy coffee. "Where'd Uncle Randall go? I thought he was with you?"

"No, he left," Judith said. "Really, dear, I'm fine by myself. I don't need anyone fussing over me."

"Mom, I don't think you should be by yourself," Francesca told her. "I know perfectly well someone pushed you off that wall."

Judith said harshly, "I didn't say so."

"Mom—" Francesca sighed. "Someone needs to be with you, all the time."

"It doesn't have to be you, you know. Savannah and Ben were talking of going to town. You should go with them."

Francesca's face shut down. "You know I'm not going there."

"Whatever you say, dear," Judith agreed, her dark eyes limpid under her arched brows.

Francesca lay back on the chair, looking seriously at her mother. "I wish you'd tell me what happened."

Judith smiled. "I think it's better if I don't remember, dear. Why stir up trouble?"

"One of the family tried to murder you, Mom. You need to tell me, at least, what happened," Francesca demanded.

"I simply don't remember, Francesca," Judith said. She lay back into the cushions and closed her eyes. "I'm tired."

"Oh, Mom," Francesca sounded as exhausted as the invalid. She watched Savannah and Ben walk past on their way to town, and waved. She swallowed hard, feeling trapped in this sunlit villa. She turned another page of her book, forcing back tears of frustration.

Diane slept, falling on top of the soft comforter with relief. She didn't dream, but fell hard into a hot, dark space that trapped her. She tossed from side to side in the dark cocoon, not waking.

When she woke, two hours later, she felt more tired than before her nap. Last night had been a long one. She'd sewed on a button, and did what repairs she could to Judith's clothes that she'd worn in her fall. It was probably a waste of time, since Judith would certainly just replace them as soon as she got home. Diane had tried to read, but the light had been dimmed for Judith to sleep. It gave her a headache to try to see the words on the page.

She felt wrung out by Judith's accident, and her decision to restart school. The little white chair was fine for sitting on for a few minutes, but wasn't a chair to sleep in. Every time she'd fallen asleep, her head had lolled, and she'd woken quickly to a sharp pain in her neck.

She stretched and yawned. Francesca was taking care of Judith. Diane would be expected to sleep until after lunch, but she was ready to get up now. She showered and changed, then cautiously entered the kitchen, looking for food.

"Signora Teresa?" she asked.

Teresa smiled, stirring a heavy copper pot on the massive stove. "Signora Parker? I knew you would want breakfast when you came down. I have coffee and a brioche waiting for you."

"Call me Diane, please," Diane told her, taking the tray. "Would you mind if I sat in here while I ate?"

Teresa glanced at her acutely, her bright dark eyes searching Diane's. "Not at all." She continued cooking, stirring the impressive pot.

Diane sat at the scarred wooden table, clearly the centerpiece of the kitchen for generations. The polished brass knobs of the Bertazzoni range shone. Heavy copper pots were stacked high on a shelf, with more hanging underneath on the white tiled wall. An old wooden door led to a pantry, where Diane could see neat glass jars of passata sitting on shelves, alongside canned jams and jellies from the villa's gardens. French doors opened onto a little patio rimmed with rosemary, oregano, and thyme, all the herbs a cook might need in a hurry. Sunlight streamed in the windows, lighting the old, dark beams and the plaster walls with a golden radiance.

Teresa poured some water into the pan she had been sautéing, then poured herself a coffee and sat at the table. "You had a good sleep, yes?" she asked kindly, stirring a large spoonful of Demerara sugar into her cup.

Diane nodded noncommittally. "I feel better than I did," she added truthfully. Having a little time to herself made all the difference.

"Signora Parker is out on the veranda," Teresa told her. "It will do her good to be out in the sunlight."

"It will," Diane agreed. She took a bite of the crisp brioche. The buttery flakes melted in her mouth. "Have you worked here long?" she asked Teresa.

Teresa laughed, her round cheeks balling up. "I was born on the estate," she told her. "When I grew up here, all of us children, ran in and out of the house all day long. Signora Schiavon, Signore Pietro's mother, had three people cooking in this kitchen alone, to feed everyone. Now, there is just me and Anna, with maids and gardeners coming from the town."

"Why did it change?" Diane asked.

"Pietro had several sisters. They married and left. They didn't want to live on the estate here—too boring. They moved to the cities, Bologna, Turin, one even to Paris. I have been to visit. It was very nice, with a view over the city, all I could see was rooftops."

"But you stayed here?"

"I like the countryside better. The Villa Bella Sorgente is my home," Teresa said simply. "When Pietro decided to open the villa to guests, Salvatore and I were very excited. I to cook, and him to show off his gardens to the visitors." She laughed. "Pietro is very dull to cook for. He always wants the same things."

"I guess he knows his favorites," Diane said with a laugh.

"Yes, but I like to try new dishes, or old ones in new ways," Teresa said with a rich chuckle. "I can experiment with guests."

"I've certainly been enjoying your creations," Diane told her.

"Good." Teresa paused, then asked, "The man who died, Jeffery? He was your cousin?"

"He was," Diane agreed, thinking about Jeffery. Jeffery as he was, that last night, biting and vindictive. Jeffery as a teenager, taller and very superior to her, teaching her how to play croquet at a family gathering, impatiently striking her ball with his own, and telling her she'd lost a turn. Jeffery bent over his computer, not bothering to look up as she dropped paperwork off at his office.

Jeffery and she had never really been friends, but they had been cousins. She said slowly, "He's always been there. He was family."

"It's hard to lose family, always. You will miss him."

Diane said nothing. She didn't think she'd miss Jeffery, but she regretted his death.

"Do you have any idea who killed him?" Teresa asked, curiosity bright in her eyes.

Diane slowly shook her head. "No. I wish I did."

Teresa nodded. The thought that the murderer was certainly one of the Parker family showed in her eyes, but she was too polite to say so.

Anna ran a casual cloth over the bathroom counter the couple were sharing. She ran her eye over the multitude of cosmetics the American woman had. She opened the lid of one she'd seen in ads and touched her finger to it, rubbing the expensive lotion on the back of her hand. Nice, she thought, very nice. Money really did buy you better things.

Anna put a dab on her other hand, then replaced the lid, shoving the cosmetic containers to the back of the counter. A little swipe, and it looked clean enough.

She removed a crumpled towel from the bathtub, and glanced around the room. It would do.

Placing the towel in her cart's dirty linens bag, she got the cleaner to polish the mirror. Admiring her face in the reflection, she thought about what it would be like to have money, real money. Like these Americans. The Parkers, they had money to spare.

She thought of the other girl, Savannah, looking down her nose because Anna was a maid. The girl was dressed like an extra in a bad vampire movie, and she was looking down on Anna.

Well, Anna had to take the job she could find, right? She certainly wasn't going to be a maid for long, just until something better came along.

She idly moved the hangers in the big wardrobe. Chichi clothes the woman wore, just like her cosmetics.

She pulled out a particularly slinky sequin dress in hot pink, and whistled under her breath.

That was a dress for the club, if ever she'd seen one. Matteo would sit up and take notice, if she wore a dress like that. She'd make him notice her. She held it up against her in the mirror, admiring the brightness.

She thought about Matteo, with his laughing dark eyes and casual grin, those eyes never lingering on her, just passing over her like she didn't exist. If she had money, and a dress like this, he'd pay attention to her.

She sighed and put the dress back. She'd go to Milan and do some shopping, as soon as she got the money tonight. She'd agreed to meet the—she should say the customer, that sounded most respectable. She'd agreed to meet the customer in the villa courtyard tonight at midnight to get her money. These Americans would be asleep then, she was sure. But if she screamed, with all that had happened, they would all come out to see what was wrong. But there was no way the customer wouldn't pay up, and handsomely, too. Otherwise Anna would go to the police and tell what she knew.

She'd rather have the money than tell. What did she care of that American's death?

And then she'd buy a dress like that one, but in red. Anna's eyes danced at the thought of Matteo choosing her—choosing her from the giggling line of girls waiting to dance. He'd notice her, for sure, with lots of money and a sexy dress.

She pulled out the cord, plugging in the little vacuum. She gave the middle of the floor the same lackadaisical attention as the counter, striving only for good enough. She pulled the machine into the tiles of the bathroom, clattering behind her. She bent to pick up a fallen piece of paper from off the floor. Straightening up with a tug at her brief skirt, she met her murderer's amused eyes in the mirror, but it was too late.

Candace came back to the room, still annoyed. After lunch, Judith had gone to her room for a lie down. Kevin sat in Judith's living room, "For protection." Candace couldn't blame him for taking care of his aunt. That had been a horrible fall she'd had yesterday. Candace shivered and sat down abruptly on the bed.

Someone must have tried to murder Judith yesterday. She didn't know how they hadn't succeeded. That had been a long fall for an elderly woman.

Candace hated Judith. She always had, from the time they'd met. Judith constantly demanded so much from Kevin. There were so many 'if you could stop by and'—they added up to all his meager free time spent over at Judith's house, Judith's business, away from her and Ben. Kevin hadn't been able to coach Ben's mountain biking team because of all the times Judith needed something. He had missed date nights to the point that Candace quit making reservations, because Judith would always call with some emergency she needed Kevin for. And Kevin would always go.

Candace loved that Kevin was a good person. And he should take care of his aunt, who had pretty much adopted Jeffery and him when they'd been orphaned young. He was a good man, and he was looking after someone who'd taken care of him. It was the right thing to do.

But did it have to take so much time? Every weekend she could remember, he'd run over to Judith's house to do something. She'd tried having a house a little too far from Judith's to drop in, but all that had meant was Kevin spent more time in the car. She'd bowed to circumstances, and when they could afford to, they'd bought a house nearby so Kevin could run over without it taking all day.

And Candace resented all that time. She knew she shouldn't. After all, Judith had showed up for Ben's school plays. She'd taken them on vacation when they hadn't been able to afford fancy trips. Judith had even offered to lend or give them more money during expansion hiccups. They hadn't taken it, but it had been kindly meant.

And still, Candace resented Judith.

Judith hadn't liked her, right from the start. She'd thought Candace too flashy, not from a good enough family for Kevin. She had been polite to Candace, but there were invariably little cutting remarks that still hurt her, though she'd learned not to show it, like when she was a teenager.

Back then, Candace had flounced out of the room in hurt and fury, knowing Judith would be innocently asking, "What ever could be wrong with Candace?" Now, older and wiser, she'd laugh off Judith's barbed comments.

But they hurt, because she felt the truth of them. She hadn't been from a rich family—nothing like the Parkers. She hadn't been especially smart, but she had always worked hard. But Kevin—Kevin had chosen her. He was smart, and brave and so kind to her. He was a good dad and a good husband.

And Judith was tearing him apart.

He tried to do the right thing. He just didn't have time and energy to do it all. He was going to have a heart attack like his dad, if he kept trying.

Candace stood up. She was going to have to do something soon to keep Judith from destroying Kevin's life. It was up to her.

She went into the bathroom, and screamed.

Tenente Zanatta surveyed the assembled Parker family in the sitting room. The family was seated in the same places, but there were definite differences from the same assembly a few days ago. Candace Parker, who had found the body, was huddled next to her husband. Her previously impeccable makeup had been scrubbed from her face, which was beet red from crying. Not having access to reapply her makeup, her face revealed smooth, perfectly tanned skin, and eyes that looked bigger, than when they'd been rimmed with eyeliner. She looked less polished, but infinitely younger and prettier, crying and clinging to her husband's arm.

Kevin Parker had aged twenty years in the past days. His skin had a grayish tinge now, and Zanatta wondered uneasily about his family history of heart attacks. Kevin's arm encircled around his wife protectively. He looked out defiantly at the Tenente. Zanatta wondered why he was defiant?

Why would Kevin have killed his brother? His wife had seemed extremely upset at Jeffery Parker's death, even before she had found Anna's body. Could they have been having an affair, and Kevin Parker found out about it? That was a possible motive for his murder.

Ben slumped into the soft sofa next to his parents, his big hands hanging limply off his knees, and his lanky legs sprawling. His jaw was clenched, and his eyes narrowed and wary. Did he know something?

Judith, her back rigidly straight, asked with forced dignity, "Are you going to keep us all here? Do we have to keep staying at this murderous hotel?" she demanded.

Zanatta thoughtfully turned his gaze onto her, examining her ivory silk pantsuit and concluding she certainly had money to spend—and would have seemed to Anna to be a good candidate for blackmail.

"Yes, Signora Parker. There have been two murders now, so we must conduct a full investigation."

"How do we know it's not the staff, or that hotel owner who's killing off guests?"

Diane looked up sharply, but said nothing, pleating her skirt between her fingers.

Zanatta said icily, "Because there has not been a murder anywhere in the vicinity in a decade. And even then, it was a simple domestic matter." He shifted position, "No, your family brought murder here with you." He looked at each of them in turn, and they quickly dropped their eyes from his steady brown ones. "Did Anna say anything to any of you during the past few days, since Signore Parker's murder?" He tapped his black pen on his notepad.

Randall offered, "Anna was not very talkative to guests." He shrugged. "She obviously wanted to do her job, then go back to her actual life."

"I talked with her," Savannah said unexpectedly. "I was working out by the pool, on my laptop, you know?"

Zanatta nodded, "Go on, Signorina Parker."

Savannah thought about what to say. She remembered the hot sun on her skin, enjoying the novelty of working while wearing a tiny black bikini by the pool, instead of the windowless office they'd assigned back in Atlanta. Anna had brought her a glass of lemonade. It had felt so refreshing.

"She talked about money," Savannah said. "She asked why was I working, if I was rich?" She shook her head, her lips trembling. "I told her I was working because I wasn't rich."

"Go on," Tenente Zanatta urged.

"She said, if she was rich, she'd go to Milan and shop where the movie stars went."

"That's more money than Anna would have made working at the villa," Zanatta said. "Did it seem like she was expecting to have that kind of money?"

"I don't know," Savannah shrugged. "Maybe." She brushed her long black hair back from her face, her dark eyes uncertain. "I think maybe. She thought she was going to have money, and she wanted to talk about it, girl talk, you know?"

"Anna didn't have many friends left in town," Zanatta told her. "She went to visit them some, but she stayed here, because working at the villa is a good job, and jobs and apartments are scarce in the city."

"It seemed like she just wanted to talk," Savannah agreed.

"Hmm," Zanatta's pen tapped. "That is interesting, the possibility that Anna was expecting money. I had already decided the most likely reason for the girl's murder was that she was blackmailing the murderer," Zanatta said. "This confirms that theory."

Savannah sat back in the chair, her hair falling over her face in a sleek dark curtain.

"Did anyone else speak with Anna?" Zanatta asked. He was answered with silence. "Well, that is that, then."

Candace said in a very shaky voice, "I'd really like to lie down, but I can't...I can't..."

"Hush, honey," Kevin told her. "No one could possibly expect you to sleep there." He looked around.

Zanatta answered him, "The police have sealed the room. They will go through everything first, of course." He smiled kindly at the distraught woman, while wondering if she had murdered the girl Anna. "I am sure there will be no objection to Signora Parker getting a change of clothes, and what she needs for the night. If you tell me what it is, I can tell the forensics team."

Candace burst into tears. Kevin patted her shoulder, murmuring and looking helpless.

Diane stood up. "I'll find out about a spare bedroom," she said, but no one heard her.

She escaped from the sitting room, feeling her chest relax. She breathed in a great gulp of air, untainted by the scent of fear. She glanced up the grand staircase. She could hear the carabinieri moving around the rooms, hunting for any clues. Diane shivered. Whose room would hold clues to a murderer?

She didn't know where to find Teresa, so she started in the kitchen. It was a good guess.

Teresa sat at the massive wooden table, her shoulders slumped, crying into her hands. Diane called her name softly. "Teresa?" Then again when she didn't hear her, "Teresa?"

Teresa looked up, too much in shock and grief to be scared, in a house where a murderer roamed free. "Yes?" She started to stand up. "I need to..."

Diane came over and put her arms around the older woman. "No, Teresa, you need to sit right here. Can I make you a cup of coffee?"

Teresa's usual cheery round face had drooped, sagging into folds of despair. "Sí, un espresso."

Diane surveyed the complicated machine, trying her best to act as if she knew what she was doing. "May I have one with you?"

Teresa had started sobbing again. Diane tried her best to combine what she did at home, and what Teresa had done the other day. She placed a steamy diminutive cup in front of the housekeeper, and another for herself, and sat down, running her fingers across the scarred, scrubbed surface of the table as she sipped her coffee.

After a minute, Diane tentatively asked, "Anna and you were close?"

Teresa looked up, tears running freely down her face. She shook her head. "That is what is so terrible. No one, but no one could have been close to Anna. I felt sorry for her, yes, she is my cousin's daughter. So I gave her a job."

"I see," Diane said softly. "Well, she seemed happy here."

"That girl would not have been happy anywhere she had to work," Teresa said, with a twisted smile. "She was very lazy." Tears flowed again. "She was my cousin's only daughter, her only child."

Diane said nothing, since there was nothing to say.

Teresa drained the small cup and started to stand up. "I need to..."

Diane came around and held the small round woman tightly as she sobbed. "Please, let me help." She suggested, "Another coffee?"

Teresa shook her head, "No, otherwise I won't sleep tonight."

"My cousin who found the—found Anna, she wants to go lie down. Is there an unoccupied room she can change to?"

"Oh, that poor woman!" Teresa started to get up.

Diane firmly stopped her. "Tell me where the room is, and if it needs bedding. I'll take care of it."

Teresa looked at her doubtfully, without energy left to argue.

Diane reassured her, "I'm basically Judith's housekeeper, you know. She calls me her assistant, but this is really what I do."

Teresa smiled through her tears. "There's a downstairs bedroom, and the linen closet is next to the laundry, down the hall."

"I'll be right back. This won't take a minute," Diane hurried out, found the crisp white sheets, snapping them into hospital corners—she'd learned that, at least. She found Candace, and showed the family into their new room. It was smaller, without a grand view, but she doubted they cared. The family huddled together, Ben collapsing in one of the chairs, not wanting to leave his parents.

Diane got back to the kitchen in record time. Teresa was still sitting at the table, but she had run out of tears. She stared blankly at the stove, as if willing herself to get back to work.

"Where is Salvatore?" she asked. "Do you want me to get him?"

Teresa shook her head. "No, he and Pietro are going over the grounds with the police. Checking to see if someone broke in."

"Well," said Diane practically, "I doubt Anna was murdered by an outsider, but I suppose it has to be done." She looked at the beautiful stove, all shining brass knobs and serious looking grates. "What can I help with?"

Teresa smiled at her, "You're a good girl, Diane." She looked around the kitchen a little blankly.

"We will all need to eat," Diane said. "There's no point in us going around starving."

Teresa told her tartly, "No one has ever starved in my house, and they're certainly not going to start now."

Diane went over to the counter, the backsplash lined with square white tiles, like a restaurant kitchen. She surveyed the ingredients Teresa had laid out, before the horror began. "Bolognese sauce?" she deduced.

Teresa nodded agreement.

"Oh, good," Diane said with relief. "I can't do anything fancy like you, but at the very worst, they'll have the same thing I cook at least once a month." She smiled at Teresa, "Maybe I can learn some tips from an expert."

She turned the flame on the heavy pot and started slicing the pancetta into small cubes, throwing them into the hot pot. The sizzling smell of frying pancetta filled the room. Diane sliced the onions, celery, and carrots into tiny pieces, throwing them into the oil the pancetta had made. She stirred with a big wooden spoon, and managed to get Teresa another espresso as she cooked.

"The meat, next?"

"Yes, ground beef." A trace of interest appeared in Teresa's eyes. "Sometimes I use the traditional veal, but it is very fatty, more than Americans like."

"I sometimes make it with part ground pork," Diane said. "I don't know if that's the right thing to do?" She placed the ground meat in the pot, watching it sizzle.

"That works, too," Teresa agreed. "There are as many variations as there are grandmothers."

Diane laughed. "I barely remember my grandmother, but most of my memories of her were in her kitchen." Diane suddenly realized that Teresa reminded her a little of her grandmother, small and round, with sparkling dark eyes. Her grandmother had always smelled like gingerbread, from the spices she spent her days around. Diane blinked in the hot steam and stirred harder.

Teresa got up and looked over her shoulder. "Now, the milk," she told her. "Always whole milk." She poured it in while Diane stirred.

Diane smelled the rich scent of beef and vegetables from the garden. She stirred until the milk was absorbed.

Teresa brought a bottle of red wine and poured it in. "Now, stir harder!"

Diane stirred like mad, scraping up all the rich goodness as she deglazed the pan. "I thought you used white wine in Bolognese?"

"No, no," Teresa told her. "Always red." She gestured, "Red is more..." her hands moved expressively. "Much more."

Diane nodded. "There, I knew I'd learn a tip." She stirred hard, under Teresa's watchful eye.

After the wine cooked off, Teresa poured in a large container of veal stock, followed by one of her homemade passata. She turned the flame to a faint blue glow down as it started to boil. "It will need to cook for at least two hours," she told Diane. "I usually cook it for longer, but..." her voice trailed off.

"What pasta do you have with it?" Diane asked. "I usually just buy egg noodles."

"That is fine for quick," Teresa said. "But what Bolognese needs is tagliatelle. That is the traditional." She sprinkled the table with flour, then placed a prepared disc of dough on it. "You must always let the pasta dough rest first."

Diane nodded, watching in fascination as Teresa rolled out a paper thin sheet of dough, covering the entire table. Her round hands moved quickly, sliding the dough sheet as if it was indeed, paper. She took a round cutter out, making quick, neat slices through the dough. She took the ribbons of pasta, placing them under dampened cloths. "There, that is done." She looked like she had felt better by moving, accomplishing her normal tasks, but was suddenly exhausted.

Diane put a chair under her, and Teresa sank into it. "Now it's my turn," she told her. "If there is one thing I know how to do, it's dishes." She stacked pans and started scrubbing.

Diane had just sat back down at the table when Pietro came in the kitchen. He looked quizzically back and forth between her and Teresa, then he hung his battered hat on a hook, fixed himself an espresso, and sat down next to Teresa.

"Bolognese?" he asked, sniffing the rich aroma.

"Yes," Teresa confirmed. "Diane made it."

"Diane?" he looked at her.

"I just did what Teresa told me to," Diane told him. "Really, that's all."

Pietro looked at the pot, smiling. "Thank you."

Diane said quickly, "Teresa rolled out the dough. I've never seen dough rolled out that thin," she added in amazement.

"I will teach you," Teresa told her with a smile. "It is not hard, it is just practice."

Diane laughed, "You could say that about anything!"

Pietro and Teresa laughed with her, and he agreed, "You could indeed."

Teresa pulled a platter of biscotti, placing it in the center of the table, and they each took one of the long cookies. The companionable sound of crunching filled the kitchen.

"So, I heard you say you were going to school to train for nursing," Pietro asked Diane.

"I was in nursing school, when Mom got sick. I've always meant to go back..." she trailed off.

"But you weren't sure it was the right place for you anymore?" Pietro astutely guessed.

Startled, Diane looked at him, her amber eyes glinting in the sunlight. "That's it exactly. I don't really know what I want anymore." She shrugged, her ill fitting top hidden under a neatly tied cheerfully flowered apron that emphasized her curves. "But I've decided I can't keep drifting along, scared to move forward."

"Do you think you'll like nursing?" Pietro asked, as if he actually cared about the answer.

Teresa cocked her head, saying nothing, but clearly enjoying the game.

"I don't know," Diane admitted. "I know I love taking care of people," she said with certainty. She looked down at her capable hand, lying on the table. She looked up into Pietro's kind brown eyes. "I need to do something," she told him, "and I think I would be good at nursing."

Pietro looked at her amber eyes, smelling the simmering pot on the stove, and thought how beautiful she was. "I know you'll make a success of it," he told her, honestly.

She looked at him, her wide lips curving. "Thanks."

Pietro suddenly thought Diane hadn't had many people, none of these Parkers, telling her how capable she was. He was suddenly very angry at their easy dismissal of this beautiful woman.

The three of them sat there laughing and chatting, talking about recipes and gardens, and about all the good things in the world that had nothing to do with murder.

Mia came into the kitchen, wondering if Teresa needed any help. She found Teresa sitting at the table and Diane stirring a pot on the stove. "Hi, ladies. I just wondered if Teresa needed any help?"

She sniffed the appetizing smell coming from the simmering pot appreciatively. "I see dinner is going to be delicious."

"It is," Diane agreed. "Teresa gave me some cooking tips too." She got up to get Mia an espresso.

Mia sat down at the table, looking sympathetically at Teresa. "I'm so sorry for your loss. Is there anything I can do to help?"

Teresa shook her head. "No, I am fine."

Diane chuckled, "She knows you're fine, Teresa, Mia just wants to help."

"Well, Anna was going to pick up groceries in town this afternoon. I need things for breakfast." The words dragged out reluctantly, but Teresa was in no condition to walk to town today.

"A nice walk, and shopping in a new place. That sounds like my favorite kind of task," Mia told her warmly. "That will be fun."

"Thank you for the offer, Signora Spinel."

"Please call me Mia," Mia told her, as Teresa handed her the list. It was, naturally, in Italian, but Mia was certain she could handle that. She'd ordered in enough Italian restaurants, after all.

Mia had a quick word with Tenente Zanatta, who must not consider her as very good suspect, as he obviously didn't care whether she went to town or not. She was escorted to her room by a handsome young carabinieri, who supervised her collecting her handbag. He checked the handbag thoroughly, commented appreciatively on the expensive quality of the brand and sent her on her way.

She waved goodbye with a "Ciao," and walked down the villa driveway, through the elegantly pollarded trees. At the end of the drive, a single carabinieri stood guard, stopping all entry and exits. He called up to Zanatta, got approval and opened the gates. Mia escaped from the confines of the beautiful villa with a newfound sense of freedom.

She took her time walking to town, enjoying the dappled afternoon shadows on the road and the birds singing in the trees. Neat, stucco houses in warm shades of ochre clustered tightly together behind walls, with vineyards and fields beyond. Mia wondered if they were family compounds still, since they must have been at some time. One section of wall had a grape arbor stretched over the sidewalk, providing shade to pedestrians and sun to grapes. Unripe grapes hung, heavy with promise. Bright geraniums bloomed at entrances to driveways, and cascaded down from windows. Chickens scratched next to the road, giving a new meaning to road hazards.

The town felt cheerful with activity this afternoon, especially in contrast with the fear hanging over the villa. The little shop on the piazza had its door open wide, and the tiny elderly lady was behind the counter again. Mia greeted her, and asked how Ryan was.

"He sits in his room, most of the time," the woman said, her mouth turning down with disapproval. "I tell him to go take some walks in the sunshine, get some fresh air. But no, he shuffles papers and types. He is looking terrible, the silly boy." She cocked her head quizzically, "You have had some bad things lately, at the villa? Poor Anna," she sadly shook her head. "Her mother is heartbroken."

"It's terrible when someone so young dies," Mia agreed with sympathy. "The carabinieri are working very hard to find out who killed her."

"You are not related to the family staying at the villa?" she asked curiously.

"No, I'm merely a family friend. I went to school with one of the ladies of the family," Mia offered the information. "A long time ago, but we've always been close friends." She wondered if her close friend had had a reason to kill Jeffery or Anna. She sincerely hoped not.

"Ah," the woman said knowledgeably. "Anna was —how should I say? Anna was a difficult child. She loved nice things, and would steal them as a child, from the shops. I think that she had stopped doing that, but she always did like nice things. If she had seen something when that man was killed..." she broke off speculatively, her bright bird-like eyes looking at Mia.

"I think so too," agreed Mia. "She must have seen something."

"She was talking in here, the day before when she went for groceries, about how much money she was going to have soon. Bragging," she added, her face disgusted.

"Did she say why or where she would get the money?"

"She hinted," the woman told her, straightening the folds of her scarf. "She was always a hinter, that one. It always came to nothing. Nothing at all. Just talk." She held out her hands, gesturing. "She talked about the oleander poison, said it would be easy to make." She shrugged expressively, "Well, we all know how dangerous ammazza l'asino is."

"Indeed," Mia agreed. If she hadn't known before this week, she'd know it now. "Did she see someone making the poison?" Mia asked.

The woman shrugged again. "Maybe. Probably. That, or she guessed."

"When did she seem to think she'd have money to spend?"

Deliberately, the woman took a cold drink out of the refrigerator for herself and gestured to Mia. Mia nodded, putting a much larger bill than the cost on the counter, clearly indicating no change was needed. They both sipped the icy Crodino with enjoyment.

After a minute, the woman put hers down with a clink. "Anna said she would have money tonight. She talked of getting a new dress for next weekend, going to the club."

"We went to Vicenza yesterday," Mia said thoughtfully. "I doubt any of us would have had enough money to pay Anna off without going to a bank."

"Did anyone go to a bancomat while you were there?" The woman took another swig of Crodino.

"Yes," said Mia unhappily, remembering Kathleen's asking about ATM's.

Mia ascended the narrow stairs and knocked at the door. "Entra," Ryan called, clearly assuming it was the elderly woman from below.

Ryan sat at the table, using the sunlight from the window to read documents, while he took notes on a big legal pad. "Ms. Mia? I didn't expect to see you." He looked even worse than a few days before, with his hair standing on end, and wearing wrinkled gym shorts.

Mia sniffed disparagingly, then regretted it. The room smelled very much like unwashed boy. It was definitely time for her to take action.

"I don't know if you've heard the news from the villa? she asked.

"I heard it was poison," Ryan said dully. "I wish Francesca would get out of there."

Mia told him the rest of the news, of Judith's fall and Anna's murder, and his face turned white. "I didn't know any of that," he said. "Francesca, where her family is killing each other..." he shook his head. "I can't stand it." He stood up abruptly, slapping the legal pad down on the table. "I have to do something."

"I don't like it either," Mia told him. "It's time for Francesca and you to have a long talk. Jeffery's death puts everything into a different perspective."

"I think we should talk too, but she won't see me." Ryan shuffled through papers. "What am I supposed to do about it?"

Mia told him.

She smiled at the shopkeeper when she came back down. "I've convinced him to get himself together, and go outside." She wrinkled her nose. "He'll need to shower first, of course."

"Good, young men take love hard, don't they?" She grinned, her wrinkles deepening into well lived laugh lines. "He seems like a good boy."

"I've always thought so," Mia agreed.

"I've been thinking about poor Anna," the woman said. "I am sure now that she made an appointment with one of those Parkers. She was too excited about it to keep it to herself."

"Like something good was going to happen, perhaps?" asked Mia.

"Like she was getting money," the woman said bluntly. "Money and men was all that girl thought about. But she didn't seem scared." She shrugged. "If I was blackmailing a murderer, I would be scared, no?"

"I would be too terrified to brag about it," Mia agreed, trying to put herself in a stupidly greedy young girl's shoes. "Of course, she was very young."

"So, I think she would have been scared of a man, like the victim's brother or that Army man. One of the women seems more likely."

"And poison is usually a woman's weapon," concluded Mia. "Very interesting."

10

Reflections

Francesca swam with a slow, steady rhythm, covering the length of the rectangular pool in just a few strokes. Her long hair was tucked on top of her head, but strands fell down as she swam, floating in the water behind her. Her classic white one piece suited her, and showed off her perfect figure. She had been on the school swim team, and it had left her with an easy grace in the water.

Savannah sat sunning herself on a nearby lounger wearing her brief black bikini. She'd closed up her laptop, saying she was done for the day. She lay absolutely still, her headphones on, relaxing to music.

Francesca called, "You know, you're going to lose that Goth look entirely if you're not careful. You tan too easily."

"Yeah, a little more time here, and I'd be brown as anyone," Savannah agreed. "Black looks good on tan skin too, though."

"True," Francesca said, treading water next to Savannah. "I wish I could tan. I slather on sunblock, and just hope I don't turn lobster red."

Savannah laughed. "Yeah, remember when we went to the beach that time? After the first day, you had to hide in your room, smeared in aloe, while the rest of us enjoyed the sun. You looked like some green, goopy monster."

"I know," Francesca said, scrunching her face in memory. "Well, I can swim for a few minutes outside anyhow." She sighed, "When we get back home, I'm starting a routine swimming in Mom's pool. She keeps it heated, so I could go all winter long even. Maybe first thing in the morning."

"You know that will end up last thing at night," Savannah told her. "You've never been a morning person. Might as well admit it." She shifted onto her side. "Look, Fran, I've been thinking," she paused.

"Really?" Francesca said sarcastically, lazily twisting around in the water.

"Look, Fran, don't be mad. I'm totally on your side, no matter what. But I've been thinking..." Savannah said warily.

"Uh huh?" Francesca's tone was not inviting.

"Look, the whole thing doesn't make any sense at all. Ryan didn't have to steal money. Judith would have given ya'll anything you wanted. And he adores you, he always has." She held up a hand, "No, hear me out,

240

then I won't say another word. I never have, this whole time, you know? So hear me out, Fran."

"Fine," Francesca agreed resentfully.

"Ryan didn't kill Jeffery. He plain couldn't have. Not possible." Savannah sat up, gesturing forcefully. "So, unless you think we have a thief and a murderer, both of them, in our family, then he didn't do it. He didn't do any of it."

Francesca swam a minute, absorbing the novel thought. Finally, she warily asked, "So what's your theory?"

Savannah leaned forward. "I think Uncle Jeffery knew who the thief was, and he came to demand money. All that stuff at dinner was him threatening the thief. So the thief killed him."

"Then, why did he say Ryan was the thief? I mean, there were bank accounts in Ryan's name."

"Anyone could set up bank accounts now. It's all online." Savannah warmed to her subject, her bare toes vibrating as her theory spilled out. "I mean, you and Ryan were going to control the company next, we all knew it. Uncle Jeffery always thought that was unfair— he hated Ryan's guts. I've seen him look at Ryan like he wanted to kill him."

"But Uncle Jeffery is the one who got killed," Francesca objected.

"Yeah, so he was threatening the thief. Probably blackmail, like Anna."

"So, who could be the thief if it's not Ryan?" Francesca asked.

"Well, any of us have access to the accounts. We all own shares and check in on the finances, at least we're supposed to," Savannah said, a trifle guiltily. "I never have before what happened, but I could have. It would be easy for me to do a big ad purchase order or some equipment, pass a fake through the system." She wiggled uncomfortably. "I didn't, but I could have."

"Yeah, I really don't think it's you." Francesca propped her arms on the side of the pool, kicking her legs out.

"Thanks a lot..." Savannah drew the words out. "I don't think it's you—or Ryan—because it was basically your money. There's no motive."

"And couldn't be Mom, since it actually is her money. She didn't need to steal it."

"Yeah. I think Ben's too young. I mean, he could have used the passwords since he helps with the business, but why would he? He's planning on going in with his dad."

"What about Uncle Kevin? Could he have?"

Savannah said slowly, "I think he could have— like I said—the system is secure from outsiders, but not protected at all from family. Uncle Harold purposefully made it that way, so any of us could step in, if we needed to in an emergency." She shook her head, her sleek black hair swinging with the movement. "I don't see him wanting to—he's always been pretty hyper about not taking extra money from the business, besides that seed loan."

"I don't see how Uncle Kevin could have killed his brother. Or Uncle Jeffery exposed his own brother as a thief. He'd have gotten the money back quietly."

"Maybe," Savannah said, adding, "but he sure liked needling Uncle Kevin."

"True." Francesca thought. "So who else? Diane could have, but she wouldn't."

"Diane is the only one of us that's broke, but if she asked Judith for college money, Judith would give it to her in a minute. I don't see why Diane would steal it." Savannah sat on the edge of the pool, dangling her feet in the water. The blood red nail polish on her toes darkened to deep purple in the water, and she stared moodily at her toes, kicking her feet. "The problem is, all of these people wouldn't. They're all family." Savannah finally stated. "But one of them did. One of us."

"It's all so crazy," Francesca said. "I feel like I'm walking in some sort of nightmare."

"I know," Savannah agreed. "What about Uncle Randall?"

"There's no way," Francesca said, then dropped her eyes. "I guess he could have. Same with Aunt Kathleen. They both have account access." She thought a minute. "Maybe that's how Uncle Jeffery found out, they could have forgotten to use a VPN or something."

"That makes sense." Savannah kicked her feet.

"What doesn't make sense is either one caring enough about money to steal it. You know Uncle Randall. He lives in military housing and usually flies military too. But he'll spend tons on other stuff, like that scuba trip. And Aunt Kathleen just doesn't notice money the same way other people do. I think she has what she wants. Neither makes sense."

"Aunt Candace?" Savannah asked.

"She'd like nothing more than to get Uncle Kevin all to herself," Francesca admitted, "but killing Uncle Jeffery wouldn't do that. It'll probably do the opposite, since he'll have to do all the stuff Uncle Jeffery did, too."

"True," Savannah said. "Well, we've come to a conclusion. No one did it." She looked at her cousin, her kohl rimmed eyes serious. "If I were you, Fran, I'd go talk with Ryan. Hear what he has to say." As Francesca glared at her, she added reasonably, "Because whatever he did, he's definitely not a murderer, and someone here is."

Francesca pushed off the wall, and took a few strokes to the steps. "I'm getting out before I turn into a lobster." She gracefully stepped out of the pool, and stood drying her long hair.

"Fran?" Savannah asked in a small voice.

Francesca waved a hand at her cousin. "It's fine, Savannah. You've given me a lot to think about."

The other girl sat back on her lounger, looking relieved.

Francesca added, "Love you, too."

She went to change. Savannah smiled, and put her headphones back on.

Francesca let the hot water beat down on her head and shoulders, stretching out the time, so she could think. All of her thoughts had snarled into a giant ball of pain and betrayal, a confused mess of everything that had happened over the past few months, and especially the past few days.

She'd been blissfully happy with Ryan, being Ryan's wife, living with Ryan. When they'd first met at the office, they'd had an instant connection, laughing at the same jokes and liking the same things. They'd fallen head over heels in love, and everything had been perfect.

That love had seemed real, a solid foundation to build a life on. Had it really all been a fraud? Had Ryan been just faking his love the whole time? He'd danced with her, made dinner with her, made love with her. They'd been sick with the flu together, and if that didn't bring out the worst in a person, she didn't know what would. They'd packed office lunches together, going together to picnic at a little park when the weather was nice. Their little bubble of happiness in the day, alone together. Had it all been fake, just Ryan manipulating her?

He'd talked about children, their children. Oh God, Francesca thought, clutched her stomach and crouching on the shower floor, rocking and crying under the pelting water.

She didn't know what was real anymore. Had someone else stolen the company money, and set up Ryan to take the blame? Could Uncle Jeffery have found out, and kept his mouth shut? Would Uncle Jeffery really have stooped that far?

Tears ran down her face, mingling with the water, burning into her skin.

Francesca didn't know what was real anymore.

She got out of the shower, and dried her hair, taking her time. She needed time, time to think. She put on a plain white dress that floated around her in a soft cloud. It wouldn't be polite to wear bright colors, with the deaths in the house. The murders, not the deaths. They were brutal murders. Someone in this house, one of her family, was a murderer.

Francesca felt like she was trapped in a nightmare.

She mechanically brushed out her hair until it was a soft mass, then twisted it up on her head with one practiced move, holding it in place with a tortoiseshell clip. She put on comfortable shoes, some she could walk in the garden with. At home, she would have hiked in the mountains, but not here, she didn't know the countryside.

Next, there was something she needed to do. Oh yes, she needed to check on Mom. She had left her talking with Aunt Kathleen earlier, and gone for a swim. She had needed to move her body, get out of this muffled cocoon she was trapped in.

She took a deep breath in. She needed to stop feeling all her decisions, and start thinking about them instead. Because feeling everything, feeling so much all the time was emotionally exhausting, and she simply couldn't handle any more.

Uncle Jeffery was dead. Anna was dead. She needed to stop feeling sorry for herself, retreating into overwhelming emotions, and start thinking clearly. Because there was a killer in the house.

She breathed in. First, she would make sure Mom was okay, and didn't need help. Make sure she was safe —someone had tried to murder Mom by pushing her over that wall. Mom wasn't admitting it, because she'd never admit one of her family had tried to kill her.

Francesca padded down the stone stairs, thinking that if Mom and Aunt Kathleen were still talking, she'd just slip quietly out the back door, and spend a few minutes in the garden. Smell the roses, and listen to the birds. Calm her mind.

She went softly to the door, and listened a minute, hearing a deep male voice. Uncle Randall was with her. Good, Francesca thought, I can take a few more minutes to clear my head.

She turned away, then heard her mom exclaim, "No, you can't! That would kill me!"

Francesca turned back, uncertain if she should intervene.

Uncle Randall said furiously, "I'm Francesca's father, Judith. I have a right to tell her. It's not right not to tell her, now that Harold is dead. She needs a father."

Francesca's world froze. She held onto the door frame, for balance. Taking a deep breath, she slowly walked outside, and into view.

"What did you say?" she asked, looking at the man she knew as Uncle Randall.

Judith stood up, stretching her arms out pleadingly toward Francesca, "He has no right, no right at all." She glared at Randall. "Shut up. You're ruining everything."

Francesca ignored her mom. She repeated, looking directly into Randall's silver eyes, "What did you say?"

Randall stood up awkwardly, hanging his head down and slumping. It was odd to see the usually confident man so unsure of himself. He mumbled, looking at the floor, "This wasn't how I wanted you to find out, Francesca." He added inconsequently, "I thought you were swimming."

"I came in," Francesca said dully. "What did you say?" she insisted.

Judith said, "I demand..."

Randall cut her off. "No, Judith, this has gone on long enough."

Francesca looked at her. "Mom, don't worry. I want to know what's going on. I need to know."

Judith sat down, holding her hand to her chest as if her heart was broken. Francesca patted her thin shoulder. "Don't worry," she repeated. "I need to know."

Randall sat down, leaning forward and steepling his hands. He looked directly at her, his cropped silver hair shining as it caught a ray of light. "You're my daughter, Francesca, but you're much more Judith's and Harold's daughter than mine, I know that." He looked back down at the floor, then into Francesca's grey eyes.

"Your mother, my wife, Nora, she was amazing. Just amazing. You look a lot like her, you know." He sighed heavily. "She died when you were born."

"Oh no," Francesca gasped.

"No, honey, don't feel like that." Randall paused, "It was just—nothing anyone could do. I was deployed. Out of contact. It was a week before they could get to me and tell me. I couldn't leave, people would have died." He looked down, "Frankly, I hoped I'd die, with Nora gone. She was my life."

He fell silent, his bright eyes suddenly dull with pain.

Judith took up the story, her eyes pleading with Francesca for understanding. "I was there, with Nora, the whole time. You know that Harold and Randall were best friends? Well, we were close. She was staying with us, while Randall was deployed. We had plenty of room in that big house."

She looked at Francesca, her dark eyes filling with tears. "We couldn't have children. We both wanted a child of our own, so much. The house was filled with kids, but they were all other people's kids. Family, but not ours. Not really."

Francesca held out her hand, and Judith gripped it tightly. "Nora went into labor early. She died before the ambulance could get there." Judith's face was white and drawn at the memory.

Randall choked a little, and she looked at him sympathetically. "I'm so sorry, Randall."

"When you were born, you were the most beautiful baby." Judith smiled at Francesca. "Nora named you after her mother, you know. She died holding you. She got to hold you." Judith swallowed hard.

"Emergency services were pretty confused when she died—a storm, so they were overwhelmed. There was no way we would have let you go into Child Services. Not have some stranger taking care of you.

She smiled at Francesca. "So we just kept you, of course. No one asked about you. So we took care of you." She squeezed Francesca's hand tightly.

"It was months before I could get back," Randall said. "I was doing some pretty sensitive stuff, and—well, I wasn't allowed to leave at the time. When I did come back—"

Judith smiled at Francesca. "It was months later. He held you like you were the most precious gift in the world." Her eyes were full of pity. "Francesca felt like our child by then. We had told everyone you were, just to avoid—complications," she told Francesca. "We were terrified you might be put into the system. Randall couldn't really communicate, or show up in court. We decided to straighten everything out when Randall did come back. Harold talked to a lawyer, who had it all lined up. But when the time came—"

"I was a mess," Randall told her bluntly. "I had PTSD from some pretty bad stuff, I was drinking too much, and my heart was broken."

"I looked at you, so happy with those round little cheeks and big gray eyes just like my mom. You were in that cute, pink nursery that Judith had done up with frills everywhere, surrounded by a big family who loved you. And suddenly, I knew I wasn't the right person to take care of you, right then. Judith and Harold were."

"So we adopted you. I was so happy when all the legal stuff was done with, and you were really mine." Judith held onto Francesca's hand. "I'm so sorry, dear. I kept meaning to tell you, but I didn't know where to start. I was worried that Jeffery might be mad about the business, might try to sue for control of the company, if he remembered you weren't actually related by blood, and Harold did so want you to have his legacy. He always considered you his daughter and heir, you know. I was just trying to look out for you, dear." She squeezed Francesca's hand. "I'm sorry if I did wrong."

"It's okay, Mom. It's just a shock." She looked at Randall, seeing the broken man he had been, back then, in the slump of his shoulders.

Francesca said firmly, "I grew up in the best family ever. This is just—" she stood up. "I'm going to go for a walk." She needed to clear her head more than ever.

Judith watched her white dress float out of sight, behind the colorful flowers.

She turned to Randall, tears in her eyes. "I'm going to lose her, now. Oh, why did you have to tell her, now?"

"She had a right to know," Randall told her. "I didn't mean to then, not like that, not when everything is so bad. But I do think she needed to know she had a father she could count on."

"Harold was her father," Judith said, her voice icy.

"Of course Harold was her father. He was a much better father than I ever could have been. He was my best friend." Randall paused. "But Harold's dead, and she has another father. And I can help her get through this stuff she's going through, be there for her like I wasn't able to do when she was little."

"Oh," Judith sobbed, "You've ruined everything."

"Judith, you're her mom, by every count that matters."

Judith shook her head. "I'm going to lose her now. She's all that's ever mattered to me." She got up, suddenly a very old woman. "I'm going to my cottage." She looked out at the distant figure of Francesca.

"Can I help you?" Randall stood up.

"I think you've helped quite enough," Judith told him acerbically. "I'm going to go lie down." She made her way back to her cottage with slow, faltering steps. It seemed like a very long way.

Ben moodily walked through the vineyard. This was the worst vacation ever. Then he stopped, and gave a harsh bark of laughter. Well, of course it was. People had been killed.

He'd planned on going swimming, but Savannah had basically glued herself to that lounge chair, and Francesca was swimming laps. He wasn't in the mood for them whining at him if he got their hair wet jumping in. So he'd veered off, as far away from people as he could get.

The grapevines stretched to the horizon were in rigidly controlled rows. Tight little green grapes dangled down, but they weren't ready to eat yet. It was dry, dusty, and hot. He probably should have stayed by the pool with the girls, but he didn't want to be around anyone right now.

He idly kicked at clods of dirt, watching the dust fly up. It was crazy how much they pruned the grapevines. Only nubs left, really, then the leaves came out and grapes grew. Sometimes pruning was a good thing. Necessary for growth.

Ben had never liked Uncle Jeffery. He didn't think Uncle Jeffery had ever liked Ben. He always seemed to be examining Ben for signs of flaws, like an inferior metal that might break, if he probed hard enough. Uncle Jeffery would never just say, hi, how's it going? No, it was twenty questions about his grades, with a superior air of disinterest in school sports. Which was rich, coming from someone who could bore you about marathons for hours on end. No, he'd never liked Uncle Jeffery, but murder—that was something else.

At dinner that night, Uncle Jeffery had basically attacked his dad, telling him he was calling in that loan. Ben knew exactly how much paying back that loan in a hurry would have hurt Dad's business. Dad had just bought those new trucks, and hired staff, getting ready for another expansion. They'd even been looking at moving to a new building to hold the extra equipment.

Ben planned to be one of the new people, in a year or two. Dad had always planned on bringing him into the business. Right from the start, Ben had handed Dad tools, and fetched stuff from the truck. He felt like it was his business too, or would be.

He swept his bangs out of his eyes. They flopped back down again. He needed a haircut. There hadn't been time before they came.

Uncle Jeffery had threatened his family. It just wasn't right.

Kathleen sat on her balcony, looking out over the rich green fields of the Veneto. It was beautiful here, like some kind of a dream. It didn't seem like a place where something as ugly as murder could happen.

Kathleen knew that was ridiculous. Humans were humans, everywhere they went, and pent up rage, greed, or fear, resulted in murder. It just didn't seem like it was possible for that horror to happen in her own family. The shock of it was surreal.

Kathleen's life was full of carefully ordered plans, meaningful tasks to accomplish, filling up her days with rigid schedules.

When Judith had called, and told Kathleen about Francesca's failed marriage and her depression, Kathleen had offered to have Francesca live with her for a few months to get far away from her troubles. Make a clean break.

Judith had refused, wanting her daughter to stay with her, where she could take care of her. Well, that was natural enough.

Kathleen smiled a little. Judith had always been overprotective of Francesca. Of all the kids, really. Kathleen remembered Judith insisting on an automatic pool cover, at vast expense, so Francesca couldn't fall in the pool accidentally. Harold had laughed, and pointed out that Francesca swam like a fish already, to no avail. Judith had gotten her expensive pool cover. Which wasn't actually a bad thing, Kathleen agreed. Kids were always in and out of the house; not all of them could swim. Still, Judith had always treated Francesca like she should be carefully swathed in cotton wool, when she'd never been the least bit delicate.

Kathleen was surprised Judith had ever let Francesca out of the house long enough to get married. Judith had always encouraged Francesca to date, but all of the boys and later, men, she brought home had never been good enough for her little girl. Of course, Francesca had met Ryan at work, where Judith didn't really have a choice. If Francesca was going to take over Harold's legacy, she'd have to know how it ran. And Ryan had seemed like an extraordinarily upright young man. Kathleen was shocked at how badly she'd been fooled.

Kathleen missed her brother, Harold. He would have known how to handle all this. Murder certainly wouldn't have been committed under his roof.

Harold had been the older brother everyone wanted, kind and patient, generous with his time and his words. He'd paid for Kathleen's graduate school, long ago, after her husband had died. She'd decided back then that she had had her great love. After his death, she had no choice but to move on. She buried herself in the logic of science, making a difference to the world. Kathleen remembered sitting down with Harold, and trying to figure out how she'd afford school.

He'd told her, "Quit talking about getting a job, Kathie. Worry about your studies. I'll take care of the money. You'll do us proud."

And he had. Kathleen had graduated without owing a dime, planted firmly on her feet in her new life. She'd repaid Harold some later, by giving him all her meagre savings—which he had made possible anyway. He'd traded her savings for shares of Parker Perches. He'd made everyone who'd believed in him, and helped him so rich, in so many ways. His support, courage, and optimism had pushed her to succeed beyond her expectations. Kathleen missed her big brother, and the way he laughed at life.

After Harold's recent death, the ties that held the family together started to unravel. When Judith had called, and they'd settled on this trip to refresh Francesca, Kathleen had noticed an uneasy note in her voice. And Judith was never uneasy—she was always imperturbably composed.

That uneasiness made Kathleen decide to invite Mia. Mia was more sensitive to people's moods than she was. Kathleen preferred the absolute facts of science, rather than the nuances of other's feelings. But Mia had a knack for reading the mood of a room and changing it, well, to suit her, really. There was no such thing as an awkward gathering for long around Mia.

Kathleen thought that was probably one of the secrets behind the phenomenal success of Mia's husband, Leo. He had always listened to his wife's practical suggestions. Kathleen wondered if Mia's daughter, Nicole, had the same talent. She had been a lovely young woman, when Kathleen last seen her at Francesca's wedding. Well, if she'd inherited Mia's organizational skills, Nicole would do well.

Kathleen had hoped Mia would be able to smooth over the problems with their little villa gathering. With two murders, and a near miss, so far, that approach hadn't worked out. The problems were too deeply entrenched.

The Parkers were adrift without a head of the family. Judith was indomitable, but also immutable as granite. The head of the family needed to give people room to grow. Jeffery had been an unpleasant little boy, and had grown into an annoying man. He had never been a leader.

As far as the head of Parker Perches, Harold had been preparing Ryan for that role. Even the best leaders make mistakes.

Kevin now had the best chance of growing into Harold's role. He was successful in his own right. Candace was little prissy, but a nice woman underneath the high maintenance facade. And Ben seemed like a good kid.

Yes, Harold had been proud of Kevin, but that still left the Parker Perches company without a leader. Kathleen sighed. A lot had changed, too fast.

There was a soft tap at her door. "Come in," she called, expecting the maid. Then she realized the maid wasn't coming any more. Her heart beat fast, suddenly terrified.

To her relief, Randall's head popped around the door. "You busy?" he asked.

"Not at all." She swallowed hard and gestured at the other chair. "Take a bench."

Randall sat down with a heavy thud. Without preamble, he told her, "I've messed up. Big time."

Kathleen turned to look at him. "What did you do?"

"I told Francesca." His voice was glum.

"You told Francesca?" Kathleen sounded grim. "Exactly what do you mean by that?"

"I told her she was my daughter."

"Ah," Kathleen breathed out slowly. "How is Judith taking it?"

"Francesca overheard me arguing with Judith. I wasn't planning on telling her then. Too much happening now. I was going to tell her later, pick a good time. Maybe a visit to Germany." Randall pounded the chair arm with his fist. "Too late now."

"And Francesca overheard?" Kathleen's voice was sharp.

"I know, I know," Randall said contritely. "I messed up."

"How is she taking it?"

"I don't know," Randall said. "She doesn't give much away. Like her mom, that way." He coughed and his eyes darted out at the hazy blue mountains on the horizon. "She went for a walk in the garden."

"She'll be okay," Kathleen said. "She's always been close to you."

"Yeah, I guess," Randall said uncertainly, running his hand across his hair. "I hope so."

"How's Judith?"

"Mad. Big mad at me." Randall paused. "She went to her cottage to lie down."

"You let her go alone?" Kathleen asked with concern.

"She definitely didn't want me around. That's why I came to get you. I don't think she should be left alone," Randall said. "She needs someone with her all the time, after yesterday."

"I'll go," Kathleen said, but she made no move to get out of the chair, staring out over the fields.

Randall said hesitantly, "I think," he cleared his throat. "I think Judith is very scared about losing Francesca. Judith loves her so much."

"She's not going to," Kathleen said, brushing that aside. "Francesca's a good, loyal girl. Always has been."

"I know, but I think Harold's death made Judith feel, well, a little lonely. This didn't help."

"No, it didn't," Kathleen snapped. "Okay, I'll go see what I can do." She left him sitting on her balcony, his silver eyes restlessly scanning the fields.

Kathleen knocked on her sister-in-law's door, "Judith?"

There was no answer. Kathleen tried the door and it opened. Judith must have been too upset to lock it, which was insane to forget, with a murderer running around loose.

"Judith?" Kathleen said again, softly, when she saw the huddled woman in the chair. She looked like a wounded animal, something small and delicate, huddled up for comfort in her den.

Judith looked up, her usually perfect makeup streaked, tears running rivulets through her foundation. Her face was swollen and blotchy and her eyes red with tears. Her usual rigid grooming was gone, shorn of all pretense. She gulped a breath, but said nothing, just looked up at Kathleen, pleading to be left alone.

Kathleen came in anyway, locking the door behind her, saying, "You really should have had that locked, Judith. It's not safe."

Judith attempted a smile, but it crumpled abruptly, tears running down her face in an uneven stream. Her thin legs were awkwardly askew, not arranged with their usual elegance. Her bowed shoulders shook with silent grief. Her body protectively curved on itself, mere bones draped in expensive clothing, emphasizing her fragility.

Kathleen soaked a washcloth in cold, clear water, wrung it out, and brought it to Judith. "You need this," she told her gently, and sat down in a nearby chair.

Judith took the washcloth and held it to her face for a long moment, covering it completely. She felt the cold cloth easing the hot pain of her tears, soothing it. When she had calmed slightly, she started deliberately cleaning off the ruined makeup.

"Thank you, Kathleen," she told her sister-in-law. "I just..." she broke off with a gulp.

"Don't think about it," Kathleen ordered her. "A lot's been happening. We're all overwhelmed right now."

"Yes..." Judith drew out the word, cleaning her face. "I have to get some cold cream, and redo my makeup," she commented after a minute. "I must look awful."

Kathleen smiled kindly at her. Judith looked young and vulnerable without her polished facade, much like the pretty girl Harold had brought home, all those years ago. Judith had tried to smile and laugh with the family, but it had always been an effort for her, never easy and natural.

"Just leave it for now," she told Judith. "No one's coming in with the door locked. Take a few minutes to gather yourself."

Judith nodded in acquiescence. She carefully placed the washcloth to one side on a coaster, then leaned back in the chair, stretching her neck to either side, then closing her eyes. Kathleen looked at the dark purple circles under the thin skin under her eyes, looking like bruises in the half light of the room. Even with that, she looked strangely young. Kathleen felt an ache in her heart, and wished Harold were here.

Judith said nothing, only her thin chest moved with each breath.

Kathleen didn't push her, in her turn, relaxing into her chair and closing her eyes.

Finally Judith shifted, deliberately straightening into a parody of her usual refined posture, crossing her legs and running her hands over her hair. "I'll have to go make some repairs," she said, with an unwise attempt at a laugh.

"Leave it for now," Kathleen said. "You look fine, anyway. You got most of the smears off."

"Good," Judith didn't look like she had the strength to move. "You know what happened?"

"Randall told me. He didn't like you being alone."

"A lot he cares," Judith said harshly.

"You know he does, Judith."

"Randall knows you're here then," Judith said. "So he won't worry," she added.

"Yes."

"I never wanted to tell Francesca."

"I know." Kathleen agreed. "But it was his right to tell her, you know. He is her father."

"Harold and I were her parents," Judith said.

"You are," Kathleen agreed. "Francesca knows that. But Randall is her father too. He's tried to be there for her, especially since Harold died."

"He wasn't in any shape to be a father back then," Judith spat out. "I'm the one who stayed up at night with her, changed her, took her to ballet class, was there when she was sick. He wasn't there."

Kathleen gently chided, "He was there as much as you'd let him. He didn't want to interfere, you know. He knows how much he owes you."

Judith subsided. "I know," she admitted, diminished. She breathed in and out, the bones of her chest visible moving, making her single gold chain sparkle in the sunlight. "It's just not fair." A single tear welled up, sliding down her face slowly.

"I know," Kathleen agreed, "It's not fair." She sighed, "But it wasn't fair when Nora died, either."

"That was a long time ago," Judith stated. "Francesca has been mine ever since."

"Not to Randall," Kathleen said gently. "To Randall, it happened yesterday."

Judith looked at her, a little startled. "Harold always..."

"Harold always did his best to hold the family together," Kathleen told her. "Randall's part of our family. You know it."

"I know." Judith leaned back. "I'm scared she'll reject me now, when she needs me the most," she admitted reluctantly.

"Francesca's a good woman," Kathleen said. "You and Harold did well. She's not going to do that. You don't need to think like that."   She looked seriously at Judith, holding her attention. "You really don't need to worry about Francesca not seeing you as her mother, in all the ways that matter. She loves you."

Kathleen sighed. "Right now, what I'm worried about are Jeffery and the maid, Anna's, murders." She added, "And the attempt on you. It's a very serious situation, Judith. I don't think you're giving it the attention it deserves."

"Oh, what does any of it matter compared to Francesca?" Judith said, closing her eyes.

"It matters a great deal, Judith," Kathleen said deliberately. "I'm trying to think of what Harold would have done."

Mia walked briskly down the main garden path, looking to each side. She found her quarry huddled in a corner of the rose garden. "Francesca, there you are! We're going for a walk. Come on," she ordered.

Francesca looked up, startled, "No, I'm good."

"No, you're not," Mia said bluntly. "Let's go."

Francesca shook her head. Mia told her, "I won't accept any excuses. I need you—you're coming."

"Fine," Francesca said huffily. She unfolded her legs and stomped them on the ground.

Mia ignored that. Francesca was coming. She didn't have to be polite about it.

Mia started down the drive at a brisk pace, forcing the girl to quicken her pace to catch up. After a few minutes of fast walking, Francesca complained, "Hey, where are we running to?"

Mia slowed marginally. "Just my normal pace." She liked walking fast. "So what's going on, Francesca? Randall told me the mess he'd made."

"Yeah," her steps slowed. "He's my dad, huh?"

Mia walked faster. "No, Randall's not your dad. Harold Parker was your dad. And you know it."

Francesca hurried to catch up. "But..."

"You're a very lucky woman, to have a fantastic dad like Harold, and a father who let his best friend take care of you, because it was the most loving home for you that he could think of."

Francesca stopped in the middle of the road, accusing, "But they lied to me!"

"Don't be such a baby, Francesca. You know perfectly well your Uncle Randall has always been in your life as much as possible between deployments. He loves you."

"I know," she said, starting to walk again. She tucked her long hair in a quick knot. "But..."

Mia stopped, and looked directly at into Francesca's beautiful gray eyes. "You had a great dad. You're lucky that even though he's gone, you still have your father there for you. You're very blessed, Francesca, and don't you forget it."

"I know," Francesca said weakly.

"Now, we're going to clear up the next problem. You and your husband are going to talk."

"What?" Francesca stopped again. "Mia, how could you?" Her voice quivered with utter betrayal.

"Francesca," Mia said gently. "You know I love you, and want the best for you, just like your family."

Francesca nodded, but her jaw was clenched with anger.

"It seemed to me that Ryan had been accused too hastily," Mia told her. She chuckled, a wicked gleam in her bright blue eyes, "If I was embezzling from a company, the first thing I would do would be open a numbered bank account in someone else's name, with a small percentage of the stolen money."

"Mia!" Francesca said sharply.

"Wouldn't you?" Mia asked persuasively.

Francesca said nothing, just walked faster.

"That didn't mean Ryan wasn't guilty, of course," continued Mia blithely. "Just that a small percentage of the money in his account wasn't enough to convict him."

"But..." Francesca wailed. "He yelled at me when I accused him!"

"Well, really dear, did you think he wouldn't?" Mia asked reasonably.

Francesca's footsteps slowed, her attention on Mia's words.

Mia continued, "After Jeffery's death, I thought it was critical to look into the matter. So I convinced Ryan to give me the company records in his court case."

"You what?"

"I have," Mia smirked broadly, "quite a team of accountants working for me, dear. And Nicole can be quite voracious about tracking down fraud."

Francesca hung on her words. "And?" she demanded.

"While it is impossible to be one hundred percent certain who a thief was without access to the company computers directly, they are fairly certain Jeffery Parker was responsible for the embezzlement."

"How certain?" Francesca asked sharply.

"Certain enough that we are walking down this road right now for you to meet your husband, and discuss the matter with him, dear," Mia told her firmly.

"Jeffery was murdered," Francesca said. "Could Ryan have?"

"Francesca, get your head straight," Mia told her with acerbity. "While it is completely possible for Ryan to have sneaked onto the villa grounds, and hit Jeffery over the head while he was outside, it is highly unlikely Ryan poisoned Jeffery's pipe, which he kept on him or in his room."

"Anna was hit over the head," Francesca said.

"Yes, upstairs in the villa. The staff does notice if strangers are wandering around, you know. Especially when there has been a murder."

Francesca breathed out a heavy sigh. "So Ryan isn't a murderer."

"Ryan's not a murderer, and the odds are extremely slim that he's a thief," Mia said tartly. "Where you go from there is up to you two."

They turned the corner and Francesca's heart leapt as she saw the tall young man waiting for her, under the shade of an olive tree. He paused in his restless pacing as he saw her and stood still, looking at her.

"You go talk to your husband," Mia said. "I am going to walk very slowly back to the villa."

"You're never slow," Francesca told her, but her eyes were on her husband, as she walked to him.

Ryan stood waiting for her. "Francesca?" he asked with a question in his voice. His hair glinted gold from the afternoon sun. He'd washed and shaved, but his shoulders still slumped with defeat.

They just looked at each other. Finally, Francesca broke down. "Did you?"

He asked harshly, "Did I what?" forcing her to ask.

"Did you steal that money?" she asked.

"Of course I didn't!" he said scornfully.

"Mia says you didn't," Francesca admitted.

"But my own wife believes I did," he said bitterly. "Look, Francesca, you either believe me, or you don't. I didn't steal that money."

"Why are you here?"

"In Italy? Here?" Ryan shrugged. "I had to tell you. You never gave me a chance to tell you I didn't do it. Well, I'm telling you now. I'm not a thief, Francesca," he spat out the words accusingly.

"Uncle Jeffery said—" Francesca broke off. "He's dead, you know."

"I know," Ryan said. "I didn't kill him either."

Francesca tried to laugh, but it came out as a harsh grating sound. She swallowed, feeling her heart pounding in her chest. "No, I know you didn't."

"How do you know that?" Ryan said harshly.

"Well, you just wouldn't," Francesca told him.

"But I'd steal?" Ryan asked, more gently.

"I...it was all this terrible nightmare," Francesca said.

"Yes," Ryan agreed harshly. "Yes, it is."

"Uncle Jeffery told me you'd stolen from the company. And Mom said I'd better get a divorce quickly before it all came out."

"And you didn't think to ask me?" Ryan asked. "You didn't bother to ask your own husband?"

"The lawyer said I shouldn't talk to you," Francesca told him, eyes tearing up. "So I didn't."

"Well, Francesca, what do you think now?" Ryan's voice burned coldly. "Do you think I'm a thief?"

She looked at the ground, tracing an arc in the dirt with her foot.

"Well, Francesca?" he demanded.

She didn't raise her eyes. "I think," she paused. "I think I was wrong. Really wrong." She looked up, her gray eyes fearfully meeting his blue stare. "I think Uncle Jeffery stole the money and blamed it on you."

He nodded. He had come to that conclusion a long time before Mia had proven it.

They stood there for a minute, both uncertain.

Finally, Ryan looked at Francesca and asked gently, "Well, Francesca, where do we go from here?"

"I don't know," she said wretchedly, refusing to meet his eyes. "I messed up so badly."

"You did indeed," Ryan agreed, feeling his heart break again. "I don't know where we go, either."

Francesca looked down at the ground. She didn't have the right to decide this. She had betrayed her husband, accusing him of a terrible crime. She hadn't even allowed him to deny it.

"I don't know where we go next," Ryan repeated. "However, I do know that you can't sleep in a house with a murderer on the loose, alone." He pointed to a worn travel bag waiting in the shade of the tree. "I'm going with you. Or I'm going home. It's up to you."

"I can't ask you to—" Her eyes met his hard face, and looked away.

"You're my wife, at least for now," Ryan told her firmly. "So I have a duty to protect you. I've been—" he swallowed hard, "concerned about you in a house with a murderer." He added harshly, "After all, we were friends, before."

Francesca nodded acceptance. "Thank you," she said meekly.

They walked back up the road together, leaving an open space between them.

Mia had walked slower than she was accustomed to, but still had sat down in the shade of the pollarded lime trees to wait at the end of the drive. The birds sang in the trees, familiar, yet novel songs, and the bees buzzed in the white clover by the side of the drive.

Salvatore paused, trundling out of the bushes with a wheelbarrow load of hedge trimmings, when he saw her sitting on the ground. "You are okay?" he asked curiously.

Mia smiled in greeting. "Thank you, I'm fine. I'm waiting for Francesca."

"I see." Salvatore politely did not ask more.

"Is Teresa feeling okay?" Mia asked. "I know she and Anna must have been very close."

Salvatore set the wheelbarrow down with an abrupt squeak, and tipped his battered Panama hat back. "They were not close, but they were family," he told her. "It is a great shock to her." His tan face set solemnly, lines carved deep and his mouth firm.

"I know it is," Mia said. "Murder is a terrible thing, especially murder of a young person."

"The police, they still do not know?" Salvatore probed.

"I haven't heard any news," Mia told him, and his face fell slightly.

"I know it must be one of our family here," she said sadly. "But I don't know who would do such a dreadful thing."

Salvatore gestured at the wheelbarrow. "Someone climbed over the wall, down there," he pointed. "Not very long ago."

"After you locked the gate?" Mia asked.

"To be sure," Salvatore flashed white teeth quickly. "Why climb when you can just walk in?"

Mia looked up as Francesca and Ryan came through the gates, walking slowly, with an arms length of space between them.

"That's her husband?" Salvatore asked Mia. "The one who caused the trouble on the piazza?"

"That's the one."

"They don't look happy together," he commented dryly.

"No, I foresee another awkward evening," Mia told him.

"One of Teresa's best meals would certainly be wasted today." Salvatore added with a smile, "I heard that your Diane is a good cook."

"I'm not surprised," Mia told him. "Diane does most things well."

He nodded agreement. After the two young people walked through, Salvatore put his hat firmly on his head. Tipping it to Mia, he closed the gate, securing it with a massive, antique padlock. "No more visitors are expected today," he told them. Whistling, he picked up the wheelbarrow handles and strode away, the squeak of the wheels a high pitched chorus.

272

Ryan nodded to Mia. "We've discussed the situation," he told her. "I don't know what we will do when we get back to Atlanta, but I'm staying in Francesca's room tonight to protect her."

Francesca said nothing, biting her lip in thought. She was looking down at the ground, not meeting anyone's eyes.

"Another man in the house will be welcome," Mia agreed. "It's a bit unpleasant having a murderer roaming freely around the villa."

"I can see that," said Ryan dryly. He clenched his jaw as they neared the villa. "I don't know what we're going to say to the rest of the family, though."

Judith spotted them as soon as they crossed her line of sight on the courtyard. She stormed out of her cottage, screaming at Ryan, "Get out of here, you murderer. How dare you set foot on this place after what you did to my daughter?" She didn't even seem to realize Francesca was standing there beside him, but she saw Mia. "Mia! You brought him here? How could you? How could you do that to us?"

Kathleen took Judith's arm, "Let's not be hasty, Judith. Mia must have a reason." She tried to lead Judith back inside.

Mia gritted her teeth, but spoke calmly. "Judith, there's something you need to know, before you say anything you might regret."

Judith cut her off, "He's a thief and a murderer. A viper in our midst. He shouldn't be here. I demand that he leave. Now!" she screeched the last word, running out of breath.

Mia announced in a loud voice, "Judith, you need to know—"

"He has to go!" Judith flung out, then swallowed hard, taking a breath, and seeming to stumble. She clutched her chest. "My heart...I can't..."

Kathleen put her arm around her. "Come and sit down, Judith. This isn't doing your injuries any good."

Francesca stood still as a statue in the middle of the courtyard, unsure whether going to her mother would make things better or worse.

Judith collapsed into a chair, looking drained. Kathleen brought her a glass of water. "Drink this," she ordered her, sympathetically.

Judith drank, then placed the glass down. Her face started to regain color and return to her natural reserve. She took a few deep breaths, then accused, "Mia. Of all the people, I can't believe she'd take a thief's side over ours..." Her voice shrilled with fury.

Kathleen told her forcefully, "Mia would never take a thief's side. You know her better than that."

"But..." Judith said weakly. Her hands dangled from the armrests, limp and helpless.

"I suggest we have her tell us what's going on." Kathleen held up a hand at Judith's heartfelt protest. "Without Ryan, of course." She sat down on the sofa. "Let's take a minute to calm down, then we can find out the truth." Kathleen herself was perfectly calm, but she didn't need Judith having a heart attack. One hospital visit was enough for a vacation.

"How would Mia know the truth?" asked Judith, furious. "We all know the truth about what happened."
274

Kathleen refused to speculate, just picked up her book, turning the pages slowly, without reading, as she waited for Judith to take the next step.

After a few minutes, Judith nodded. "Fine. Just Mia, mind you. Not even Francesca. After all I've done for her," she added bitterly.

Kathleen went to the door, and called, "Mia!"

Mia's small, neat figure trotted briskly toward her. Francesca started to follow, but Kathleen motioned her back. Francesca's face fell, but she sat back down with the others.

At the door, Kathleen looked directly into the bright blue eyes of her old friend. Her own eyes pleaded for Mia to soften this blow as much as possible. Mia nodded, understanding. Kathleen opened the door and Mia entered, sitting on the sofa.

"I know that was a terrible shock for you, Judith, but I wasn't sure what else to do," Mia said, contritely. "Are you feeling better?" She cocked her head to one side, birdlike, and watched Judith intently.

"A little," Judith acknowledged sourly.

"I'm glad," Mia told her sincerely. "You've been through a lot this week."

"Mia, how could you bring—that man into the house? He's probably the murderer," Judith's voice was now rigidly under control, but it quavered at the edges.

Mia shook her head, "Judith, Kathleen, I have very good news." She smiled benevolently.

Judith arched her defined eyebrow in disbelief, but said nothing.

"I sent all the financial records disclosures to my accountants." She said aside, "You know Nicole works in Spinel's accounting department." Mia was very proud of her daughter's financial skills.

"You what?" Kathleen said with surprise.

"Those records would be on public record soon, with a trial," Mia reassured her. "But luckily, there's no need for a trial. Ryan is absolutely innocent."

Judith's face drained of color, and she leaned against the cushions as if they were all that held her upright.

"Innocent," Kathleen's face went white. "You mean, all along, Ryan wasn't a thief? He was telling the truth?"

"Ryan wasn't a thief. Jeffery was the thief." Mia's lips thinned. "He set up Ryan."

"Oh," Kathleen whispered. "Oh, poor Francesca."

"You're positive?" Judith almost croaked the words. "Jeffery?"

"I'm sure," Mia told her. "Once we knew what to look for, we were able to get the original bank records, times of deposits, the whole thing. We even found Jeffery on video at one of the banks." She smiled at them, "Ryan is, thankfully, completely innocent of those thefts."

She continued, "And even more good news is that my accountants were able to track down most of the stolen money." Her eyes shone beneficently, "Once Nicole heard about Francesca, she was on the case like a honey badger." She said in a quick aside, "She's never forgotten how sweet Francesca was to have her be a bridesmaid."

"It sounds like Nicole is a lot like her mom," Kathleen commented. "You must be proud."

"I am," Mia told her, beaming with pleasure.

"Well," Judith said, dully. "This is a shock."

"I know it is, Judith. I'm sorry about that," Mia said with sympathy. "But it's a good thing, you know. A very good thing."

"It is," Judith nodded. "I appreciate you doing— all this." She spread her fingers out, then dropped them like she'd run out of energy. "It's been a difficult week," she acknowledged.

"I'm very sorry, Judith."

"What is Ryan doing here?" she asked Mia, curiosity emerging. "I thought he was staying in the town?"

"He's going to stay here—there's no reason for him not to. He's been very concerned about Francesca and the murders, of course," Mia added matter of factly.

"But—" then Judith subsided. "I'm feeling very tired," she said. "I think I'll have an early night, and talk with them in the morning."

"I think that will be a very good idea," Mia agreed. "You'll feel better in the morning."

11

Down the Garden Path

Mia wasn't happy. Dinner tonight was uncomfortably polite, replete with sparse conversation along the lines of "Please pass the salt." Francesca avoided looking at, or even speaking to Ryan.

Kevin's family hadn't bothered to appear, huddled in their new quarters, secure under a siege. Savannah had eaten very quickly, then left, not bothering to say a word.

It had been one dinner Mia hadn't even attempted to enliven. She simply didn't have the heart to.

Ryan had sat like a statue, his jaw granite, unspeaking, shoveling the rich Bolognese in his mouth, not tasting it at all. He examined the intricately patterned white tablecloth, unseeing.

Diane had efficiently served dinner, then taken her place at the table. She sat across from the portrait of the gentle, but indomitable lady again, and looked at the portrait for guidance. She straightened her back, feeling the slump of despair ease, and ate with dignity. She was proud of the meal. Teresa had guided her through it, but she had made most of the food—and had learned techniques to take home with her.

Diane glanced over at Ryan, and smiled shyly. She had always hoped it had all been a terrible mistake, and it had been. His eyes flickered her way in bare acknowledgment, but that was it. Poor Ryan—and poor Francesca. They had been so happy together before this.

Diane hoped Ryan would give Francesca another chance. She didn't know if he understood how hard it had been, with all her family mad at her. Francesca had bowed under the guilt.

And Jeffery had been the thief all along! Diane's memories flickered through her head. It really wasn't so surprising it had been Jeffery, she thought. He had always been greedy, wanting the largest shares, the most praise. He had been as jealous of Ryan as he had been of Kevin. He had reacted the same as when he shoved his brother down as a boy, racing to get to cookies. People didn't really change, Diane thought sadly.

Randall sat at the head of the table, remembering his friend Harold. Harold would never have let things get this far. Two people dead. He rephrased in his head.

No, two people brutally murdered, and Judith's fall. Francesca's marriage in ruins, because of Jeffery's plotting. Harold had always liked Ryan. Randall's own declaration to Francesca. None of this was meant to happen—and wouldn't have, if Harold hadn't died.

In his last letter, Harold had told Randall that he needed Randall to watch over his family if anything happened to him. Ryan and Kevin would eventually take the responsibility of heads of the family, but it would be several years before they had grown into the role. When he'd received Harold's letter, Randall had immediately called his old friend, but it was too late. Harold had already had a heart attack. Harold was gone. Randall still carried that letter in his wallet, his very last communication from his best friend in the world.

Randall had tried to do his best for Harold, these last few months. But it had been more difficult than he could have dreamed, lately.

Mia sat in the dark on her balcony, listening to the night sounds and waiting. An owl hooted, soundless wings sweeping through the cool air as he hunted. A small animal rustled in the bushes near the villa, scuffling as he turned over leaves, abruptly noiseless, as the soft, silent shadow of the owl passed over. The sweetly cloying scent of oleander hung in the heavy air.

Mia felt on edge. Every clink of silverware and slosh of a glass had grated on her nerves at dinner. She felt sure, absolutely sure, that there was something she had missed.

The murderer was still out there, and had to be caught, so the Parkers could live a normal life again. No family could survive under this level of strain for long. Mia had to do something to end it. The only way forward was to completely unmask the killer, otherwise there would always be a question in their hearts.

Though her life had entwined with the Parkers for so long, she was the only true outsider here. The only one free to act without shattering the family.

It was odd, how much more sounds carried in the night. During the day, all the routine noises of the countryside were unnoticeable. Grass mowing, a hedge trimmer, the stuttering of a tractor engine or the roar of a car blurred into an unceasing hum. At night, each small crunch of leaves magnified into the importance of a lion stalking its prey.

A sharp crunch of gravel cracked like a whip in the dark, the sound of someone trying hard to be quiet. A lingering squeak, then she heard the stealthy footsteps of someone walking in the courtyard. Mia heard the familiar squeak, and guessed at Salvatore's wheelbarrow.

Time for her to go and see. Carrying her shoes, she moved furtively through the silent villa. The chill of the stones froze her stocking feet. Pausing by a fireplace, she removed the poker. She didn't feel safe out there with a killer, without a weapon of some kind.

Mia had strategically placed tape in the latch of one of the side doors earlier, and she slipped outside, closing the door behind her. Fastidiously brushing her feet off, she put on her shoes, and quietly walked in the direction that she'd heard the footsteps going, down the garden path.

She followed the squeaking, heavily laden wheelbarrow down the long walk, moving as silently as she could, praying she would not be too late. Once, she dimly saw the figure turn, and she froze, like the small animal in the bushes, hoping the dark would shield her. Mia brushed past the oleander bushes, inhaling their intoxicating scent. She would never feel quite the same about oleander again.

She hesitated when the figure entered the rose garden, grunting with effort, as the wheel turned. There were no dense bushes to hide behind, in that high walled space. Plastering herself to the wall behind the bushes, she waited for the figure to emerge, her heart thumping hard in her chest.

The figure came out after a few minutes, still pushing the wheelbarrow, squeaking less with its load lightened. The wheel crunched through the gravel. When it passed Mia at a mere arm distance, she slitted her eyes so the whites wouldn't show and held her breath in fear, but she wasn't noticed. The figure hunted other prey tonight.

After it disappeared, she hurried to enter the rose garden. A woman lay on the bench, unmoving. Her heart in her throat, Mia ran. Quickly, she felt for her pulse, and she found it. Thready and weak, but there. She breathed out a hiss of relief. Mia had been worried she hadn't acted fast enough. She needed to be quick now, so she could get help.

The high pitched scream of a woman rang through the night. The fear and panic of it tugged at her, urging her to hurry.

She lovingly smoothed the woman's hair back from her brow, then left, stalking the hunter. She clenched the cold brass of the poker firmly, holding it like a weapon. The dark figure screamed into the night still, at the edge of the courtyard.

Men's voices thundered as the villa doors sprang open. Randall and Ryan ran out. "Where is she?" they frantically called.

Mia heard a soft chuckle as the figure withdrew to another garden room off the walkway. This one, she knew, had two doorways. Quickly, she made her way around to the opening of the far entrance. Here, there were thick bushes screening her.

The woman screamed again, intense pain radiating through her voice. The men yelled and ran for the injured woman.

Too fast for Mia to act, she saw the hidden woman lean back, and strike hard with a shovel, as Randall burst in. He fell, unconscious, and the woman leaned over, straining hard as she dragged him to the side, dead weight. She repositioned the weapon, as Ryan came through the doorway. Mia screamed, as the blow started to fall on his unprotected head. He turned, and the shovel glanced off his shoulder, striking him down.

The woman pounced like a cat, pulling back the shovel for a killing blow. Mia ran out, and hit her arm with the poker, wincing as she felt the fragile bone break.

Judith screamed in agony, dropping the shovel with a clang. Ryan rebounded, and held her hands behind her.

Judith screamed again, as if his touch burned like fire. Kevin ran through the doorway. He saw Randall down, and Ryan hurting Judith. He swung at Ryan, and Ryan dropped Judith's hands.

Quicker than you would have thought, Judith picked up the shovel with one hand. She attacked Ryan again, trying for a killing blow. Kevin caught the shovel on the way down, ripping it out of her grasp, his mouth open in shock.

Judith screamed in pain and fury, holding her broken arm.

Ryan, panting hard, said, "She hit Randall with that."

"She couldn't have," Kevin said angrily. He looked at Judith, her face snarling in fury, trying to wiggle out of his hold. Control was nearly impossible without hurting her arm. "She hit Uncle Randall with that shovel?" He tried to reposition for a less painful hold, as she struggled wildly.

Judith spat, "He's not your uncle. He's nothing. Nothing!" Her wide set eyes burned with hatred. She had become a furious creature in the dark night.

Pietro and Salvatore ran in, moving fast. "What happened?" asked Pietro, stopping to stare at the little group.

"He tried to kill me!" accused Judith. She clutched at her thin arm, clearly broken. She might have looked pitiful, the frail, elderly woman, but her face was distorted by hate and fury.

Mia stepped forward. "I saw everything. She hit Randall with the shovel, then tried to hit Ryan. I broke her arm," she added, waving the poker. The men moved back a step. She continued, "And Kathleen's unconscious in the rose garden."

Judith tried again, "Kathleen admitted it all, I was just trying to protect her. Mia hit me with that poker."

Mia broke in, "She hauled Kathleen there in a wheelbarrow. She's barely breathing." She admitted, "Judith was about to hit Ryan with the shovel again."

"I'll call the doctor," Salvatore told her.

"And the carabinieri," Pietro told him.

Judith stood alone in the middle of the garden, as her family slowly encircled her, staring at the murderer in their midst. Francesca came last of all, entering, then standing behind Ryan.

When she saw her daughter, the lines on Judith's face softened. She held her hand out to Francesca. "I did it for you," she told her daughter. She leaned her head to the side, and smiled maternally. "It was all for you."

Francesca burst into tears and hid her face in Ryan's chest. He put his arm around her, and led her away.

Judith collapsed then, the insane strength that had kept her going melting like a spent candle. She crumpled inward, and Kevin caught her as she fell. Pietro came forward, and between them, they carried her into the villa.

Mia hurried to the rose garden, gesturing for Diane to follow her. They laid Kathleen in a more comfortable position, but her pulse was so thin, they didn't want to jar her by moving her more. Salvatore brought blankets and they wrapped her in them. They held her hands until the ambulance came.

As the paramedics deft, gentle hands moved her to a stretcher, and a piece of paper fell to the ground. Mia picked it up and held it out to Diane. "A suicide note signed Kathleen," she said. "Judith must have written it to be found with her body."

Diane's face was white. "Wicked."

"Yes, she was very wicked," agreed Mia. "And we might even have believed that note, if Judith hadn't been caught in the act."

The air in the sitting room hung heavy and still. Disapproving portraits stared down at Judith, crumpled on the white slipcover of the sofa. Kevin sat next to her, half turned away, sick at the sight of the woman he loved like a mother, fallen so far from grace. His hands gripped the carved arms of the chair, leaving deep indentations in his palms, as if the pain would take him out of his nightmare.

Pietro stood, hovering near the room's doorway. He wanted as little to do with the distasteful business as possible, but he was not going to allow this madwoman to escape. Diane came and stood beside him. With a natural movement, he put his arm around her. She huddled into him for comfort. Pietro's face was grim, as he stared in at the woman who had murdered in his home, and he held onto Diane tightly.

Mia handed him his poker back with a smile. He took it in his other arm, looking curiously at her, then nodded. He said nothing.

Kevin looked up at Mia as she entered the room, then dropped his gaze back to the floor, lost in his own vision of the netherworld. He refused to look at the woman who had murdered his brother.

Judith didn't look up as Mia entered. She half lay on the sofa, her slight figure wrapped in thick blankets, like an ailing child. She held her broken arm tightly to her chest.

"Judith," Mia said, and the woman looked up, her dark eyes looking at Mia blankly, almost without recognition. Judith was a stranger to them all, now, trapped in the hell she had created.

Her eyes moved to Kevin, then to Randall, shambling like an automaton into the room, a bloody streak livid in his silver hair.

"Judith," Mia repeated, then asked what they needed to know. "Why did you do it?"

Her lips parted, "For Francesca." Her stunned eyes looked at Mia, not focusing.

"But why?" Mia asked gently. The room lay quiet and still, waiting for the answer.

The dam suddenly burst, and Judith whispered to Mia, like a child telling a terrible secret, "Francesca was going to leave me. Leave me all alone."

"Francesca would never have done that," Mia protested. She clenched her hands in her lap until her nails dug into her flesh, but kept her voice calm and even.

"She got married. She left me," Judith told her, her eyes alight with fury. "She barely came back home."

"They were newlyweds, Judith," Mia said, helpless to understand. "They wanted some time together. They'd only been married a few months."

"She would have had kids and a home, without me." Judith nodded. "After all that she owed me," she added, self-righteously. "She owed me everything. She'd have had nothing without me."

"She's your daughter," Mia told her. "Your child."

"She was a Parker because I wanted her. I made it happen. She's mine, my child, the child I always wanted. My beautiful child."

Mia felt Randall shift behind her. With horror, she suddenly understood.

Judith straightened on the sofa, holding her broken arm close, and said with pride, "She didn't have a chance without me. And now, she was leaving me. Leaving me all alone," she trailed off. "All alone," she whispered.

"What did you do, Judith?" Mia kept her voice steady, but she felt the storm breaking around her.

"I told Jeffery if he stole the money, and made it seem like Ryan had taken it, he could be CEO." She laughed, a grating, tinkling sound in the silent room. "That was easy. He'd always hated Francesca. And Harold wanted Ryan to be CEO, not Jeffery. So Jeffery hated him."

She leaned a little towards Mia, confiding in a soft whisper, "Of course, I planned to kill Jeffery all along. I could see that night, he'd gotten too full of himself to let him continue. He would have come after Francesca, as soon as he'd been made CEO." Her lips curved rapaciously. "I couldn't have that. I had to protect her."

"I see," Mia kept her voice neutral. "So you poisoned Jeffery?"

Judith nodded, pleased at her cleverness. "With oleander from the garden. I hate oleander. When she was little, I was always afraid Francesca would eat some, but Harold told me his mother had planted the oleander. He wouldn't let me get rid of it. So that's how I killed him." She nodded proudly.

Mia said carefully, "That's how you killed who?"

"Harold, of course. I thought it a fitting end." Judith nodded to herself. "I showed him—he let Francesca marry that horrible man. It was really his own fault I had to kill him," she informed Mia.

"Why was Ryan so horrible?" Mia asked. "You just said he wasn't a thief."

"He took my Francesca away," Judith said simply. "So I wanted him put away. He should rot in jail," she hissed vindictively, then looked up at Mia, "He has to go to jail. It's all his fault, you know."

Mia left that statement hanging. It was unanswerable. She asked, "What about Jeffery?"

"Oh, that was very simple. I snipped up some leaves and dried them with my hairdryer. They looked just like that stinky tobacco he smoked," she said proudly. "But Anna noticed the stains and leaves on the towels—I had to use towels so the hairdryer didn't blow them away. She thought she'd blackmail me." Judith chuckled, smirking. "She was greedy—and wrong."

Mia said precisely, "I see." She added, "And you faked your fall?"

Judith agreed, "I knew if I was attacked, no one would believe I had killed anyone. All I had to do was scream and turn a wheelbarrow over." She frowned, "I ruined one of my favorite blouses." Then her lips suddenly widened, intense glee lighting her wide set eyes. "Francesca seemed so scared for me. She must love me, if she cared about me being hurt."

The room lay silent in still horror.

Judith announced, "I want some water." She smiled in a parody of politeness, "If it's not too much trouble."

Mia motioned, not looking away from Judith. She heard Pietro leave to get it, his footsteps echoing in the silence.

"Could you get Francesca for me?" Judith suddenly pleaded. "I need to see her, before—before they take me away." Her voice cracked.

Diane said uncomfortably, "I'll tell her, Judith, but..." her voice trailed away.

Judith shifted her position, pulling the blanket around her and tucking her hands underneath, still cold in the early morning light.

Mia felt the anger radiating off Randall, standing directly behind her. He shifted from foot to foot like an angry bear, saying nothing.

Pietro came in, handed the water to Mia, and quickly retreated out of the room. Mia handed her the glass, and she took a sip. Then, Judith looked around the room at her family, staring at her with horror. "I did it all for the best." She cocked her head to one side. "You'll all thank me later."

No one said anything. There was nothing to say.

Slow footsteps on the stairs, and Francesca came into the room, hesitating near the door. Ryan stood protectively behind her. "You wanted to see me, Mom?" Her voice quavered on the last word.

"Francesca, I wanted you to know how much I love you," Judith said passionately.

Francesca told her, her beautiful gray eyes heartbroken, "I love you too, Mom."

"I did it all for you," Judith told her, her proud dark eyes intense, gazing at Francesca. "All of it." She made a quick movement towards her mouth, but Mia was waiting.

She grabbed the older woman's arm, forcing it away from her mouth. "Randall, get that pill!" she ordered. "No, you're not taking that way out, Judith."

Judith threw the water, glass and all, at Mia. It hit Mia's arm, making her stumble back. Judith swiftly rose, coming at Francesca, arms outstretched, face distorted.

Randall blocked her and forced her back on the sofa. "You're not getting off that easy, Judith. The law will punish you."

Judith started laughing, laughing without joy or mirth, the laughter of a madwoman.

Francesca turned and buried her face in Ryan's chest, and he led her away.

12

Emerging

After Judith had been taken away by the Tenente Zanatta, Mia suggested, "Let's go outside. I need some fresh air."

Diane commented, "And sunlight."

Everyone came outside, collapsing into the comfortable chairs.

Ben said what everyone was thinking, "Wow, Aunt Judith was really nuts, wasn't she?"

Kevin frowned, but Mia quickly agreed, "Yes, Ben, she was."

Savannah added meditatively, "She was way darker than I'd ever be." She tapped her deep red nails on her chair arm.

Francesca told her, with a chuckle, "We all know you just think you look good in black." She shrugged, adding with a small smile, "And you're not wrong."

Everyone laughed, more than the little joke deserved. It felt good to be outside in the warm sunlight. Diane and Teresa had supplied them with brioches, then sat down to eat, Salvatore joined them after distributing a most welcome tray of coffees.

They nibbled and sipped coffee, relaxing after their long ordeal.

Finally Randall spoke, his tone flat and dull, "She must have—" his voice broke, and he swallowed hard. "She must have killed Nora. That's what she meant."

Francesca's face went white. "She killed my real mother? For me?"

Ryan's arm tightened around her, and he glared at Randall. "It's not your fault, Fran. Don't think about it."

Randall said heavily, "Of course it's not your fault, Francesca. Of course not. She killed Harold and Jeffery, and poor little Anna, too. She was crazy."

Francesca said slowly, her hand tightening on Ryan's, "I knew she wasn't—quite right. She always wanted everything her way, nothing else was ever good enough for her." She shook her head, "When Dad was alive, it was okay. He'd point out how absurd something was. Or suggest an alternative when she asked too much. Dad kept everything reasonable. But after he died—" She couldn't continue.

Randall added, "There were no checks on Judith after Harold died." He rephrased, "After she killed Harold. There was just Judith, getting more and more extreme."

Mia said, "After all, she'd killed once, and gotten away with it." With a glance at Randall, she added, "At least once. There was nothing to stop her killing for increasingly petty reasons." She sighed, then added, "She wanted to own her child, not rejoice in her independence and love. To a lesser extent, she did the same to the other children under her care, even as adults. She wanted control over Diane, Kevin and Jeffery. When she knew Jeffery might be a threat to her, she killed him."

Francesca said slowly, "I was terrified, since Jeffery's murder, that it was Mom—I don't know what to call her, now." She went on, "She had been so insistent on everything. I wouldn't have believed her about Ryan," she glanced up at his hard expression, "but Jeffery said so too and showed me all the documents. I was so angry, felt so betrayed, and guilty, too. Like if I didn't denounce Ryan immediately, the thefts would all be my fault. I'd let down my entire family. I only had one option to make it right. She had a lawyer waiting right there in the office, and everything just happened so quickly."

Ryan squeezed her hand.

"She never liked me going out, meeting people. And she hated me having boyfriends. She wanted me all to herself, all the time." Francesca looked down. "I felt like I was trapped in a cocoon, cutting me off from the rest of the world. I knew she loved me. It was just too much."

"I was so relieved when Dad insisted I go work at the office." Francesca smiled wryly, "She had to let me go, because otherwise I couldn't run the company. Then I met Ryan." She looked up at him. "And I thought everything would be okay." Her eyes filled with tears. "But then Dad died, and the nightmare began."

Randall came over and patted her shoulder, then backed away a step. He cleared his throat, then said, "I knew something was wrong with Judith. That last letter Harold wrote to me, he—" he paused, "Look, let me show you." He got out his wallet and pulled a worn, folded letter out, smoothing the creases and placing it on the low table at the center. They all crowded around, reading the last words from their beloved mentor.

To my dear friend Randall,

I hope you're doing well, in the middle of whatever war torn hellhole they've sent you into. I am sure it will be better for your attentions.

Francesca thrives in her new marriage. Ryan is good for her, a good man all around. In a few years, I will hand over the company reins to him, and I can't think of a better choice. I've tried to make Jeffery see he is best suited to his current role, but I fear that is beyond me. He is too petty to be a sound leader.

Kevin's business is seeing great success, as rapidly as could be achieved. I like to think he is a 'chip off the old block.' And Candace has raised my grandson to be a fine young man, as you saw at the wedding. Ben looks more like her side of the family, but perhaps that's just as well.

You'll be pleased to hear that Savannah's new marketing campaign has hit record numbers, so we have another fine businesswoman in the making. If she'd leave off that hideous lipstick and quit dressing like a vampire, she'd be a beautiful woman, too.

Diane is having trouble returning to normal life, after Sadie's death. I have almost decided to send her away to nursing school, but I'm unsure whether that is the best place for her, after her experience. I think she has too gentle a heart for the painful necessities of nursing. She needs a change soon, nevertheless. It's not good for her spending all her time running after Judith.

I've recently had some concerning things come to my attention that I'd like to discuss with you in person, since they involve you, as well. I know it's difficult for you to make a spur of the moment trip back home, but please come, as soon as you are able.

If anything should happen to me, Francesca will need her father, more than ever. Don't think this is a rash decision. I have thought, for some time, that she needs to know what you are to her, and that you should spend more time together. I have no fear that that will change her love for me, but rather, give her a second father she can depend on.

Also, I hate to ask this of you, especially under the circumstances, but I need you to look after Judith for me and prevent her from making hasty decisions—as she's all too prone to do. If I am not around, she will need your guidance and protection.

Hoping this finds you well,

Your friend,

Harold Parker

They read silently, with tears pouring down their faces.

Kevin broke the silence, "He really loved us, didn't he?" He held Candace's hand tightly. "Fine young man he said, Ben. That's you, in a nutshell."

He cleared his throat. "I'll make sure Aunt Judith gets a lawyer, and all that." He shrugged a little, "It's what Uncle Harold would have wanted."

Francesca sat on the balcony in her room overlooking the green vineyards, unseeing. Her mind reeled with all that had happened over the past few days. Her mother wasn't her mother, but was a murderer. And she was still her mother, who had been there for her for so many years. She didn't know what to think.

Mom had deliberately destroyed her marriage. Gone about it deliberately! She had killed Dad, who would always be her dad, no matter who her father was. Francesca was glad Uncle Randall was in her life. She wanted him to be a bigger part of her life, but he could never take her dad's place.

That was an easier mental shift, since she had always known Uncle Randall loved her like a daughter.

But for Mom to murder Dad, to destroy her marriage—she was still in shock. How could her mother have done that?

Francesca had always known that Mom was jealous of Ryan. She'd always been jealous of anyone who took too much of Francesca's time and energy. Mom liked to be the center of everyone's attention, particularly Francesca's, and she had made her displeasure known in a myriad of little ways. Francesca had felt that she was trapped inside a cocoon of intense motherly love. She needed to escape, so she could live her own life.

Francesca had always known something was wrong about Mom's intensity, but it was a far step from that to murdering Dad, and then Jeffery. Had she actually killed Nora, her real mother? And Mom had done all that to keep Francesca with her?

Francesca felt lost, adrift on pain and heartbreak. She couldn't go back. She couldn't change the past. She'd never see Dad again. She'd lost Ryan. She could only go on from here, but she didn't know where to go, anymore.

She heard the door creak open, and Ryan's footsteps. He came over, and sat next to her. She didn't turn her head to see him. What was the point?

"Francesca, we need to talk," Ryan told her, his voice serious.

She still wouldn't look at him. "There's nothing to talk about, is there?" Francesca said forlornly. "I messed up. I ruined our marriage over lies."

"Francesca," Ryan paused, then sighed heavily. "You did mess up. I wish you had believed me, not Judith's lies. But we can't change what happened."

Francesca felt hot tears burning, but she would not cry. Not now. Not in front of Ryan.

He paused, then said, "We can give up, let our marriage go or," he stressed, "we can move on, and learn from this. Build a stronger marriage."

She looked at him, but said nothing. How could he trust her again?

"I love you, and you love me, Francesca. That's too important to let go, even over really big mistakes, you know." He swallowed hard. "I'm willing to try again, if you are."

She turned to him, and he saw her grey eyes were luminous from unshed tears. She held out her hands to him. He grabbed them and pulled her into his lap, holding her tight.

Tenente Zanatta knocked on the heavy, oak door. In his mind, he reviewed the scene of a few hours ago. Judith, looking like a very proper matriarch, surrounded by her family, all of whom looked shellshocked. To find out that this well dressed woman had murdered several people, and be told she'd admitted to murdered her own husband also.

It was a shock to him, as well. He had believed the killer was Kevin Parker, because he would inherit substantially under Judith's will, and had been threatened by his loan being called in by his brother. Zanatta had been waiting on the police in Atlanta to confirm the man's financials. Frankly, until Judith had begun talking, he had wondered whether the lady was admitting to a crime she had not committed, to protect her nephew.

Of course, once the woman had begun talking, there was not a question of anyone else committing these crimes. She was crazy, and he had immediately requested a psychiatric evaluation from the pubblico ministero.

He was grateful, under the circumstances, that he had acted promptly.

Pietro opened the door, and frowned as he saw Zanatta. "Is there more trouble?"

"Yes, unfortunately. I need to speak with Francesca Parker, per favore."

Pietro asked no more questions.

Francesca came down the stairs, closely followed by Ryan. "What's going on?"

Randall entered from the library. "You're back? We've told you everything we know."

Tenente Zanatta addressed Francesca formally, "Signora Parker, I regret to inform you that you that Signora Judith Parker suffered a heart attack, and died on her way to the hospital. I am sorry for your loss."

Francesca's face turned white, and she started sliding to the ground. Ryan caught her just in time. Randall pulled over a chair. They both stood on either side of her, supporting her.

"Mom is dead?" Francesca asked.

"I'm very sorry," Zanatta repeated, not actually sure whether he was sorry or not. Judith Parker would have been tried as a murderer of two people in Italy, and found guilty. She would have gone to prison, or to a mental hospital. There was nothing anyone in this family could have done about it, except to visit her, imprisoned for her crimes in a foreign land. It was perhaps better for it to all be over, before the ordeal. They had been through enough, the Parker family.

"She died in the ambulance, and was pronounced dead on arrival." He did not say the ambulance had started out for the mental hospital, making an abrupt detour when Signora Parker had shown signs of a heart attack. That information could come later, if the Parkers even wanted to know.

"Mom's dead," Francesca said. "A heart attack? She didn't..." she trailed off.

"It was a heart attack," Zanatta stated, though privately he was not sure either. He had the pill she had tried to commit suicide with earlier that same day, after all. But a heart attack would be easier for the family, so there was no point in looking further.

Randall reflected, "She was pretty determined to die, so she didn't go to prison. I guess Judith always had to have her own way."

No one said anything, because it was the truth.

Diane sat in the car next to Pietro. The hospital had called to say Aunt Kathleen was being discharged. Diane had been relieved, then realized she had no idea how to drive in Italy. She'd haltingly asked if there was a taxi she could take to the hospital.

Pietro had laughed. "You don't want to deal with a taxi all the way there and back. Let me drive you," he offered.

"Oh, but I couldn't ask you to..." Diane began, then stopped. She looked up into his soft brown eyes, looking on her with warm approval. "Thank you, Pietro. I'd very much appreciate you taking me."

He gave her a quick grin, suddenly looking a decade younger than his usual scholarly self. "Then go get your things," he told her.

Diane quickly ran to her room, and brushed her hair. Looking thoughtfully at her reflection, she added lipstick and a little eye makeup, thinking how much nicer that made her look. More polished. She grabbed her handbag, and ran down the stairs.

Pietro waited in the hall, smiling up at her. Suddenly, she felt that she had been here, running to meet him, a million times before and seen his smile, just for her.

He had led her to the garage, opening the big green doors to the beautiful curves of a deep red Alfa

Romeo Guilia. He held the car door open for her, and she slid into the soft leather seat.

He got in, and the engine roared, whisking them down the filtered sunlight of the drive and onto the open road. He grinned with pleasure as he drove the car expertly along the curving roads.

Diane sat back in the seat, enjoying the ride. This was good, driving fast on these smooth roads, with the changing views of mountains and vineyards. She didn't have to think about anything that had happened, anything she had to do, just enjoy the man's smile, the fast car and the scenery.

She glanced at Pietro, and saw him dart a quick glance at her, then back at the road. He was a handsome man in profile, with his high arched nose and grin of concentration. His dark hair, threaded with silver, sprang back from his forehead, in a neat, glossy wave. She liked the way he drove, with complete attention and deft skill. Fast, but under control.

Diane suddenly realized how much she was going to miss Pietro, when she left Italy. Walking in the garden and talking with him had brightened her days here. She'd made a good friend here, at least. More than one friend. Teresa and Salvatore, as well. She wondered if she'd be able to visit Kathleen, maybe see Pietro again? Probably not, she thought with a sigh. She would need to restart school, and there wouldn't be time or money for anything else for a while.

Pietro suddenly pulled to the side of the road. "You want to see the view," he told her.

And it was glorious, putting all her petty worries out of her head. High mountains, blued by distance. Undulating, forested hills, lush and green. And lush green vines just out of reach, heavy with purple skinned grapes. Diane breathed in the clean, crisp air and laughed with delight. Italy was a beautiful country.

"I have been thinking, Diane," Pietro said beside her, and she turned to him with a smile. "I've been thinking I would miss you a great deal, if you left."

She said in surprise, "I was just thinking the same thing."

He smiled suddenly, and she realized he'd been nervous. "You fit into my life well, Diane. It won't feel like my home any more, without you in it." He looked at her and asked, "Will you marry me?"

"Oh," she breathed out, in amazement. "You want to marry me?"

"More than anything in the world," he said simply. "Will you?"

And in her head, there ran so many thoughts, of dark, lonely nights and utter exhaustion, of Judith's beckoning, constant demands, of the long, weary dreariness.

Then, looking into Pietro's eyes, she saw his quiet happiness that she was there beside him. She saw a future of long walks in the garden, of welcoming guests, helping Teresa in the kitchen, and reading together in the library on cold winter nights, with a roaring fire in the fireplace warming them. She saw sunlight and flowers, and laughing children in the garden.

Diane said, "Yes."

He swept her into his arms and kissed her. She felt like she would burst with happiness. She leaned into him, knowing that together, they would both be stronger than they could ever be apart.

Drawing away a little, he put his hand in the pocket of his trousers and pulled out a worn leather box, with gold tracings around the edges. "I did this wrong," he told her, with a chuckle. "I meant to give you the ring. My mother wore it, and my father's mother before her, back several generations." He handed it to her. "If you want something different, we can get it," he told her uncertainly.

She opened the box and saw the deep red of an exquisite ruby, flanked by two mine cut diamonds. Gold filigree delicately held it in place. "It's beautiful," she exclaimed.

"Three stones meant, at that time, love, commitment and fidelity. And a ruby, for passion," he told her, with a grin.

She laughed, and he put the beautiful ring on her finger. It fit perfectly. She looked up into his kind brown eyes, and smiled.

Pietro wrapped his arms around her. Diane felt loved and protected, full of joy at their future together. She had found her place in the world, at last.

They met on the veranda, with Randall pushing out the gleaming bar cart. Kevin laughing, played bartender, mixing drinks with a flourish.

Mia reflected that there was a tact agreement to not mention, or even think about the terrible events of the past week, not for tonight, at least. With Judith's death, the affair was closed. It would never truly be forgotten by this family, but this evening would be full of the joys of the moment and hopes for the future.

Francesca and Ryan came downstairs, hand in hand. Mia smiled to see them clearly reconciled. It had been obvious that they loved each other all along. Francesca's face showed recent tears, and Ryan had circles under his eyes. All marks of stress that would take time to heal, but their faces were alight with happiness, now.

Diane looked out the windows on to the veranda as she came down the stairs, smiling at the lights of the party outside and the laughter heard through the thick walls. She had dressed with extra care, putting on the terracotta colored dress, which swirled around her like an unfolding flower. Her ruby ring sparkled. She had added her mother's pearl earrings, thinking what how happy her mom would be to see her married to a wonderful man.

She walked past the party and into the kitchen, where Teresa was cooking. She got an apron down from the hook, tied it around her, and asked, "How can I help?"

Teresa looked at her, and a beaming smile spread across her round cheeks. Pietro and she had told Teresa their news earlier, and she had been full of enthusiastic —and elaborate—plans for their wedding.

Teresa nodded to a pile of rich purple radicchios, "If you could quarter those, please, then take in the spunciotti, that will be enough." She added, "My sister's daughter will come to help tomorrow. She is a sweet girl, and a hard worker. You will like her."

"I'm looking forward to meeting her," Diane told her.

Diane chopped until the radicchios were the perfect size to sear, then carefully arranged a large platter of appetizers. Baccalà on thick slices of bread, the little pickled Sottaceti, with onions and zucchini Teresa had grown, and big, round green olives. Wafer-thin pieces of Sopressa Vicentina and Asiago, Monte Veronese and Taleggio.

Pietro came in, and said, shaking his head in mock frustration, "Diane, this is your party. You need to come and enjoy it."

"I am enjoying it," Diane said with a grin, as she arranged the last slices of cheese.

Teresa told her, "Go, Diane, there will be plenty of parties to cook for. Shoo, go and see your family." She waved Diane out.

Diane took one tray, and Pietro another. They paused in the foyer, and kissed briefly. He opened the door to her, and they swept out.

"Here come the appetizers," Diane called gaily.

"Oh, yum!" Ben dove in.

Diane was glad she'd piled the platters full, with the avid gleam in his eyes and ready plate.

Pietro told Randall, "I found her working in the kitchen, of course. She needs to learn to have fun."

Diane came over, putting her hand on his arm. "I am having fun," she said with a laugh.

"Good," he smiled.

Francesca came over, "Let me see the ring!" Candace, Mia, and Savannah clustered around, admiring the antique sparkle, while Diane beamed proudly. She looked up at Pietro, and saw something in his eyes that meant much more than a pretty ring.

Mia looked between the two, and saw a light and happiness between them that would make this villa a beautiful home. She asked Diane, "What are your plans now?"

Diane said, "Everything is so new," she glanced at Pietro. "I'm not sure yet." They had had little time to talk in the car ride, before they had picked up Kathleen.

Pietro stepped in, "Diane will live with Kathleen, for a little while." He nodded to Kathleen, ensconced pale, but upright, in a comfortable chair in the center of the group. Randall sat at her side, in close attendance on his old friend.

"Kathleen will need some help for a few months. She's anxious to not leave her work undone while she's in recovery, since it's so important." The sleeping pills had been a very heavy overdose. It was a miracle Kathleen had survived, but it would take time to rebuild to her full strength.

"Pietro has promised me driving lessons, so I can take her to and from work," Diane said. "And just look after her, in general."

"And for yourself?" Mia asked.

"I'll need to take the Catholic corsi prematrimoniali, of course," Diane told her. "Also, a lot of Italian lessons. And then we'll get married."

Pietro told Mia, "I hope that you, all of you, return for our wedding. Teresa is already planning the festivities."

Salvatore opened the door, flourishing a silver bucket, filled with ice and several bottles of Prosecco.

"Now, it's time to celebrate!" Pietro expertly uncorked a chilled bottle, and its sharp pop rang in the night.

Teresa stepped forward with a silver tray of champagne flutes, and he filled them with fizzing bubbles, not spilling a drop. At Pietro's gesture, they all took a glass, toasting to Pietro's bride and their future together.

Cheers and laughter rang out. The Parkers would be back.

Ms. Mia Murder Mysteries
Lighthearted and Fun Mysteries
with Satisfying Conclusions.

A luxurious private island paradise, with palm trees and white sand beaches, sets the stage for this classic cozy mystery.

A Gilded Age mansion on a secluded Maine island, perched on rocky cliffs overlooking the ocean, sets the scene for a classic murder mystery.

A priceless discovery. A glamorous desert resort. And an unexpected mystery... At the Desert Sunrise Resort, Ms. Mia is preparing to host a dazzling exhibit featuring an ancient flute unearthed on the property.

In a sun-drenched tropical paradise, Ms. Mia chases a vanishing corpse and a cunning killer in this delightful cozy murder mystery.

Coming in February 2026:
Ms. Mia uncovers a deadly plot
in New Orleans.

About the Author

Jennifer Branch writes classic mysteries set in glamorous destinations.

Her Ms. Mia Murder Mysteries follow an elegant amateur sleuth as she uncovers secrets and solves murders at luxurious resorts around the world—from Georgia's Sea Islands and remote Maine retreats to sunlit deserts, tropical islands, and historic European villas.

Often compared to a modern Miss Marple with champagne, the series blends traditional puzzle-solving, gentle humor, and richly drawn settings for readers who enjoy classic whodunits with a strong sense of place.

A lifelong landscape painter, Jennifer brings an artist's eye to every setting. She lives in Northwest Georgia with her husband, their sons, and two adventurous dogs.

Discover more Ms. Mia Murder Mysteries, exclusive art, and behind-the-scenes insights at www.JenniferBranch.com.